Unforg

The Forgotten Secrets of a Family's Ruin

By

Yusuf T. Woods

Taking You beyond The Read

www.MasterExpressionsPblications.com
MasterExpressionsPblications@gmail.com
www.MasterExpressionsStore.com
MasterExpressions.Me@gmail.com
Instagram.com/masterexpressions.me
Authoryusufwoods@gmail.com
Copyright © 2019 Yusuf Woods
ISBN: 978-1-7343406-0-0
Printed in the USA

1 2 3 4 5 6 7 8 9 10

DEDICATIONS

This book is dedicated to special people

Beatrice E. Woods

And

Ida B. Hales

You would never be forgotten we promise

1

On a brisk October evening, just minutes passed midnight inside a corner store on 145th street in Harlem. The ceiling light flickered wildly swaying back and forth sending pauses of darkness throughout the room as the butt of a P39 automatic slammed once again upside the owner's head. The blow sent him back against the wall forcing him to fight to remain conscious.

"Just give it up, how many times I gotta tell you this is not a fucking game! Now where the hell is it?" demanded one of the three intruders wearing gold and black warrior masks.

"And I'm told you there has to be some kind of a mistake. I don't have anything...look." Mr. Patrick quickly opened the cash register revealing a hundred and twenty-two dollars. "That's all there is, take it and go... please."

"Alright if this is how you want to play it, let's play!" The masked man without sparing a second brought his weapon back across Mr. Patrick's face. He collapsed down onto one knee. The cold steel sliced the corner of his eye sending the warm moisture of his blood trailing down the side of his face dripping onto the freezing tiles.

The display of his own blood awakened a wave of intense anger that Mr. Patrick thought he had buried deep within him centuries ago. The day he made a mistake that would alter his life forever. He slowly rose his head to meet the intruder's stare declaring through tightening teeth, "You young pill-popping punk! In my day you wouldn't have dared look at me wrong let alone come in my establishment on some bullshit. I was known to kill suckers like you for breakfast and then tell your family I did it at lunch just to see who really wanted to get busy for dinner."

The small grin concealed by the mask slowly vanished from the intruder as he bent down whispering into Mr. Patrick's ear.

"Well old man, it's my day now and I'm doing this to you so let's get busy."

He threw a hard right hook at Mr. Patrick's face, distinguishing the stare of a true killer. *"This man had downed a few people in his day I know it. So I'm definitely not going to lunch on him."*

The strike sent Mr. Patrick's in shape frame head first into the floor. He attempted to stay calm, taking deep breathes slightly disorientated. He again glanced upward gathering his mind looking towards the man that he now vowed to murder at all cost. He focused, committing to memory any distinctive details of his eyes and mouth. For he knew if he survived this moment the
Devil himself couldn't match the rage he would unleash.

"If you don't kill me I swear you will die in the palm of my bare hands. If so someone still will repay you for this I swear to it."

"Is that so?"

"Son If I tell you there's cheese on the moon go get your crackers because my word is my bond. And nothing happens to this family without repercussions." Mr. Patrick mumbled a threat he received himself many years prior.

He observed the masked man's finger tightening around the trigger and thought back to just moments before; at how he got here......

"Ding-dong!"

The store's door chimed as it opened making Mr. Patrick pause from jotting down his daily records. He swiftly slid them underneath a set of newspapers while turning to face his customer with his usual smile. Out of sight, his right hand gripped onto the 9mm placed in the cigar box just beneath the cash register.

At the age of sixty-five Mr. Patrick never thought in a million years he would ever have to touch a firearm again after all the blood he once shed. Let alone in his own neighborhood. His store was a cornerstone of Harlem for over 30 years. This is where he was born. The place that made him a man before he went off to war. This was home but lately, his store had been burglarized four times within the last six months, all occurring after closing time. Now on behalf of his daughter's wishes, he refused to take any chances on there being a fifth with him present.

The display of a familiar face calmed his impulse as he released the weapon back into its place. He chuckled to his surprise loving the feeling of it being back in the depth of his palms.

"Yes, how can I help you Son?"

A returned smirk came from the young man who was singing something Mr. Patrick couldn't understand while rocking back and forth, doing his own version of the two-step.

"Kids," Mr. Patrick uttered before glancing at his watch, 11:40 pm. The time compelled him to wonder about his own son

Amir, "Where is that boy? He knows he's supposed to be here to help clean up before I close."

Drew, who was high on Molly and liquor looked at Mr. Patrick's mouth moving but couldn't hear what he was saying and didn't care to be honest as he continued to sing along with Lil Baby and Gunna blasting through his Air pods.

"Drip too hard, don't stand too close...You gon' fuck around and drown off this wave."

The sight of Mr. Patrick's hand waving back and forth got his attention.

"What up Popp's?" He questioned looking down at his black and white Jordan's 9 making sure they remained spotless.

"Can I help you with something, you know I'm about to close in ten minutes and I don't want to rush you."

6

"Yeah, that's my bad I'm all lit and shit... Aaahhmm lemme get aaaaa...two vanilla dutchy and uuuhhhmmm..... Some sour cream chips and a gold magnum."

"Okay, that will be four dollars and seventy-five cents."

"Here's a twenty old head, keep the change I'm eating out here why shouldn't you."

"Thanks," Mr. Patrick reviewed his watch again, lifting the phone off the hook following the "Ding-Dong" informing him that Drew had departed.

The caller picked up on the third ring.

"Hello."

"Sherry."

"Hey Dad, how is your night going?" Sherry questioned in high spirits, happy to hear her father's voice.

"I'm fine for an old soul, I can still move a bit." Mr. Patrick threw a double jab at the air while moving his head slipping the imaginary punch returned. The military had instilled in him how to keep his mind conditioned to working-out and eating healthy and for that, he didn't look a day over 50.

"Dear the reason I'm calling so late is to ask if you have seen that brother of yours."

"Why, Amir didn't show up again?"

"I'm not saying that he didn't show... I'm saying he hasn't arrived as of yet and maybe he is just running a little late that's all."

"Running late my as-"

"Sherry!"

"Sorry dad but I just don't know why you keep making excuses for him. When all he wants to do is keep running those streets with Damon and them pretending to be some kind of gangster boss until he ends up dead or in jail like half of his other friends. You know they just locked Tom's ass up. The one who's always over our house said he robbed that bank downtown. And

I bet you it's not his first one either."

7

"I'm sorry to hear that about Tommy he a good kid remind me to have someone go down there to see him."

"See that what I'm talking about you always got an excuse for them. The man robbed a damn bank at gunpoint."

"Wait! I didn't say if he did it or not... either way, he going to need someone by his side knowing his family. But as far Amir goes it's because he's my son and giving up on him isn't an option. Hell, you were hard-headed at a time also. Myself included before going off into the military."

"Yeah dad I know and they showed you what kind of a man you truly could be. You only told me just a thousand times." "Ha...Ha... Sherry, you know I'm starting to think that you have incorrectly taken my hopefulness for excuses."

"I'm sorry dad but I see the anguish on your face every time Amir lets you down and that stress isn't good for your heart. I guess what I'm trying to say is don't give up on him just lower your expectations a little and then maybe he won't let you down as much."

"I hear you dear but wait... I think I see him coming now."

"Okay, love you dad, and if that's not him call me back and I'll come down there to help you."

"Love you more princess," Mr. Patrick hung up the phone smiling. *"I knew my boy wouldn't let me down."* He quickly turned to gather his notes hearing the doorbell chime. He concealed his smile, *"You're late but I knew you wouldn't let me down."*

"The hell with you, I couldn't let my-my- myself down," The drunk man's words slurred as he bumped into the freezer. *"Shit I need me a drink now! An- an and if I don't get it from here I gotta walk all the way to 125th stree- street. Pl- plus it's cold and it might start raining again and my feet are killing me. You know they aren't built for that much walking anymore from what happened when we were in the war."*

Mr. Patrick turned to witness his old pal struggling to keep his balance leaning against the chip rack.

"Sorry, Dave I'm closed."

"No don't you try that one on me, you got me with that the last time. It's 11:59 and you close at 12:00 which means I'm early," Dave contested, pointing to the wall clock as he adjusted his dirty Yankees hat.

"Ain't this something the man can't even stand upright but he can tell time," Mr. Patrick whispered.

"Yeah and I sure can hear you too, don't think jus-just because I take a few sips every now and then that I'm not on point.

Hell, I'm like a number two pencil right out the sharpener... like that red van that keeps riding around here as if nobody sees it.

But I'll tell you one thing they won't be getting my drank I'll bet you that."

"I know Dave, now what can I get you?"

"Pat you know I'm old school lemme get a double duce can of ole E and a brown paper bag because I got to keep mine on the low key. The boys are watching."

"Okay, but how about you help me clean up and I'll give you a large turkey hoagie to go along with that but you must leave right after because I'm running late."

Mr. Patrick always wanting to make sure Dave ate while hating to be so harsh with his military buddy and friend for over 40 years but to see him rehabilitated back into his old self he knew tough love was the only way.

"Make it two double deuces and a small hoagie and you got a deal." "Same old Dave."

"Hey, you gotta love me! I work cheaper than the Mexicans and I'm going to be hereafter Trump kicks them out."

"That's not right, but let me run in the back and find out where this boy put the broom and you can start by sweeping up." Mr. Patrick disappeared into the storage room.

"Yeah, you do that while I go and secure my cart so nobody takes my precious belongings."

"Okay."

Dave eased the door back stumbling onto the welcome mat making the door alert his presence when a gloved hand occupying a black automatic Glock came through the threshold stopping in the center of his face.

"Don't you fucking move you hear me?"

Dave wanting to warn his comrade but having seen the damage first hand of what the weapon could do to men at pointblank range. He knew he would have been issued a closed casket in a split second. Reluctantly he agreed.

The masked man without removing his weapon lightly placed his foot onto the welcome mat next to Dave's, slowly feeling it out. Content, he lowered his aim giving a short head nod.

Dave suddenly sober as the day he was born let out a deep breath of relief. Then the door swung open fully with another masked man pulling him off his feet and out into the darkness of the night.

The masked men quickly repeating the foot trick until two of the three men were standing on each side of the storage room door due to the information provided by Dave. The one remaining on the mat received a head nod.

Ding Dong!

"Dave I'll be right there." Mr. Patrick yelled, not finding the new broom he snatched the old one and headed out. "Dave this will have to d- what the hell."

The men grasped hold of Mr. Patrick withstanding his attempt to break loose. "Get your damn hands the hell off of me!"

"Don't worry we will as soon as we get what we came for."

"Came for, there must be some kind of mistake I have nothing but pennies and scraps."

"Sshhh," The leader of masked men placed his finger onto Mr. Patrick's lips, "The gig is up old-timer. You know why we're here just hand it over and we'll be gone as quickly as we came."

"Okay... Okay, I know when I'm in a no-win situation...may I." Mr. Patrick pointing behind the counter. With a quick nod, the men released Mr. Patrick.

"You two check the back just in case the old man is pulling our leg."

Mr. Patrick trailed by the barrel of a gun walked behind the counter. "Now where did I put those keys?"

"Now that's what I'm talking about."

"Here they are." Mr. Patrick retrieved a gold key ring from an empty candy jar placing one into the cash register when he was hit abruptly.

"Aaaahh!"

The corner store ceiling light shook wildly back and forth as the force from the butt of the P39 automatic slammed upside Mr. Patrick's head again knocking him back against the wall as he fought to remain conscious. "I'm telling you this is not a game! Now, where is it...?"

"Get up!" The masked man yelled interrupting Mr. Patrick's thoughts as he was brought back to the present moment dragging him onto his feet.

The invader looking Mr. Patrick dead in the eye stating, "I'm about to demonstrate to you how serious I am about this. So

I'm going to ask once more and if I don't hear the right answer I'm going to take this mask off and you will surely die. Do you understand me? Now, where is it?"

Mr. Patrick took several short breaths through his nose as trained to preserve energy, before raising his slumped head high returning the man's stare. He locked onto his green eyes slowly parting his lips hating what he had to do. Now knowing all he'd worked for in life, would be taken like this. Sadly he had forgotten one of the main rules he was taught as a kid. *That anyone could become prey.*

"Well let me see that ugly mug of yours and I just might piss on it for you fagot. Will that make you happy tinker bell."

Mr. Patrick having nothing left to lose threw a fast right jab at the man's face grazing his chin as he dipped to the side just slipping the punch.

"You want that work old-timer I see, well let's get it!" The masked man snickered knocking down Mr. Patrick's follow up blow. He returned with a brutal gut-shot sending it hard to the left side of Mr. Patrick's body.

"Aaaahh!"

He watched Mr. Patrick double over and on instinct he clutched the back of his head with two hands, cocking back his knee aiming for Mr. Patrick's forehead.

"Yo yo... son, what the fuck are you doing?" Grilled the second masked man rushing out from the back overhearing Mr. Patrick's cries. He aggressively pulled his partner apart from Mr. Patrick.

"Remember the man is not to be touched!"

"I know but this nigga is acting like he wants that smoke."

"I don't care what he wants you're not going to be the one who gives it to him. We found the safe so you just be cool and play your position until we're clear you hear me, none of that Rambo shit son word not on this one."

"You found it?"

"No doubt and its loaded nigga we lit." The two high fived with a quick embrace as Mr. Patrick's hand inched toward the cigar box.

"So put him in one of those freezers then come in the back and help unload." The second masked man uttered rushing off.

The one remaining stared off in a daze thinking of the Range Rover he was soon to purchase. He rubbed his hands together visualizing the African girl Mojica from down the block who only dated ballers giving him dripping wet head in the comfort of the plush leather heated seats in the new car he would buy.

"Yeah, bitch eat all of that." He thought rotating to face Mr. Patrick with a big smile that instantly disappeared.

Mr. Patrick's finger tightened around the trigger of his weapon aimed at the masked man's heart.

"Come on old-timer don't do anything stupid." He pleaded as his own weapon eased upward.

"The only thing I did stupid was not kill you soon enough punk."

The masked man's perception of a murderer was accurate for he made his livelihood off of it. Therefore he knew the owner's words were anything but a bluff. He quickly jerked his gun toward Mr. Patrick's direction as a shot ripped through his chest followed by another.

"You old Baster-!" The masked man's body tightened on contact unknowingly he returned fire inevitably feeling the soul that possessed his life, leave him.

With the echoes of gunfire in the air, the two men quickly took cover in the doorway, one high and the other low.

"We move on three, I'll go first you cover me," The masked man moved with caution into the storefront prepared to kill. The point man paused infuriated as rage bolted through his veins at the vision of his partner and store owner lying in a mixed puddle of blood motionless.

The sight of death has become the norm for these men so he recognized immediately they were gone. He turned to place a hand on his partner's chest, saving him from the gruesome memory that he knew he would never forget.

"Don't... it's too late, they're gone."

"What, nook!" He shouted dropping his weapon running to assist but the grip on his forearm was too powerful?

"Listen, I need you to pull it together we came here on a mission and we got to finish it, that's the way he would want it."
"Okay just give me one second to say goodbye."

"We don't have it, the shots went off 30 seconds ago which means the cops will be here in five minutes or less. It's going to take two minutes to reach the wheel."

The man snatched his arm free, "I don't care if the cops were standing right the fuck there, the man's going to get the respect he deserves. You got a problem with that?" He clenched the handle of his back up weapon lodged in the center of his back waiting on an answer.

"Alright, just make it quick." The other agreed thinking *to himself "I don't care if it was his family... this guy is getting soft."*

He watched his partner just stand there in a 'daze for a few moments before saying some limited words then closed both men's eyes. The time was four minutes and fifty-eight seconds when they evaded the block as swiftly as they arrived leaving nothing behind but an enemy that always kept his promise.

2

"**D**ispatch this is detective Heather number 13 exit-"

"Rising up, back on the street, did my time took my chances?" The Rocky ringtone erupted from Heather's phone reminding her that she would be missing yet another girl's night out with her BFF and sorority sister Stephanie.

"Shit!"

"Pardon me?"

"Oh sorry, not you Dispatch 13 exiting the vehicle, over."

"Roger that, 13 we have you and that nasty mouth of yours back at the base, over."

Heather departed her Lexus LS stepping out into the brisk night air. She took a deep breath before answering, "Stephanie dear I was just about to call you."

"No no no...Heather please not again! I can't take another day off going out by myself. You know me, I always end up combatting off every man that hits on me because I'm too busy reading their shortcomings. Therefore I need my wing bitch there with me to bring out my inner Hoe as only you can."

"So what are you trying to say I'm a freak and it takes one to bring yours out?"

"No not at all bitch...but then again yes." They both laughed. "Girl after that third drink you can make me look past all that he's not the perfect man shit and just get my panties out of this knot they been in for the last three months. Plus you keep working at the rate you are your pussy may not open when its time."

"In other words, I'm locking everything up even my kitty cat ...Ha...ha... But Stephanie I'm coming don't worry, you don't have to lay the guilt trip on me. All I was going to say is that I'm running a little late and I will be at Gotham before you have time to take down your second drink."

"Heather that's why I love you because you always speak from the heart but your mind tells a different story. So we both know you're not coming and my night will consist of me watching our favorite movie with a pint of strawberry ice cream alone."

"No that's the farthest thing from the truth. I'm at the office now, I'm just going to run in and hand in my report. Give my authorization on a few things I'm behind on and then I'm on my way."

"That's nice but as a criminal psychologist let me tell you what your brain informed me of without you knowing it. First, you let the phone ring four times meaning that you didn't want to answer but the loyalty you have for our friendship impelled you to do so. Second, the long exhale before you began speaking let me know there was something disappointing to be spoking whether you said it or not. Thirdly the fact that you never started walking and still standing at your car means you're in no rush but to get back to work. I'm not mad at you girl another time I'm sure, love you bye-bye."

"You know what, I hate you hussy bye." The phone disconnected with Heather now comprehending why nobody wanted to go up against her friend's in court. She smiled readjusting her jacket around her slim model 34-24-34 physique. She sprinted up the steps to the sound of her heels tipping as she headed into the special homicide division building on 130th street.

Inside, she found her newly assigned rookie partner Jake standing in the wing. He had been waiting for her arrival for hours holding a stack of files, with a pen and iPad eager to learn.

"God, why me?" Heather thought, running her hands through her shoulder-length brown hair.

"You're late."

"When am I ever on time and what's up with your face why are you looking at me like that?"

"Overjoyed I believe."

"It's that but there's something about eyes every time I see them I could swear I know them from somewhere? But I never forget a face?" Heather stated without stopping. She walked at her up tempo-pace while Jake struggled to keep up.

"Heather you know that statistics show that 73 percent of great people who are often late can't handle everything that's on their plate and will eventually substitute their attention from one thing to the next until they completely lose focus all together of what once made them great in the first place?"

"Well, you tell whoever did that statistic that I have everything under control and they need to mind their own damn business and stay the hell out of mine." Heather contemplating, *this little shit is trying to read me.*

"Point noticed, boss."

"Oh and have some flowers sent to Stephanie."

"What, you missing another ladies' night out?"

"And what makes you think that?"

"Because you're here with me and if I'm not mistaken this is the day you had me schedule you off to replace ya'll last gathering you avoided."

"Jake has anyone ever told you you're a fucking prick."

"As of lately no."

"Well, I am."

Heather picked her pace back up while scanned the large office observing if anything had changed within the last 15 hours she was away on a stakeout.

"I see Alex has rearranged his desk again for the tenth time... I've got to find him something to do. He's too skillful of a detective to have his talent forced to rot at that desk for being a little rough... Shit! Only three cases have been solved out of the seventy-four homicides that's one every five hours... we have to do better."

Heather stopped with her eyes centering on a picture pinned to the bulletin board of a 13-year-old girl that was murdered two months prior while walking home from dance class.

"Jamie we will find your killer, I promise." She whispered meaning it to her soul.

Unconsciously her stare shifted to the name Barbara Evans as it did every time she walked through the double doors. It was the only case to date she has yet to keep her promise of finding the killer within a year. Actual several years had passed since Barbara was murdered however Heather refused to allow anyone to mark it as a cold case because she always kept her promise. She worked on the case mentally every day though her body was needed elsewhere. "Barbara I will never forget you …we are going to do better."

"Excuse me, boss did you say something?"

"Yeah, anything new on Barbara's case-"

"Yo cop get ya hands the fuck up off of me I didn't do shit!" Yelled a man in cuffs being roughly pushed through the front doors.

"Yeah…yeah, that's what they all say now keep walking."

"I can't speak for nobody else but me pussy and you just ran up into my mom's crib for nothing other than I'm black faggot. But don't worry I was on live when it happen everybody saw you."

"No, we ran up into your mother's home because you killed Darrel Marion because he moved in on your pill operation," corrected detective David.

"Fuck you, you bitch ass cop. All you mother fuckers do is lie. I didn't do shit and that's all the fuck I'm going to say. This ain't going to be no first 48 shit where I tell on myself in the whole hood. You can miss me with that shit word son. I want to see my lawyer right the fuck now."

"You remember this and don't come snitching to me later when you realize I got your ass for life." Detective David pushed the man into the holding cell.

"I guess David is going to close the Marion's case."

"I hope so. Now, what's on my plate for today? I know you weren't waiting on me for nothing."

"Yes, there has been a lot going on around here lately. To begin with there are no new leads in the Barbara case at this very moment but I'm making sure someone is working on it around the clock."

"Okay."

"The Captain has a suspect in the interrogation room and he's waiting on you."

"Me?"

"Yes, and he won't permit anyone else to speak to him. Also, the head office downtown keeps calling requesting a copy of the search warrant you used in the Johnson's case somehow their copy has been misplaced. I expressed to them that I don't know how that could have occurred but you would get it there as soon as possible."

"Nice lie. At least they heard it from you this time and not me."

"Excuse me I don't understand."

"Believe me if you make it long enough in this profession you will."

"I hope so boss I hope so."

Jake who majored in criminal justice at Syracuse while minoring in psychology; believing it would help him identify with the mind of a criminal thought he noticed a particular bitterness hidden within Heather's statement, *"I wonder why."* He continued to update her,

"And last but not least this just came in through dispatch and I thought that you might want to hear about it. A store owner in Harlem on 145th street was murdered just a few hours ago and it seems he killed one of his invaders."

"That's my old neighborhood."

"I know, I had this e-mailed over… do you know him?"

Heather placed her hand over her mouth, "My God that's Mr. Patrick. He would give my mother groceries for free when I was a kid after she lost her job. Finally, months later she found one but if not he still would be giving her groceries today with no problem. That's just how caring he was." Heather was back in that moment with just the thought of her hard upbringing. The sour dry tasted of an empty stomach was fresh in her mouth. "Boss are you okay."

"I can't believe someone would do this to him."

"Boss for what it's worth I'm sorry for your loss? You need me to get you anything."

"No I'm fine but you're never okay when someone you care about is murdered like a dog. All you can do is make those who did it pay and in time the wounds will heal."

"That has been recorded but I, on the other hand, agree with Rose Kennedy when she stated that, *the wounds remain but in time the mind protecting its sanity, covers them with scar tissue and the pain lessens. But it is never gone.*"

"Odd, not too many people think like you but we`ll see,"

"So we're taking the case?"

"Yes, it's the only way I can show my gratitude."

"Yes!"

"Don't be so happy, a man is dead."

"Sorry."

"Now call and find out who is in charge of that crime scene and tell them I want every one of Mr. Patrick neighbors' interviewed at his store and his home within a two-mile ratio and don't touch another thing. Then send Alex down there to see that my orders are followed correctly."

"But he's on desk duty."

"Let me worry about that you just do what I ask of you."

"Right away boss."

"Oh and before I forget change the case number to 70."

"So you solved the Bricke's case, wow! Who did it, the husband?"

"No, it was the mistress."

"Wow, she had me bamboozled."

"Bamboozled?"

"Shocked"

"Jake always remember a crime scene that screams out pure violence..." Heather paused at the sight of several quick flashes in her mind of the bloody crime scene. She shook her head to clear her thoughts then continued. "Nine times out of ten the killer is going to be a woman for that is an emotional act of rage. Now in the case of a man, even when he is killing out of pure fury he still tries to maintain his reflex control to have some order.

You just got to make the connection with the two."

Heather watched Jake's hand aggressively move over the keys of the iPad taking down her every word knowing he wanted to be just like her. Hell, what true detective didn't. She couldn't deny that she appreciated the power that her job provided her. Nevertheless, the stress and nightmares were indescribable that came along with it. Being the prime investigator meant that Heather outranked any other homicide detective in Harlem if not the whole city which meant she had to work twice as hard.

"Consider it handle," Jake answered, placing his phone to his ear while concealing his smirk, for deep down inside he was ecstatic. This would be the first investigation he would be permitted to attend a crime scene in the past nine months he'd been working with Heather. Normally he did the paperwork after the case was solved while memorizing each document anticipating this very moment when she believed he was prepared for the deadly streets of New York.

Jake, in his mind, was ready since the day he was born. His childhood wasn't all peaches and cream he too had his days of starving and sleepless nights. However, he didn't let this discourage his dreams of being a detective. He graduated from the academy at the top of his class with scores so extraordinary that they shortly became classified. After refusing the CIA and

FBI offers Jake was given the opportunity to serve anywhere he pleased.

He was educated at an early age that in order to be the best, he had to be skilled by the best. Therefore he studied Heather's actions to a tee. Who, also graduated top of her class with scores that instantly became classified. She majored in criminal justice with a minor in psychology. So when questioned where he would attend, he just said her name because she was the very best anyone had seen in years.

He removed Heather's jacket while handing her the file on the Captain's suspect which she declined with the wave of a hand. "No, debrief me."

"Well, the perp's name is Antonio Cruz 38 years of age, accused of killing his wife Maria Cruz and her lover Robert Gray by way of a gunshot. He allegedly shot them several times to the upper body in their 7th-floor apartment on 132nd street."

"So Mrs. Cruz liked a little chocolate for dessert."

"I believe so."

"Nothing wrong with that, a girl should have her choice of flavors but once she says I do she needs to stick with that… if not it could kill her."

"In her case literally, both victims were found dead this evening lying in bed together. Officers believed that Antonio shot the victims through the bedroom window which is connected to the fire escape which he used to getaway. There's no positive I.D but some witnesses believe that they may have seen him in the area around the time of the shooting." "Was the bedroom window broken or not?" Heather asked while picturing the crime scene.

"Yes scattered."

"Inside or out?"

"Inside."

"Where were their clothes?"

"In the living room on the floor next to two glasses of wine."

"Did he die while… you know or beside her?"

"I don't understand."

"Come on Jake was he fucking her when he was killed, or were they done and then killed."

"It says here that… the bodies were next to each other and there were traces of semen inside Mrs. Cruz."

"I bet there was."

"But it could be her husband's which would refute your two other implications of during and after. It's possible that it happened beforehand," Jake smiled, happy to be bringing insight to the case that Heather hasn't thought of.

"That's impossible, for one the drinking glasses and clothes indicate that the foreplay happened in the area of the living room. So by the time they moved to the bedroom, it was all or nothing. Jake if you knew anything about a female then you would understand that once a woman's oven is turned on there is no turning it off until the cookie is baked. Therefore it could only be during or after. Two… if the killer was to hit his target before they fucked as you believe that gives him about 5 seconds between kisses to hit them both making him or her a sharpshooter. However, there is no record of Mr. Cruz having a military background is there… No." Heather answered her own question not stopping her point of view. "Because that would have been the first thing you stated for the reason that you and I both know it makes him more likely to kill."

"No he doesn't and a sharpshooter would have used fewer bullets making the before sex impossible."

"Now that we know that he fucked her Jake. Do you know how I acquired this information before stepping into an interrogation room with a person I know is going to feed me more falsehood than truth?"

"Because you worked it out by eliminating what could and couldn't have happened."

"Wrong you only get the truth by becoming one with the crime scene, and not just looking at it...Oh did you just hear that?"

"Hear what?"

"Mrs. Cruz just had an orgasm."

"Funny, the report also said th-."

"That's all. I've got enough."

"But that's only two paragraphs... there are six more papers of Intel."

"Then you read it," Heather opened the first door to the interrogation room to hear a heated argument between Captain Matthews, Assistant District Attorney Cain, and Defense Counsel Baitz.

"I don't care where you have to go, counsel nobody is going in there to see that man until I say so."

"Well let me just state for the record Captain that you're holding my client on nothing but some uncertain hearsay."

"And that nothing you're speaking of gives him the right to hold your client in that chair for 72 hours, thank you." Corrected Assistant D.A. Cain.

"Boys can't we all just get along?" interjected Heather playfully.

"And where the hell have you been?"

Heather paying the Captain's question no mind walked up to the large two-way mirror to get the first glimpse of her target. Antonio was seated in an uneven chair with one handcuffed to the table. She gradually let her eyes trail over his body taking in what a file could never reveal to her. Where he was a cold assassin or not.

She examined his rich black curly hair, thick eyebrows, and moist lips that he seemed to repeatedly lick due to nervousness. She keyed in lastly on his rough hand. *"He's cute."* Heather did this several times until she was certain that she knew his facial expressions and body movements by heart as he was semi-relaxed.

"How long has he been in there?" she inquired moving to the computer rewinding the interrogation room video.

"Five long hours can you believe that? An innocent man is being treated this way after the loss of his wife?" answered defense counsel Baitz.

Heather not seeing anything different on the tape than in person removed her printout knowing it was time for her performance. She grasped the file from Jake's hand turning the doorknob, "Bring me two cups of coffee and make them fresh."

"Okay, but that will take ten minutes to brew the machine is still acting up."

"That will be fine I don't think Mr. Cruz is in a rush. Oh and Counsel If he is not innocent I'll make sure he never leaves here again." *Now let's see how he reacts under pressure.* "

The sound of the door slamming hard got Antonio's attention immediately. "I'm glad you here, I did no spoken to anyone yet, how long I going-."

"Sssshhhh," Heather blew onto her finger receiving the quiet she demanded as she walked around the table several times.

"What the hell is she doing in there?" asked the D.A

"Ah –Ah, yeah Jake what the hell is she doing?" The Captain stuttered hoping Heather wasn't pulling another one of her stunts.

"I believe she is slowly building the tension in the room making the defendant nervous if you look closely you can see the sweat drops forming on his forehead and hands."

Heather at the sight of perspiration rolling down the side of Antonio's face glanced at her watch; *"Five minutes that's odd."* she sat the pictures of the crime scene around the table saving two for last. Antonio's vision became stuck to the wall refusing to look at them.

"What's wrong you're not man enough to look at the mess you left behind, your blood-soaked sheets?" Heather picked the picture up throwing it at his face.

Antonio quickly turned in the opposite direction with the picture missing him within inches. "Me no scared of nothing I don't do this, so I not want to see," Antonio explained with poor English

"Is that right so you admit you can take the sight of brain fragments on the wall if you did do it?" She threw another one.

"Si, but me don't know what you thinking but I love me, wife, to dead."

"I know that now because she's dead and you killed her." Heather threw another.

"No, no true I did nothing."

"Then where were you at the time of the murder because it says here you were walking to work alone meaning you have no alibi."

"Does this make me a murderer I walk to trabajo…ah, ah as you say… work, every day to feed me familia."

"No it doesn't and it doesn't make you innocent either. Let me ask you this Mr. Cruz, are you a racist?"

"No me have friends of all kind Blanco, Negro it means nada to me."

"Are you sure?" Heather threw another picture harder this time waiting to make her move. Antonio turned away when he came face to face with the picture of his dead wife lying on a cold steel table in the morgue.

"Mariaaaa nooo! My love my sweetheart." Antonio sobbed taking the picture from Heather's hand holding it close to his heart. Heather refusing to let him get off with just a few tears.

"I know one thing for sure Maria wasn't a racist, in fact, she loved black people like this guy, her black monster cock lover." Antonio's head turned without hesitation facing the photo snatching it with pure hatred in his eyes.

"You f-king Nigga I'm going to kill you over and over again." He spit on the picture when a knock came to the door.

"Come in"

Jake eased the door back carrying a coffee in each hand, "Here you go boss lady and one for you sir." Antonio removed his eyes from the picture to say thanks when he suddenly spits on Jake as he shot to his feet backhanding him across the face with his free hand.

Jake fell back against the glass mirror seeing stars.

Antonio cocked back his foot aiming for Jake's head when Heather's gun clicked as it pressed firmly into the center of his back.

"That's enough." She forcefully pushed Antonio's face down into the table. He raised his hand in the air releasing the picture surrendering, "Me kill you cock-a-roach."

The door flew open with all three men rushing in. Jake standing up straight, adjusted his shirt regaining his composure. He made a gun gesture with his hand saying

"I know you would try and fell poorly like the others because you will let my appearance mislead you to die."

Jake revealed a mysterious smirk before bending down picking up the pictures placing them back in the file. The smirk progressively formed a smile toward Heather now understanding the man's anger seeing a photo of himself taken the day of the office cookout.

He whispered to Heather "Excellent trick if he believes I'm his wife's lover then he's not the killer."

"True and that there wasn't an act, but the killer is close," Heather stated thinking of the few possibilities exiting the room.

"And may I ask then who the hell is it?" Questioned the Captain as he followed.

"I don't know precisely captain but if I were you I would start with the defense counsel's phone records. Because if Cruz hasn't spoken to anyone since he's been here then he couldn't have placed a phone call so who called the lawyer?"

"Maybe someone that doesn't want Mr. Antonio to go to jail for a crime he didn't commit." answered Captain Matthews when it hit him, "Hold on, what you mean if you were me."

"Sorry Captain you have to find someone else to work this one I have another case I'm already involved with," Heather stated commencing towards the main door.

"Now wait just a got damn minute Missy, another case from who, I'm the director of this show." The Captain pulled Heather aside so no one could hear him.

"Heather don't pull this shit on me now. I don't know who this lady was but I got a call from the Mayor himself asking that this case be closed quietly and not to mention fast."

"I understand Captain a call from the Mayor that sounds like some deep business but what I'm about to do is personal. But if it will help, whoever you get to handle it I will keep my eyes on them to see that it's done right."

"Heather again this is no time to be playing games, if this goes badly my ass will be in the air and you know what happens to an ass that's in the air."

"Eww, save me the image. Don't worry I promise I got you. Come on Jake I have a tab to settle."

"Right behind you boss."

"Oh and Cap, Alex will be working this one with me."

"Like hell he is, that man is on desk duty for the two people he shot last week!"

"Don't worry he'll be cleared of that also, he always is."

"Heather I'm not playing with you-." The door slammed cutting the Captain off in midsentence. "Damn it I hate that she's the best!"

3

A few hours previously, in an expensive but not too upscale apartment building. Damon and Frankie stood outside residence 8A. They waited patiently for over twenty minutes until the sound of locks being unlatched made Damon look to his
Italian friend curiously,

"Yo what was taking your people so fucking long? I don't have time for no funny shit on this move, either they got it or they don't. If you're not sure let's bounce."

"Just be cool everything is fine."

"Ok, Frankie but if this goes wrong it's on you."

"I know, but you remember when we were in the joint what I told you about this moment?"

"That you were connected and we were going to do big business in the world when you touched down."

"And I'm here now and that's exactly what we're going to do, so relax!" Frankie smiled. He knew that soon he would be back at the top of the mob in no time and this was just the first installment in doing so. He was released from the Federal penitentiary five days ago after serving a ten-year bid. From the instant he when in until now, all he could think about was taking his spot back.

He looked at the black Gucci bag on Damon's shoulder containing a hundred and sixty thousand in large bills. A bit smaller than what he was used to but for now it would have to do.

"I hope so," Damon whispered not wanting his best friend and mentor Amir to be right about Frankie as he looked to the backup 22 automatic placed inside his oversized Timberland boot.

The door slowly parted

"After you," said Damon as he once again inspected his surroundings. He looked in both directions of the dim-lit hallway checking for any signs of a setup. He paused deliberating on a bum three doors down lying on the floor sleep smelling of a mixture of piss, whiskey, and funk.

"How the fuck he get in here?" Damon tried to get a closer look at his face but he couldn't. *"He's black so he isn't with the Italians because they don't like Nigga's in their business at all. Shit if they knew this was my money instead of Frankie's he never would have gotten this meeting."*

Damon altered his vision in the direction of the only other man in the hallway. He was positioned at the far end of the hall pretending to be in a deep conversation with a female. Damon noticed the man's hands kept raising to his ear out of impulse. Which he believed was due to the bad connections with the earpiece hidden beneath his long hair. The man's hand rose to his ear as his head lowered toward the ground to gain focus for the fifth time.

"Lol another lookout, trying to become a made man." Damon laughed.

He followed Frankie into the appealing apartment immediately being searched forcefully by a 6-foot clean face Italian man in an expensive suit. He was liberated of his 45 automatic in the center of his back.

"Yo Frankie what the fuck is this."

"Don't sweat it, guns just make Sammy uneasy that's all they'll give it back when we depart I'll see to it."

"Okay, but you know I don't feel right without my baby." Damon let out a deep breath beginning to get an uncharacteristic feeling in his gut. He wondered now if he should have listened to Amir.

Though Amir was arrogant and only two years older than him at 23, Damon knew he played the game with the rules and the mind state of a true O.G. He put in work utilizing patience that many young men their age didn't have any more while matching it with the mentality to win at all cost. A skill that he learned from his father.

Amir would listen to the older players on the block and scrutinizing them as well as classic gangster movies at any chance he got. He took in the right moves and rejecting what was wrong when it came to street life. The issue was why Damon didn't get it.

Amir's principle was clear if he were going to rob a man, a plan was needed, a gun for sure and the heart to pull the trigger if necessary.

Damon, on the other hand, thought all he needed was a gun and someone to kill. While being lead into the plush living room he started to thinking of Amir's disapproval in his head....

* * * * * *

"Don't do that shit I'm telling you, fuck them Italians. The only thing they ever did for a Nigga is leaving Harlem and that was by force."

"I hear you Amir but you need to get down with this move, I'm telling you. It could be our big break."

"I highly doubt it," Amir said pouring himself another cup of black coffee a habit he acquired from his father believing it kept his mind sharp in times of putting in work. He took a seat at the table giving his young partner his full attention knowing this deal meant a lot to him. This was his chance to prove his independence.

"Come on just check it out because you never did let me tell you the whole plot of the plan." Damon tried once more.

"You didn't have too, I paid attention to what goes on around me and I heard enough to know that it doesn't sound right."

"If it didn't sound on point, do you think I'd be putting up my savings?"

"No, not at all."

"Alright then give me some credit nigga, we out here and all I'm trying to do is bake my bread and watch it rise."

"You're right Damon." The two did there special handshake as Amir continued, *"We are the streets, check in with us or get checked by us, no fucking doubt. So I definitely got to give you, your just due because you stay on a dollar. Ever since you put yourself on with my little bit of help, your drip hasn't been off but..."* Amir's face turned stone cold, *"On this one, you're not listening to the words on the play. It seems to me on this line up you're the fucking prey."*

"How can you say that?"

"Because you're listening to a so-called friend who had years to build on your intelligence for this moment. In the lifestyle, we're living there are only enemies. So if I was you I would place a backup gun in my boot something small so it won't be too uncomfortable. Trust, you will be searched. The question is if Frankie will be searched also. If not, he's in on it if something goes wrong."

"Don't be ridiculous everybody ain't your enemy, especially not me."

"Truth indeed... in parts."

"In parts what? I don't need anything from you so how can you say some shit like that?"

"Because the ones who are not your enemies are potential enemies. Because what we do involve money in every aspect or we wouldn't be doing it. The undeniable fact is that money is the essence of evil in any four corners of this world. Therefore no matter how you put it any person is still a potential enemy. It just comes down to when will they strike and for what price. But then again who knows I could be wrong about Frankie." Amir chuckled, *"He could be different from all us nigga's trying to master a dollar. Whatever the case if I was you I would put most of that money back in your safe and give your friend a coming home check. No matter if it's a hooker or some cash whatever the case call it a day. Believe me, it will end better. If not protect your body then wait on it."*

"Well your wrong on this one, Frankie is cool plus he is well connected with the respect of all the big Italians."

"Fuck if they respect him, the point is if he respects you enough for you to keep your paper, cause at the end of the day your bankroll is at stake, not mine or his. Just know in every plot there has to be a target, a stage for deception and a reason to kill for a con to work."

"Listen I understand your concerns Amir, but you should come along and I'll introduce you to him no business needed; we can all just chill."

"No thanks, it's only going to make things harder for you when I'm killing him for putting you in the crossfire. So you really don't want me around that man. I just might rob him because Trump is in office. Plus I got to help my father out at the store again tonight. I can't dip out on him he's been on my back lately about not showing up and shit."

"Now that's funny a killer sweeping floors...

* * * * **

Damon laughed knowing Amir loved his father with his all and would kill the world for him. But the thought of him talking slick with his gun on his hip and do-rag on standing at 5'11'' 195 lb. all muscle pushing a mop in Tim's. *"That's not gangster."*

Damon arrived in the living area spotting two armed men standing off in each far corners of the room while Sammy relaxed on a large white leather sofa with his back toward them watching the game. The room aroma was of luxurious cigars as the Cuban Savanna smoke slowly retracted from Sammy's lips into the ceiling. The bodyguard in the expensive suit raised his hand stopping Damon and Frankie a few feet from Sammy.

Damon studied Sammy's face pondering to himself before whispering, "Yo Frankie, I believe I know him."

"Sssshh keep your voice down he doesn't like to be disturbed, plus that's impossible he just come over from Italy a few months ago."

"I understand that but I know this guy from somewhere."

33

"Maybe in passing because prior to that, I think like over eight years ago he was in America and was about to become a Capo like his father and his father's father before him. However, he made a critical mistake and was forced to go back to the homeland to be taught our ways again from its roots now he's back."

The escort approached Sammy alone. He stood beside him in silence until a commercial, "Boss Frankie is here."

"Jerk off do you know how much freaking money I'm losing on these Knicks."

"I understand Boss but its good old Frankie."

"Yeah, you're right good old Frankie." Sammy stood to his feet slowly rotating the flame of his cigar against the marble ashtray back and forth making sure not to mark it. He turned with open arms.

"Frankie come over here and let me see you. It has been a long, long time aye."

The two embraced with Sammy kissing Frankie on his left cheek.

"Glad to see you back and my family really appreciate this. It is so sad how you caught that bad break of yours."

"It's fine Sammy that's all behind me now,"

"I understand but nobody should have to live in that fucking hole that they call jail that shit for the worms."

"Your right but now it's about the future at hand, and I'd like for you to meet a good friend of mind Damon out of Harlem."

"Nice to meet you, Sammy."

"No, I believe the pleasure is all mines."

"Thank you, sir... Frankie, I can speak to you for a second?"

"In a minute Damon I came here to handle some business with an old friend and I believe we should get that out the way first. Sammy if you don't mind, the diamonds."

"Oh yes." Sammy gave a nod and one of the armed men disappeared from the room.

"But this will only take a minute Frankie."

"Then it can wait, Damon, the bag please," Frankie extended his hand at the sight of the man returning with a black suitcase.

"Damon... Damon?"

Sammy repeated the name as it ran through his thoughts "Harlem ...you wouldn't be the same Damon that runs with that guy Amir?"

"Amir..." Damon mumbled looking Sammy dead in the eyes before answering, "No I never heard of him, Sir. There has to be another Damon. Excuse me is there somewhere I can relieve myself. I really have to go."

"Yes be my guess, Randy show this gentleman to the restroom."

Frankie shot Damon a questionable look as he was lead down the hall to a room on the right.

Inside the extraordinarily clean white on white bathroom, Damon placed his ear to the door listening for departing footsteps.

"Shit he's still there!" He quickly turned on the water letting it run drowning out the sound of him dialing.

"Come on Amir pick up." Damon pleading as if his friend could hear him. He pressed end, immediately calling back. He paced back and forth while his mind jumped through the past event in his life.

"Damn, what the hell have I got myself into?" He questioned remembering the day he was walking the track in Lewisburg penitentiary and first met Frankie....

* * * * *

The sun was beaming at its peak with the temperature at a delightful 83 degrees which meant every weightlifter, gambler and killer were present in the yard. Each trying to get a piece of the only freedom they become accustom too. Damon was on his third lap around the massive yard enjoying the nice breeze when Frankie interrupted him,

"Excuse me, fella, can I trouble you for a square?"

Damon didn't know the man's name but had seen him around companied by two in shape Italian men that permanently trailed a few steps behind him. He sensed that the man was mob connected big time.

"Sorry but I don't smoke." He replied walking around the man as if he never existed.

"But you do keep a few backup packs in the inside pocket of your windbreaker to buy something to eat or to pay for your weekly laundry and meats bill."

Damon paused, then saying without turning around "You must have me mistaken ah-"

"Frankie...the name its Frankie Alinara and I trust you're the right person. You still keep them right next to your knife?"

"Knife!"

"Yeah, why else would you be wearing a jacket in such good God-given weather?"

Damon eased his jacket open as he turned back around approaching Frankie whose men quickly stepped in front of him. Frankie flickered his hand waving them off "Let the young man through, hell we're the ones who are interrupted him."

"My jacket, it keeps me slippery but later for that, what's the deal with you Frankie and why are you watching me?" Damon prepared to strike but hesitated to ponder the man's angle more than his death.

"Just a little, fella relax. I mean you're not in any harm's way. In fact, I think I can save you some trouble."

"And how is that?"

"Take a look about twenty yards in the direction you were walking by the weight pile, what is it that you see?"

"A bunch of white dudes trying to get big, so what that got to do with m- hold on where are the blacks? Oh, shit something going down." *Damon quickly scanned the area not finding one person of color lifting weights which is like trump not having white people in the white house. It's damn near unthinkable.*

"You're correct, now focus your sights on the short Italian with grey hair getting up from the bench. He's an underboss in another family."

"Yo son what type of freaky fuck shit you on, watching that man kiss another man on the face? I'm not with that fagot shit I'm out!"

"If you were Italian you would know that was the sign your eyes were just searching for. Now, wait and continue to watch. The signature of a made-man is to greet another mademan with a kiss on each cheek meaning a solid bond of life in our world. But if there is only one kiss to the left cheek it meant the word was approved from the Boss for someone's death."

Damon continued to watch the man who received the kiss wait until the underboss was back at his seat comfortably before giving a short nod. Immediately several men began stabbing a man standing by the shoulder rack until his body stopped moving....

Damon continued to pace the marble white floor whispering into the phone, "Amir I hate to say it but man you were right, something is wrong here, I need you, man... I need you bad son this situation is all or nothing! If you come through for me this one last time I swear I'll never ask you for anything again." Damon quickly texted Amir his location, the number of men and their position as he thought of Sammy kissing Frankie on the left cheek only, "You bastard!"

Boom Boom! The bathroom door vibrated. "Hey, guy you okay, in there."

"Yeah I'm taking a shit Nigga is that okay with you?"

"Well make it quick you have people waiting on you." Damon hurriedly loosens his boot gripping hold of the gun's handle. *"I know they're waiting but I'm not going out like no sucka."* Damon cocked back the hammer sending a bullet into the chamber when the instinctive sound made him remember where he knew Sammy from.....

* * * * * *

One day while making his way home after skipping yet another day of school Damon spotted a familiar face sitting on a set of house steps. He smirked approaching Amir and Keith as they passed the Dutch between them as the day fading into nightfall.

"Yo Son was scared to death you hear me? When I jumped out that closet with the desert on him," stated Keith laughing

"Yeah I still would've downed him for getting piss on my Prada's"

"Man fuck them shoes we got forty- five bands off that sucka."

Damon as he got closer wondering why they were in his neighborhood. However, knowing their reputation it wasn't going to be good for someone. In the end, he could care less, this was his chance to speak to Amir who quickly was becoming a boss in the streets and he was going to take it. He took a deep breath while putting his pride to the side saying,

"Come on Amir let me hit that sour and get with some of those moves I know you be, making."

"Go head young buck this shit I'm on is not for you, people get hurt for real." Amir laughed passing the Duchy back to Keith.

"What you mean not for me, you got on the fake beard and that makeup shit to make your face look darker. So that means whatever your doing has to involve money and do it look like I'm not in need of a bag?"

Amir glanced at Damon's too small hoodie, ashy black jeans, and dirty sneakers. He thought of the rumors about Damon's mother being some kind of a big-time drug hustler in her day until she started to get high off the product. She now was turning tricks just to feed her and Damon.

Amir deep down inside felt sorry for Damon and wanted to go inside his pocket and give him a few thousand to help out but he just gave him a head nod letting him know he understood his struggle.

"That's it, not a, I feel you and this is what I can do for you nothing."

Amir remained silent.

"Okay, you just sit there and keep smoking with this lame ass nigga when I could be your real point man and shooting guard like Westbrook."

"Watch your mouth little nigga this shit is only for real head hitters." Keith cut in knowing the young buck was on hard times at the moment but he surely didn't want to get into business with Amir who knew loyalty but was the true meaning of going hard.

"I'm not talking to you Keith I'm talking to your boss with the funny windbreaker on."

"What you say nigga I'll blow your fucking head off." Keith jumped to his feet cocking back a chrome desert eagle from his waistband.

"Be easy Keith I know the man didn't mean any harm... right young buck and the reason for the windbreaker is it make me slippery when the action is on."

"Fuck Keith and you know what they say about niggas that's quick to pull there weapon."

"No, what they say about us."

"That you can't fight. But Keith here is double fucked because everybody knows he's quick to pull his gun and shoot up into the air but he never hit anybody, not even a stray. That's how I know he's not going to shoot me. And stop with this young *buck shit your only two years older than me and we used to be in the same school when you wore clothes like mine."*

Amir checked his watch... 7:53 pm as Keith's gun locked on Damon's face.

"Damon, you think I'm playing with your dumbass?" Keith questioned.

Damon was silent staring down the barrel of the massive gun as Amir continued to scan the area waiting on the sound of the shots.

"Look at you all scared and shit."

"I ain't bothered about shit."

"Nigga you better go ahead or you're going to force me to put a hole in your face."

At 7:58 pm Amir snatched the gun from Keith's hand demanding, "Step off, I was too busy busting my gun to even notice that you never really let yours rip into someone flesh." "Come on don't do this Amir, what about the plan?"

"That's not your business anymore now get the fuck out of here before I bang you, pussy."

"Alright, you got it." Keith uttered keeping the last part of his statement to himself but he wanted it noted, "I'm going to get both of ya'll for this."

Amir without delay looked at his watch reading 7:59 "Shit! Damon, I hope you know how to use one of these because it's show time." Amir's watch beeped at 8 sharp just as a black Benz pulled to a stop a little way up the block. An Italian man quickly exited opening the back door.

"I'm ready."

"We'll see soon enough, now the man getting out of the back seat he is our target. When he returns from that house he will have a suitcase that belongs to us."

"What, someone took it from you?"

"Nigga when I'm on the scene everything is mine. Now it's ours and that's all you need to worry about, so are you riding or nah? I can do it myself but it's just going to be

*bloodier than I would like." "Like they never made brakes,"
Damon answered with confidence.*

"Talk heavy, now what I need you to do is walk down the
block, go about four cars then cross the street as if it's just
another day. Make sure nobody is laying in the cut. At the
corner dip into the alley and race back as fast as you can to the
top of the block on the opposite side and cover me as I get busy.
No matter what happens they can't make it back to that Benz
with the suitcase. You got that?"

"I hear you but it doesn't mean anything until we have
the case right?"

"Right and always keep your head tilted down at a
90degree angle when you're working. Not too high and not to
low just in case someone is looking. You never want anybody to
know who is really putting in the work. Because when they do, it
will be the end of you."

"But I have been heard you were getting busy."
"Fuck what you hear. Nigga's will say anything once you start
getting fly and fucking their bitches. It's what they can prove
that counts."

Damon started on his way when Amir gripped hold of his
wrist. "One more thing and you can go. This is a job we do to
eat this is no games so never play with it or you will end up
being the one getting played I'm telling you. "

Damon disappeared around the corner hoping that he
made the right decision as he slid into action. He reached the
top of the block out of breath with his eyes locked on the Benz
eager to see Amir. The gun in his hand shook at the sight of the
house door opening. He spotted the man with the suitcase.

"Where the hell is Amir?" On impulse, Damon made his
way down the street toward the target.

The Italian man's head rotated as he looked in both
directions pausing on the harmless-looking kid before
continuing to his vehicle.

Damon picked up the speed of his walk but realized he
wouldn't reach the man in time unless he ran at full stride.

The driver opened the door for his boss as Damon thought *"What the fuck did Amir need me for- oh shit!"* The door opens with the passenger instructing in his Sicilian accent, *"Take me to Queens and make it quick."* Suddenly Amir slid out from beneath the car on his back with his gun locked out in front of him, *"Yeah he can take you to Queens, right after you give up that case."*

The Italian man's hands shot straight up on impulse which made the driver look in Amir's direction.

"You fucking mooley." The driver yelled.

Amir pulled the trigger twice aiming for the driver's chest. The bullets ricocheted off the shatterproof window. The driver grinned raising his firearm. *"You dumb fucking mollies can't think for shit!" "*

"Fuck that drop it or I'm going to shoot your Boss," Amir said quickly shifting his aim back to the man with the case.

"It doesn't matter without the case he will be nobody boss."

The driver cocked back his weapon applying pressure on the trigger. A shot erupting through the air.

Amir braced himself for the impact when Damon's shot exited from the driver's chest. Damon stood there in shock staring at the smoke flowing from the barrel of his weapon in amazement.

"Aaaahh" The driver yelled falling to one knee.

Amir grinned with his weapon locked on the suitcase waiting on another shot from Damon to finish the racist man off. When none came he quickly fired under the door sending several shots into the driver's frame. He wiggled out from underneath the car with ease gripping the suitcase as Damon appeared at his side.

"Give me that pussy."

The man pulled back his hand resisting, instantly the butt of Amir's gun crashed into the side of his head forcing blood onto his tailored suit.

42

"Okay, Okay, here take it but remember this face Nigger because no matter how long it takes I will get you for this."

"Who said you were going to live, young buck it's your call because it's your first mission. Either he's gone or we can wait until he tries to make good on his promise, then kill him." Damon lifted his gun to Sammy's head.

"That's what the fuck I'm talking about young bull now Nike," Amir said meaning just do it!

Sammy closed his eyes tightly waiting to die when Damon said: *"Let's wait because I think he's ..."*

* * * * * *

"Bluffing my ass I should have murdered Sammy back then when I had the chance." **Boom Boom!**

The door frame shook more violently behind the powerful fist hammering against it. "Hey, guy come the fuck out of there.

The boss doesn't like to be kept waiting."

"Okay, I'm sorry it was more in me than I thought."

"Well hurry it up."

"Alright, I'm coming out now... *time to put in that work.*" Simultaneously on both sides of the door their guns raised toward the structure.

Outside of the apartment in the hallway the bum's leg vibrated as he staggered to his feet. "Oh shit, how long have I been out?" He took half a step while stumbling from side to side crashing hardback to the floor. "Not that long I'm still drunk haha."

The lookout's hand shot to his ear. "It's nothing Boss just that bum again that's all."

"If it wasn't anything Joey then I wouldn't be speaking to you, now would I?"

"No Sir."

"Then handle it for good this time the Don wants complete silence."

43

"Consider it done." Joey pulled his long hair back into a ponytail addressing his lady friend. "I think you should go to the apartment now."

"You don't have to tell me twice."

Joey waited until the blonde vanished behind the wooden frame before setting his vision onto the bum who once more attempted to make it back to his feet.

"Don't worry pal I think I just found you a permanent home." Joey eased the Glock automatic out from his back tightly screwing on the silencer. He positioned it out of sight at the side of his leg. He held his breath as he neared, refusing to allow the man's stench to enter his body.

"Let's get this over with." He bent down helping the bum to his feet declining to the cowardly act of shooting a man in his back even if he was black.

"Get- get your damn hands up off of me. You got to pay to touch me."

"Don't worry I got something for you." Joey grinned as the bum stood to his feet slowly turning in his direction.

"It wouldn't happen to look like this would it," asked Amir resting his silencer Mack -10 in the scared Italian man's face taunting him to make a move.

"Thought you were just going to kill a bum nigga didn't you pussy? Now raise your hands slowly."

Joey's arm became shoulder length when Amir demanded.

"Don't let it hit the floor or you're a dead man."

"What?" Questioned a puzzled Joey as he watched Amir cock back the gun before hitting the side button releasing the clip from Joey's weapon. Joey dove for the clip grasping it inches from the floor. He let out a sigh of relief pleased to have caught it until he locked eyes with Amir. "What I got it?"

"What about that?" Amir pointed to the bullet from the chamber lying on the floor. "Aa-ahh."

"Don't worry about it there's more where that came from." Amir pulled the trigger twice,

"Broken dreams Nigga."

He quickly snatched Joey's earpiece placing it into his own as his leg vibrated again,

"Just sit tight Damon I got you."

Amir removed his phone from his pants pocket while closely listening to the man speak through the earpiece.

"It's time, he has kept us waiting long enough and my promise will not be stalled a moment more so you know what you have to do."

"Is that so?" Amir texted, "No brakes." He removed the clip from Joey's dead hand. He raised both weapons toward the door. He relentlessly withheld the wrath charging through his blood waiting on his cue. Emotionally it took everything he had not to bust through the entrance in attempts to kill everything moving or lose his own life trying to save his young comrade's.

Amir was taught at the mere age of eight that the team you ride with is the team you die with as he raced through the back door of his home with a busted lip right pass his father who had been watching him from the window as he drunk a cup of black coffee...

"Wo wo slow down boy. Where you going in such a rush anyway." Mr., Patrick quickly released the window as if he was none the wiser. *"I'm getting out of there, I mean going to my room dad."*

"Okay, but isn't that your friend Tommy out there fighting that you always play with?"

"Yes."

"Then why aren't you out there fighting with him."

"But dad that's his fight I was fighting Jo-Jo and he ran home and I'm going to bed my back hurt."

"Son sorry to have to tell you this but you have no choice in the matter. The people you walk within life are the people you fight for as long as they will fight for themselves you must fight

with them. If you don't you will have nobody but yourself and no one can win a war alone do you understand that."

Amir nodded his head in agreement and raced back out the door. Mr. Patrick sat back down and sipped his coffee. He didn't look out the window because the outcome didn't matter to him. Amir would have hundreds of battles in life it was the comprehension of the fight that counted...

"Bang-Bang!"

Amir smiled at the sound of the gunfire knowing that Damon had once again arose to the occasion. He knew from his research that this team of Italians all moved with silencers. He set his watch on a two-minute count down before lowering his shoulder crashing through the door.

Amir turned right on impulse catching the man in the expensive suit off guard in the kitchen at the end of the hall. The muffled sound echoed twice in the man's direction sending him back against the pearly white refrigerator. Amir adored the sight of the man's blood trickling down the colored metal as he continued to move for the bathroom. His amusement was shortlived as a sudden movement from the corner of his eye made him shift his aim.

Amir's body turned as he rotated his weapon toward the action when a bullet slammed into the wall painting just inches in front of his face. He squeezed the trigger with a thoughtless effort using the gun in his right hand hitting Sammy in the forearm. The impact knocked the weapon free of Sammy's hand just as Amir's left hand made its way around.

"Broken Dreams Nigga," Amir whispered his signature calling to the angel of death that another was on his way with all hopes of life broken, pulling the trigger.

"Bossss nooo!" escaped the bodyguard's lips from across the room as he ran tossing his body in front of Sammy shielding him as he returned fire. The muffled sound continued as Amir quickly ducked behind the threshold of the living room using its structure as cover thinking, *"I thought this kind of shit only happens in the movies. Fucking white boys are crazy as hell. I'm*

46

not throwing myself in front of a bullet for Obama let alone someone bossing me around."

Amir verifying his remaining time as a minute and thirtynine seconds as sweat began to trail down the side of his face. He recognized he was short on time distinguishing the moment shots are fired there's only a two-minute window before chances of not getting caught became extremely rare.

The painting and wall fragments flowed in the mist of the air as Amir tossed Joey's firearm across the opening. He watched as two shots missed wildly with a third one splitting the gun in

half. *"He's not used to moving targets."*

Amir popped his head out into the opening and back again to be certain. A shot came a second later.

"You got to be faster than that if you think you're going to get through me to take that piece of shit boss of yours to the hospital. Before he dies from that hole in his chest."

"Hole, boss what is he talking about? Boss... Boss" The bodyguard quickly turned to find Sammy leaning against the wall with his eyes wide breathing hard as his blood-covered hand applied pressure onto his heart. On impulse, the bodyguard dropped his weapon and swiftly aided Sammy as he was trained. He removed his shirt wrapping it around Sammy's chest pulling it tightly when a bullet slammed into Sammy's cranium.

"Oh shit!" The bodyguard yelled now remembering his surroundings. He looked to the gun by his feet as the footsteps behind him gradually got louder.

"Don't even try it you'll be dead before you bend all the way down."

The man, key on surviving dove for the gun with Amir sidestepping his action beating him to the spot bringing the butt of his weapon down hard upside the bodyguard's head knocking him out cold.

"Fifty-seven seconds until departure!" Amir quickly searched the room gathered a few things before racing for the bathroom at the end of the hall. There he found Damon with his gun extended standing over a bloody faced Frankie, who was laying on the floor next to a dead body explaining.

"I swear Damon it wasn't me who wanted you done they make me do it."

"Then who you fat piece of shit and how did they find me?"

"There was some nigger- I mean some black guy that heard that Sammy had been placing a big price on the heads of two nigg-Blacks every year for some time now for robbing him. Many had tried to claim the reward but none had the right details of the night in question. Sammy needed to be definite that he was killing the right men to restore the honor back to his name. The day I was released I was summoned by Sammy and was questioned about you. I swear I had your back. I knew nothing about it. I mean I heard the stories but when that nigger walked in the room and tossed your picture on the nightstand I almost shit myself. Come to find out your dumbass was the only one not wearing a fucking disguise and Sammy remembered you. You know the rest of the story, me walking the yard with the man who robbed my fucking boss. Gives off the appearance I had something to do with it. So either I help them kill you and pray that they didn't kill me too or don't and they'd kill you, me and our family."

"What's the name of the person that gave me up?"

"I don't know I swear."

"Well, how much did he pay him?"

"What?"

Damon detecting a bit of hesitation pulled the trigger shooting Frankie in the inner thigh just inches from his private parts.

"Aaaahh."

"How much was he paid? Depending on the amount is where I start looking for him to spend it."

"Strangely he didn't want the money he just wanted the name of the top four drug suppliers in the city. That's all, I swear to you…please, Damon, don't do this to me I had no choice."

"Will you shoot him already?" Both men turned to Amir.

Frankie's eyes suddenly widen "It's you the guy with the p-,"

Bang! Bang!

Two slugs entered his upper chest piercing his heart with the first stopping him in mid-sentence. Amir inhaled the smoke from his weapon deep into his lungs just as his watch beeped indicating the forty-fifth-second mark. "Now come on let's go I don't have all day I still got to help my dad at the store."

"But."

"But what? That man was trying to spin you fuck'em, let's move!"

Amir headed for the door. Damon started to follow then paused looking back at Frankie thinking, *"Were you lying?"* When his thoughts were interrupted by the sound of someone moving in the living room.

Damon quickly put his feet in motion making his way to the exit, not wanting to find out the source knowing Amir's outlandish ways when it came to killing.

He caught up with Amir two blocks over as he moved quickly alongside the building blending into the shadows avoiding the street cameras.

"Yo wait up…. son wait." Damon watched as Amir paused with the glossiness clearing from his eyes returning back to normal. It was during this moment he knew Amir was off in a zone.

"What's up? You know I got to change then meet up with my pops."

"Bet but we still have a half a block before the split."

"So talk."

"What's the deal with someone still moving back there? You know the rules if we down one we down them all." Damon asked for a dead man couldn't see no evil, hear no evil or speak evil's name.

"Yeah but not the Italians or Russians you always leave one alive as long as it's not the head because they take out their own. As we speak, a cleanup crew is on its way to that apartment and when they're done it will look like no one had ever lived there. They're well connected so the cops will be delayed slightly but that doesn't mean they won't come looking for our asses in the meantime to give us up to the Mob for a big payday. Oh and by the way, here." Amir handed Damon the bag off his shoulder.

"That's your savings back, your half of the diamonds and a PlayStation 4, they had two."

"Thanks and I guess your right nobody needs the extra heat. I just wish you would have let Frankie finish his statement so we would know who gave me up."

"If you believe that shit then being locked up messed with your decision process more than I thought…split."

Like clockwork, Amir turned right moving up the block as Damon turned left down the block. The two always parted ways on the third block from each mission knowing definitely if they were being followed by then. Damon still ambiguous about Frankie's words removed his phone.

"Hello"

"One last thing how can you be so sure that Frankie was lying,"

"If he wasn't then why the diamonds, which was the reason you went there in the first place isn't it."

"Yeah,"

"Alright then," Damon heard the phone disconnect, "But how did he know that it was actually me?" He said to himself thinking of the way the man looked when he saw Amir.

4

The flashing red and blue lights of the undercover Charger invaded the night as Jake repeatedly pressed down on the horn yelling, "Get out of the freaking way!"

He maneuvered the steering wheel back and forth racing through the crowded streets of New York. He abruptly pulled hard to the left with the sound of screeching tires just missing an oncoming taxi by inches that cut him off.

"A-hole,"

Jake's vision transferred from the road locking on the taxi's license plate "*5959benz.*" He memorized it while keeping his thoughts to himself.

Heather watched her new partner through her peripheral while pretending to look straight. She was certain she detected a deep rage of anger inside him that he was trying hard to suppress, "*Maybe it's the pressure of being on his first case. Whatever the reason he better lose it fast. A crime scene is not a place for emotions it's the quickest way to get yourself killed.*"

Shortly Jake parked on 145th street killing the engine.

"Dispatch this is 7 exiting the car with 13 accompanying me."

"Copy that 7."

Jake quickly exited,

"No, wait, just sit here a moment."

"For what, I been waiting my whole life to put bad guys in jail, then after putting in all that hard work you make me wait another six months to get my hands dirty. So I apologize if I seem a little eager."

"That's understandable Jake but to solve a case you must first put your feelings aside to become one with the crime scene. That's knowing it from the outside as well as within."

Heather recalling the area from when she was a kid allowed her eyes to roam. She examined the broken glass covering the concrete. The mob of faces crowding the yellow tape and the possible escape route. She then counted the steps it would take for each route multiplying them by three different speeds before dividing them by distance.

"The slowest it would take them is 5 minutes, next to that 3 minutes, and lastly 2 minutes and 43 seconds if they used the back to escape."

Heather's sight fluctuated to the large crowd several feet away trying to keep their distance from the police without missing a second of the street gossip. She gradually traveled over each face to capture the detail and emotion knowing that it was possible for the killer to be just inches away.

She paused on a rough-looking man with his hat placed over his heart and his head bowed in a military display of respect. Though it was the built-up wetness in the crease of his eyes refusing to drop that caught her genuine attention.

She raised her iPhone taking several quick photos before dialing. "Sue I'm sending you a few pictures run them through Intel and see what you come up with then get back to me."

"No problem."

"Jake now we can go."

Heather's door cracked to the horrifying sound of a woman's screams in the distance. A turmoil she knew all too well. *"That has to be a loved one of the victim either his wife or daughter the pain is too raw."*

Heather removed a flashlight from the glove compartment and headed across the street. She bent down feeling the ground,

"Jake It must've rained here earlier today because the ground is still moist which means their tire tracks may be still around here somewhere."

"I'm on it, I'll have a few officers use the machine to comb through the area within a two-mile radius."

"You do that." Heather made her way to the crime scene trying to block out the growing shouts of pain hoping to prevent it from pursuing her dreams like the many others. She raised her hand stopping two EMTs coming out the store pushing a body on a stretcher. She braced herself to face her childhood hero as she slowly pulled back the white sheet.

A slight sigh of relief escaped her lips as her brain registered data. *"Tommy Jackson 5'10, 165 lbs. A scare over his right eye a shade darker than his caramel complexion. He received during an attempted robbery at the Dr. J's store that landed him two years up north. Known as a two-bit stick-up boy from Harlem that would do anything or anybody for a price up until a year ago. That's about the time he started to run with the kid Keith and that kid Shane."*

"Come on baby girl you can't give that thug all the attention. Let him go to that sheet of metal they got waiting on him and I'll let you in on a little secret. He'll never get it up if you know what I'm saying." Alex said imposing on Heather's thoughts. He wrapped his arm around her tense shoulder.

"Come on let me get you up to speed on what I have so far."

Heather smiled at the sight of Alex, she had worked with him on several cases and trusted him with her life. It was the criminals that Heather was worried about when it came to him.

"Okay, but first have someone place an A.P.B (all-points bulletin) on Shane Peterson and Keith Jackson."

"Got it. Keith is the dead one's cousin, correct."

"Glad to know you're still sharp."

Alex stood 6'1, 253 lbs. solid muscle and has never bullied anyone that didn't deserve it. He was the sixth detective in his family starting as far back as his great grandfather. Alex was a good detective, who like the rest of his family ran the streets by one rule when it came to dealing with bad guys, shoot first and ask questions later if they survived. The rule begun after Alex's great grandfather was shot 8 times in a dark alleyway and left for dead after a traffic stop went bad. That moment changed the family's mental state forever.

Alex led Heather into the store, "Okay if you're not on

53

Heather's squad clear out, this is now the boss lady's crime scene.

Now please exit! And let the pretty lady through."

"Kiss my ass Alex I know I look terrible you would too if you've been working 19 hours straight and by the looks of this crime scene I won't be getting home no time soon. There's not a lot of things out of place meaning we're not just dealing with some crackheads trying to get a quick fix."

"Your right these men knew exactly what they were doing and what they were looking for, the thing is what was it?"

"It's that answer that will lead us to our killer."

"Well I talked with the neighbors and they all said about the same. That this Mr. Patrick fella was a family man who mostly left his home every morning around eight o'clock and walked about a mile to work opening the store up by nine. Other than that his son or his daughter would bring him."

"What days did he take off?"

"That's odd from my notes he didn't take any."

"And that's because?"

"I don't know yet but it sure as hell wasn't no petty thief involved here. The cash register still has money in it. There are three rooms in all in this location but no one has moved passed this area since I arrived, so your crime scene is still intact. All you got to do now is work your magic. Then you can return back to my sexy Heather."

"You wish Alex and I told you then that it was only going to be that one time and it was a sympathy screw for you saving my life and almost losing your job in the process. Anyway, who is the person with the body?" Heather inquired as her brain continued to examine looking in the direction of the freezers. *"I wonder if they were thirsty."*

"The woman's name is Sherry, the store owner's daughter she's the one that discovered the body."

"Did she make the call?"

"No, I believe someone heard the screams looked in, saw her and the body and place the called."

"Vibe?"

"She has been extremely hostile since we arrived but give it a minute or two. I believe she'll calm down. If it'll help I'll debrief her for you. "

"That won't be necessary I know her."

"That should make things easier...Come on fellas let's move it, we don't have all damn day here."

Alex waited until all the officers were gone to ask his next question. "Your still having those nightmares aren't you?"

"No, I'm fine." *Dammit, I never should've taken that nap on that stakeout.*

"That's great to hear," Alex's give a fake smile knowing that his friend was being dishonest. He quickly changed the subject, "Where is it you know her from?"

Heather's eyes rested onto Sherry's swollen face as her tears saturated her father's apron while holding him tightly in her arms. "Daddy please don't leave me I need you. Oooh God don't do this to me!" she continuously pleaded.

The word pain couldn't validate what Heather witnessed on Sherry's face as she answered. "We went to school together, I don't remember a lot about her because she used to be in and out of school. They said she was sick a lot back then. I do know we used to joke all the time about how I had the biggest crush on her brother."

"So did you?"

"Did I what?"

"Have a crush on him."

"What I did is none of your damn business, now if you would excuse me we have a case to solve. But if you would like to help other than standing there trying to be nosy? You can start by dusting for fingerprints. Everything in here must be processed starting with the sodas in the freezer down to the last piece of paper." Heather indicated observing all the scrap paper on the floor covered in blood. Through the redness, her eyes locked on the few notes with just numbers written on them. There were eight rows of numbers on each. She didn't know what they meant or why they stuck out to her as odd but it did.

She used a pen from her top pocket bending downing scooping up the four pieces of paper."

"Bag."

"Here's one, but come on Heather you got to be kidding me with the sodas and shit right?"

"Do it look like I'm kidding, the owner of this store was a dear friend of my mother's and he was there for my family when we needed it most, so I'm going to do right by him and find whoever did this. I want the records of every communications device connected to his name. Furthermore, if we're dealing with professionals they were in here before tonight steaking out the place. So more than likely they weren't wearing gloves. I won't dare question if the tape is still there." Heather pointed to the three surveillance cameras placed throughout the store."

"No, they even got the backup feed to the owner's phone."

"GPS tracking?"

"Stops at the front of the store. They must have destroyed it before they left."

"Alright, the hunt has begun and the only way to make up for their head start is to capitalize off of their mistake. You already know how much I hate being behind. Now get the crew started and keep me updated on anything that looks out of place while I go speak to an old friend."

Heather pushed record on her cell phone positioning it on a shelf in the corner where she had a great view of Sherry. She kneeled down next to her gently touching her shoulder.

"Excuse me my name is Hea…"

"Heather Caroni what the fuck are you doing here?"

"Yes Sherry it's me, I'm sorry for your loss and if it means anything I just want you to know I have never forgotten what your father did for my family. I'm a detective now and I'm heading this case and I promise you I will get who did this to him. I just need to ask you a few questions if you're feeling up to it."

"Ok, but if you will let me sit with him a few moments more I'll tell you what you want to know."

"Sherry you do know he's dead-" Heather paused and just nodded letting her vision drift onto the still face of Mr. Patrick

knowing she owed him at least that...

5

A few blocks over in a nicely furnished two bedroom, one bathroom apartment. Amir's phone vibrated for the hundredth time as he slept sweating profusely. He tossed and turned back and forth trying to escape his own nightmare…

He refused to weep as the darkness shielded his young 13 old frame as the ripped tank top now hanging on by a single thread once did. He tried to escape the cave he had crept into for safety. The silhouette of a gun could be seen slowly rising before him forcing his eyes to shut went the echoes of gunshots awakened him…

"Noooooo!" He shouted, his eyes shooting wide open as he set straight up in bed.

"Baby you alright… baby?" questioned a heartfelt Trina, who was Amir's main girl. She was a freak by nature and the Bonnie to his Clyde for the past several years. She wiped the sweat away from his forehead pampering him while caressing his balls in a circular motion. She knew he didn't like being helped but she had an exceptional gift when it came to tending to a person's needs in any fashion as if she knew what they needed even if they didn't. She replaced the drenched washcloth with a fresh one immediately.

A response never came, for Amir was lost in thoughts as he whispered, "Nooo don't shoot."

The sound of his breathing became harder as his arm moved upward from beneath the thick covers with his weapon in hand. He slowly drew back on his trigger finger preparing to shoot.

"Amir what are you doing! Snap out of it!" Trina yelled letting out a deep breath seeing his polished eyes, "God please not this shit again. Amir! I don't even know why you sleep with a gun at this apartment nobody even knows we have it."

She shook him aggressively needing to get his attention as she eased her 24-36-42 naked frame out from the bed not wanting to be shot again. She knew Amir visited the firing range three times a week devotedly and could hit a person dead center between the eyes with either hand from about a hundred yards away. A tradition he acquired from his uncle Robert.

Trina was attractive with hazel eyes full lips and a body to kill for which some did literally. At 159lbs and 5'7" she was known for her fast mouth and quicker hands but still she was no match for her man.

Amir's eyes progressively focused back to reality as he analyzed his surroundings trying to figure out where he was. Distinguishing his home he began to relax when he observed the weapon in his hand. "Why do I have this, niggas are scared of me not the other way around."

"I don't know but you're making me nervous as hell. Look you got my pussy all dry and shit. You know that never happens. It stays Niagara falls down there." Trina said rubbing her fingers through her pussy lips before placing two inside.

"I can't right now."

"Are you sure" Trina seductively detached her now soaked fingers running them in a circle on her clitoris then placing them into her mouth licking them bone dry one by one.

"If you ask me it taste like honey baby your favorite" Trina placed her index finger under Amir's nose allowing him to sniff her naturally sweet aroma.

"You know me all too well but I can't." Amir tossed the weapon onto the dresser and headed into the bathroom.

"Wait you're forgetting your medication." Trina held out two Prazosin pills.

"No, you're forgetting I don't take that shit anymore."

"But the dreams are coming back more and more to the point where you're having them every time you close your eyes."

"Okay but let me deal with whatever the fuck is going on in my head. I don't need any pills just because a doctor who knows nothing about me said so. Look at all these junkies running around here now because they listen to a doctor. We don't even know what the fucks in that medication."

"Calm down baby I would never wish that on you but they were working."

"And what else were they doing...exactly you don't know. Knock it off Trina for real, you're starting to sound like my damn father."

"No, I'm just trying to stand by your side like always."

Amir stared at Trina knowing her words to be genuine. He gave her a short head nod in agreement that made her smile.

Amir began having his childhood nightmares recur a little over two years ago. One night following an assignment involving Raymond McMillan, a fly talking high-profile hustler who had run off with the wrong plug's work this time who vowed to make certain that he never did it to anyone else.

The plug was known as Blind Sonny. A Jamaican killer that lost his sight in a gunfight when he was twenty-six which in turn only made him worse. Now twenty years later anybody that's anybody knows he was nothing to play with. The fact was Raymond didn't care he lived for the bag.

Blind Sonny quickly placed a hundred-thousand-dollar bounty on Raymond's head and he requested the best to handle it...

Amir dressed in all black entered the huge New Jersey house surrounded by woods located somewhere near Mays Landing. The home looked more like a fortress than a residential had one weakness due to the gardener's smoking habit and Amir used it to his advantage.

He removed the ashtray and slid through the basement window face first. He placed his hands above his head using the suction cups lowering himself down inside. He knew that it would be unoccupied from his weeks of trailing his prey but he explored nonetheless. Contained he flickered the flashlight twice out into the darkness.

Upstairs on the first floor, Amir unlocked the back door for Damon and Trina to gain access. They quickly split getting right to work. Trina took the front stairs two at a time and Damon seized the rear doing as planned. They secured the first and second floor making sure that no one was present but their target. Amir took a deep breath and calmly exhaled as he walked up the kitchen's spiral steps heading straight for the master bedroom. His watch vibrated informing him all was clear.

Raymond's eyes parted at the sound of his iPhone constantly ringing on the nightstand. He sat up in bed in a panic. He was certain he placed it on silent like usual to avoid his girlfriend arguing about other females calling so late. He grasped it to say bye when he notices a familiar face on the screen.

"How did he get this number I changed it that night... Hell, it ought to be fun." Raymond thought as he pushed accepted. "Blind Sonny my main man long time no see. How life been treating you?"

"Yeah like a year to the day star since yuh ran off with me bumbaclot thirty keys."

"Come on Sonny you know I would never run off on you. We got pulled over after the delivery from your guy. We had to throw some shots at the coppers to get some space as we torched the evidence. You know how the game goes."

"Rassclaat indeed and yuh know what me told yuh when we first begin business together." "What not to get caught."

"No, I tell yuh to treat me product like it was yuh'er life because if yuh lose one I will be forced to take the other. And yuh know my word is me bond... and now it's time to pay up."

"Pay up I got a better idea how about you go fuck yourself, Sonny. Ha...ha...ha." Raymond laughed with his middle finger pointed at the screen forgetting that Sonny was blind.

"So I amuse yuh star?"

"Hell yeah, why the fuck you face-timing me and you can't even see."

"Because I want me face to be the last yuh see before you die and for the record, I didn't call yuh, Raymond yuh called me

Star I'm just returning yuh'er call."

"Why in the hell would I do that and farther more I was sleeping you lying-" The words felt like cement in Raymond's throat because if he knew anything about Blind Sonny it was that he didn't lie. His word was good all over the world. He quickly checked his recent calls seeing Sonny's number on the outgoing list placed just moments ago.

"Oh shit, how that happened!" Raymond attentively cast an eye over the room. He could sense the danger in the air as his free hand grasped the tech 9 automatic from off the top of the drawer.

Amir eased out from beneath the bed with his silencer locked on Raymond's head just as his palm connected to the handle of his black steel. Amir whistled making Raymond look down when he pulled the trigger sending two shots into his target's skull.

Raymond released the phone falling over the nightstand crashing to the floor breaking the lamp. Amir stood gathering the phone aiming it at Raymond's lifeless body advising, *"Broken dreams nigga... It's finished."*

"I heard. Another job well done."

Amir tossed the phone onto Raymond's chest sending several shots into it destroying it completely. He declared into his smartwatch, *"Exit count down sixty seconds starting now."*

"Copy." His team responded simultaneously.

Amir examined the room one last time then made his exit. He opened the door then suddenly stopped. His eyelids connected listening to his surroundings as taught. He quickly turned around pulling the cover off the bed revealing a scared woman.

"Wait please don't shoot I don't see anything I swear."

"That's true because of the mask but it's what you heard I'm wary of." Amir leveled his weapon at the woman's heart. *He swallowed hard knowing the unwritten rule never leave a witness behind. His finger eased back on the trigger. "No please don't." "Sorry, Not Sorry."*

"Leave my mommy alone." An eight-year-old kid yelled racing from the walk-in closet jumping into his mother's arms. *"It's okay, Lil Ray Mommy's fine. You just keep looking straight ahead, baby."*

"Then mommy why are you crying and where did daddy go?"

"Baby these are good tears that's all. Now please can you be quiet mommy's talking with a friend." The woman placed her hands over Lil Raymond's ears and requested. *"Sir not in front of my son I'm begging you."*

"How are you even here I watch you leave."

"No that was his wife. I'm Blare, this house is so big he keeps my son and I hid on the west wing and nobody even knows we're here."

Amir's watch beeped indicating 30 seconds remaining to depart. He looked from his gun to Blare detesting what he knew had to be done.....

Amir turned from Trina and continued to the bathroom brushing his teeth he glanced at the wall clock spitting out the toothpaste,

"Oh shit I'm late again, dad is going to kill me." He grabbed a black t-shirt pulling it down over his wife-beater and rushed for the door. He paused staring back at his handgun resting on the top of the dresser, *"I'm bugging I'm* not that scary." He tucked the automatic in his waist.

Outside in the mist of the night, Amir walked in-between blocks using the shadows to barely be seen. He resurfaced on 145th street in hopes that his father wouldn't be too hard on him when he suddenly noticed a crowd of people standing outside of his father's store.

"What the hell is going on?" He began moving faster blending in with the people at the sight of the unmarked police cars parked across the street.

"I pray they're not there for me because I'm not going out without a fight," Amir reassured himself easing his hand onto his weapon. He lowered his head focusing on the gossip around him as he passed through.

"Yo that shit crazy how he did the man."

"Word son they said the owner hit him with that forty Cal."

A small smirk appeared at the corner of Amir's face as he uttered, "That's right pops give them hell, for just the thought of taking something from us." He stood just a few feet away from the entrance and waited patiently. The officer's head rotated to scan the crowd for the hundredth time as Amir swiftly slipped under the yellow caution tape. He approached the entrance overhearing a weeping Sherry in mid-conversation.

"I'm positive the last time I talked to my father he said that Amir had just arrived to help clean up the store. I arrived here twenty minutes later because I felt sorry for how I doubted Amir and I wanted to tell him that I was regretful for misjudging him.
That's when I found him lying here dead."

"So tell me please Sherry who you believe would do such a thing like this to your father?'

"Bitch did you hear what I just said."

"Yes, I did."

"Therefore if anyone knows what happen its Amir?"

"Dead." Amir inquired, from the doorway when his roaming eyes rested on his father's corpse. Onsight he became traumatized losing a part of himself as the best person he knew in life laid lifeless.

"Dad." He whispered with the first tear in fifteen years escaping out the creases of his eyes. He stepped forward approaching his father's body.

"Don't you dare come near him, you fucking murderer. You and your goons did this to him," Sherry screamed, snapping her brother out of his daze.

"What?" Amir couldn't believe his ears.

"Fuck you and I hope you die in jail for this, pussy."

"Me, I didn't-"

"Excuse me, sir, I'm Detective Alex from spec-"

"Man if you don't get your fucking hands up off of me. My dad just been killed and your all up in my mother fucking face," Amir aggressively pulled his arm free as he turned toward the door knowing Sherry's words had just made him their prime suspect.

Heather gave Alex a slight head nod in the direction of the bulges on Amir's hip.

"I know pal I'm just trying to help that's all," Alex replied.

Amir noticed the gesture in his peripheral and followed Heather's stare. *"Oh shit my heat!"* He thought as Alex stepped forward quickly closing the distance between them.

Amir pivoted to the left with Alex, side-stepping the move cutting off his exit route. Refusing to be boxed in for he needed answers to his father's death. Amir sent a hard right hook to the side of Alex's face followed by an even harder body shot. The blow caught Alex off guard forcing him to double over as Amir pushed him to the side generating a gap to the doorway.

"Aaaahh"

"Oh no, Alex!" Heather screamed making her way to her feet when Alex crashed into her; shoving him to the side and with three large steps she was out the door in pursuit of Amir. She yelled at Jake who was at the corner of the block.

"Stop him!"

"What?" Jake asked puzzled.

Amir dipped out the store as if he were about to run but he walked into the crowd as nothing happened. He headed straight for the other end.

"Stop him right there in the black shirt and watch it he's armed."

Amir took off at full speed knocking a man to the ground as he shot from the crowd toward the alley.

Jake spotted a man running and immediately gave chase. "Hey stop police!" He shook his head disappointed with himself the moment the words left his lips, "I don't know why I even bother yelling that, I read it only works 22 percent of the time." Jake stayed in tip-top shape knowing that the day would finally come where he would be in the field pursuing a true criminal. Now he just prayed the books were right. Jake picked up speed moving quickly over the damp concrete as he sprinted into the alley behind Amir.

Heather arrived at the tip of the alleyway to see Jake midway through disappear behind a building.

"Dammit! He's taking him through the concrete jungle gym and Jake will never be able to keep up unless he was born here." In-mid thought Heather's walkie-talkie came alive.

"Shit! I lost him, boss."

"Wait don't give up just keep running," She closed her eyes saying to herself, "Come on dammit you remember,"

The sound of Amir's voice when they were childhood friends replayed in her mind....

"Come on Heather this way I know a short cut." Amir stated in the middle of the alley as he dips behind a building looking down the long pathway, "Never mind let's go the way you been going."

The look of disappointment upset Heather, "What you want to go through there let's do it I swear I won't tell."

"I know but you're a girl and this is called the tangible jungle gym and half the boys in my school can't make it and they're all stronger than you so I know you never will."

"Yes I can, let's do it." *Heather started between the* buildings

"No, come on I don't need you wasting my time I got boxing class tonight and I can't be late again or my dad is going to kill me for wasting his money."

"I'll bet you a month of allowance that I'm able to make it and I can beat you doing it."

"You're on."

Heather at age 13 raced like she was back with her track team as Amir yelled out directions. *"Left,"* Heather made the turn scaring a dog that shot out from behind a trash can. She continued to run as Amir instructed *"Jump!"*

"Where?" Heather looked around seeing nothing but more alleyway.

"The fire escape."

She jumped up missing the metal ladder by inches. She tried again harder only to fail.

"See I told you that you were only going to be wasting my time." Amir turned to head back down the alley. *"And I want my money... girl,"*

"Fuck, you Amir." Heather retreated behind him then when they were about to exit she turned around taking off running at full speed. She jumped with all her might as her fingertips wrapped around the fire escape bar. She smiled tugging on the ladder when suddenly her grip slipped sending her face-first into the ground. *"Aaaahh!"*

"Heather get up and knock it off before you hurt your damn self."

"I think it's too late for that." Heather brushed herself off mentally giving in. she started up the alley again when it dawned on her, *"I'm not my mother I'm strong and no man is ever going to tell me what I can and can't do I'm a thinker."* Heather visualized the moment she caught her mother on her knees pleasuring a stranger without a drop of hope in her eyes. *"That would never be me."* She hastily sprinted back down

toward the alley once more jumping into the air. She passed the ladder kicking off the back wall grabbing hold of it.

She drew herself up quickly heading for the rooftop when she realized she didn't know where she was heading. "Amir you know if you go back you still got to pay up."

Looking up he smiled, "No I'm right behind you." On the roof top, Heather sprinted with Amir hot on her tail screaming,

"Jump!"

"Aaaahh" she screamed elevating over the large empty space leaping from one roof top down onto another. She landed on her feet before the momentum forced her to lose her balance falling over onto her shoulder. She refused to think about the pain shooting up her side as she listened to Amir,

"Turn!"

Heather headed for the left side of the building now realized that they were cutting through whole blocks "Jump!" She lost her balance again as she landed quickly sticking her hand out on reflex touching the cold cement pushing upward not to fall. She continued to run.

"Head for the door then go down two sets of stairs enter the hall and go into the third apartment on the right."

"What?"

"Don't worry Mrs. Richardson understands just go through the door and keep straight for the fire escape"

"If you say so." Heather finding it unlocked slid through the door." Pardon me miss."

"Just make it quick you little bitch and if the cop comes knocking you better bring me my damn money because I haven't seen shit."

Heather quickly made her way down the fire escape at the end of the alley she stepped out onto the sidewalk lifting her head seeing the street sign reading 135th street...

Heather gradually opening her eyes coming back to the present questioning, "Jake you okay,"

"I'll be damned," Jake said out of breath turning from the street sign noticing Amir walking up the street as if was never being chased.

"Heather I found him." Jake with his eyes locked on Amir swiftly closed the distance between him and his target.

Amir crossed the street in the middle of oncoming traffic while looking over his shoulder making sure he wasn't being followed. Not definite his hand slid towards his weapon as his eyes keyed in on a man a few feet behind him. He watched as the man raised his hand before disappearing inside a taxi.

"Never mind Sir I think I'll walk," Jake tossed a twenty on the dashboard the moment Amir looked away and raced off. He slammed the taxi's door rushing in pursuit of his mark spotting him dipping into another alley. Jake quickly reported what he could without losing Amir,

"Officer in need of back up I'm approaching the entrance of a side street off of 133rd in pursuit of an armed murder suspect, over."

He turned into the barely lit back street. His high tempo jog alternating into a leisurely walk while looking around. He didn't see any sign of Amir in the darkness but he knew that it was impossible for him to make it out the other end so quickly.

Jake feeling a trap could be in motion released his weapon from his holster. He moved in with caution when a sound to his right got his attention. He slowly rotated toward the source as his cheek bumped into the barrel of Amir's gun who stepped out from the blackness.

"The old come and get me trick and you fell for it so you gotta be a rookie?"

"That I am," Jake responded trying to remain calm.

"Shut the fuck up pig I should blow you're fucking head off of your neck for following me in my hood."

Be calm Jake he said I should which means he's still debating on it. "Come on young man you don't want the blood of

an officer of the law on your hands."

"Why the fuck, not pussy, you're chasing me because you believe I killed my father so what you think your better than him?" Amir smacked Jake upside the head with the butt of his gun while removing Jake's weapon from his palms. "And that back up piece on your ankle" Amir hit him again

"Aaaahh! Ok…here and no I'm not implying that in no means."

Amir tossed the guns down the alley "But you do think I killed my dad and its fine for me to have his blood on my hands but a not a cop's." He endlessly hit Jake upside the head until it started to bleed, "Pussy empty your pockets."

Jake did what he was told while maintaining his composure enough to think about how to survive his first day in the field. Amir picked up Jake's notebook

"What is this right here?"

"Oh, that is nothing just notes of previous Fed cases that in some way is connected to Ms. Heather's cases."

"I wouldn't be in there in some way would I?"

"I'm sorry to say but yes."

"You don't say," Amir's eyes raced over the pages as he memorized the stories inspecting it for his name.

"Here I am, now let's see what the big boys have to say about little old me." Amir's facial expression continued to show tranquility on the outside but he was more than shocked by what his eyes were witnessing. There was step by step accounts of two home invasions and an out of town bank robbery that he and Damon had pulled.

"If they got all of this bull shit why aren't we locked up yet?"

"That's a question you'll have to ask yourself."

"Nah nigga I'm asking you," Amir threw an uppercut to Jake's face that made his legs go weak. Holding him up by his collar, he threw another right hand then a left demanding "Stand up clown and answer me."

"Alright, alright." Jake attempted to rid the vision of stars out of his head before continuing, "The way I see it is if the actions are true or not, you're only on the street because what they have on you at the moment is just hear say."

"Hearsay."

"Yes, hearsay meaning somewhere in your circle there is a snitch."

"No we're airtight, play that trick on a different lame, not me. And for the record rookie out in these streets never take the presumption that just because someone asks you a question they don't know the answer already. And it's "hearsay" meaning the person who is telling heard it from someone else. So it's not directly from my circle pussy. Now, what else is in this?" Amir hastily glanced through the remainder of the notes in hopes of finding clues to his newly discovered information.

He instantly became furious to perceive a name he knew all too well.

"What the fuck is my father doing in here" Amir took in each factor and couldn't believe what he was reading about his father's past and murder. "Someone tried to kill him before? This shit is a fucking lie my dad was none of these things and he never ran with a gang."

"Are you sure about that, what about Philadelphia?"

"What did you just say?"

"Nothing, relax please, remember you're the one in power."

"Pussy did ya'll tell that to the man in the car before ya'll shot him in front of a kid or when ya'll shot that man when he was already down and handcuffed." Amir wrapped his arm around Jake's neck from behind pulling him close to his chest as he placed his gun to his temple. "Now it's my turn to get on the scoreboard when I push your shit back."

"Wait, please! Do nothing irrational, that was other police officers and they may have a good reason for their actions I don't know. All I was saying is that this is not a black lives matter issue and I'll do anything you want just remember you're the one in power."

"Yeah that… the one in power, your voice I know it from somewhere-."

"Jake… Jake do you hear me copy." Heather voice echoed from the walkie-talkie interrupting Amir's statement, "What's your location I'm on 133rd street debating on left or right which way copy."

"That's my boss… what you want me to say."

"Nothing."

"I got to answer her or they will activate the tracker in my walkie-talkie and have this area surrounded within the hour?"

"Man to hell with that walkie-talkie" Amir seeing a red flashing light on the top and tossed the communication device with Jake's guns. "Fuck it, they can come and get me but I'll tell you one thing I'm not going out like the others. I want that action. If I ever go up on worldstar it's going to be for firing nigga not flashing a piece."

"Worldstar what's that?"

"Something you're going to die on," Amir stated swiftly pulling Jake back into the darkness from which he came. He noticed Heather through his peripheral vision approaching the entrance of the alleyway.

"Sssshhh if you utter a word I swear that it will be your last." Amir's eyes trailed Heather's every movement when he observed her halt briefly and gaze in their direction. His muscles tightened as he closed his eyes shielding the whiteness from her. He slowly counted to ten then eased them apart seeing that Heather's vision had shifted.

Jake could feel Amir's breathing subsiding like a predator stalking his prey in the wild becoming one with the environment as Heather inched closer toward them. Jake skilled in animal Intel knew this action was only for the sole purpose that their kill would be relaxed before they died. Now he just prayed Amir's reason wasn't the same.

"Keep moving Heather please." Jake silently prayed, sweating profusely as she got closer.

Heather with her weapon locked out in front rotated it from side to side pausing for a second time having an uncanny feeling about something. She drew back the hammer believing she saw an outline of a shadow in the mix of the darkness. She considered it to be nothing and continued to move then suddenly she spun back around yelling,

"Amir, let him go and come out with your hands up and I promise you won't get hurt but I'm only going to tell you once.....one."

Boom Boom, Boom. Heather pulled the trigger rapidly stepping in with each shot waiting to hear the screams of agony. The sparks from the bullets ricocheting off of the stone wall informed her that her eyes weren't what they used to be.

The pace of Amir's heartbeat picked up a little as his life flashed before his eyes. He observed the forced hardship he brought amongst himself as well as the many deaths that came with it.

Amir deep down inside knew although he didn't speak on it that his father didn't approve of his deeds in the streets. However, he had always assumed once his need for action subsided he would make his father proud now that would never happen.

Amir not believing that he was still alive as a weapon shot at point-blank range missed him by a hair. The rip in the collar of his shirt will forever give the testimony. He for a slight second smiled thinking, his father had to be looking over him as he would always say,

"You think just because I am in this store all day that I don't know what you're doing on those streets? Well, I do and these hands that push that broom reach well beyond that door.

So just know I'm always looking after you."

Amir's rage abruptly kicked in with the thought of his father to return fire hitting Heather dead center in the face with each round. Then standing over her lifeless body reloading

73

doing the same. He took a deep breath knowing that slaughtering whoever did this to his father and every person they loved was now his main and only priority and having the blood of a cop on his hands would only make it more difficult. On the other hand, he likes things the hard way.

Amir's finger eased back on the trigger as Heather inched closer into the darkness following the trail of her shots. She strained her eyes trying to distinguish what was before her.

"If she comes a few more steps I swear I'm going to air her out then it will be broken dreams for her and you faggot," Amir whispered into Jake's ear meaning every word.

A stream of hot urine escaped down Jake's leg at the sight of Heather's devoted approach. She took another step with Jake holding his breath as Amir's weapon locked on Heather's face,

"64, dispatch officers in need of assistance on 28 and 7 street in pursuit of a black male with a handgun believed to be armed and extremely dangerous copy," echoed out from the darkness.

Heather quickly turned racing in the direction of the sound. She bent down picking up the walkie-talkie noticing Jake's initial on the side. "Shit! Jake must have chased him through here." she hurried out to the tip of the alleyway with expectations that she hadn't lost them.

"Your ticket to survival just departed now spread them." Amir pushed Jake face first up against the wall with such force the collision made blood pour from his nose. He patted him down removing his shield, phone, and shoes.

"Aaaahh shit you nasty mother fucker."

"When a man has to go he has to go ha-ha." Jake nervously joke.

"My point exactly." Amir raised his pistol to the back of Jake's head whispering, "Broken dreams," He bought the butt of it across Jake's skull knocking him out cold.

"Today is your lucky day pussy, I'll see you again I'm sure of it."

Amir disappeared out the other end of the alley. He raised his hand with a taxi coming to a stop. In the back seat, he examined the contents of Jake's unlocked phone until he saw what he was looking for.

"Thank god Jake you're okay," Heather said in relief spotting Jake's number on the screen

"He's fine just a little big-headed that's all."

"Then put him on the phone and I swear if anything happens to him I'll-."

"You'll do what Heather." Amir interrupted. "At least now I know you got the heart to pull the trigger before you were too scared to even touch a gun or has it been that long that you forgot who showed you your first piece."

Heather bit down on her bottom lip until it bled thinking back to that very night...

"Come on in girl stop playing there's nobody here. I told you, my dad's at the store."

"And your sister?"

"She's staying the night over her friend's house. Now come on with the scared shit." Amir pulled Heather out of the hallway into his arm pushing his room door shut behind her. He kissed her passionately, palming her right ass cheek firmly. Heather placed her hands on his chest pushing off to regain the space between them. She became shocked to find herself becoming hot all over. She returned his kiss pushing her tongue deep into his mouth wrapping her arms around him.*

Amir's hand lowered to the rim of Heather's skirt drawing it up above her hips. He eased her panties aside with the fragrance of her soaking wet pussy straying throughout the room. His finger trailed up her inner thigh in search of her clit making her hotter with each touch. Discovering it, he rotated his fingers in a circular motion that forced a moan to discharge.

"Aaaahh your touch is wonderful."

Amir pulled back his dripping wet finger placing it into his mouth before he gently kissed Heather again sharing the good flavor.

He parted her pussy lips when Heather grasped hold of his wrist. Thinking to herself "If this is going to be my first time it's going to be my way,"

She gripped the back of Amir's head gliding him down onto his knees. A hot pleasing sensation raced up her spine as Amir's tongue replaced his fingers. The feeling was better than Heather imaged going off the woman's factual expressions in a porn movie. Though Heather never thought it was possible.

She fought to catch her breath as her eyes rolled into the back of her head loving it. She moaned again lost in the moment as Amir abruptly lifted her up into the air wrapping her legs around his waist. He laid her down on the mattress that was as firm as his body.

"Now it's my turn." He thought to himself quickly removing his clothing placing them neatly on the dresser. He eased above her looking down into Heather's vibrant eyes kissing her tenderly permitting her another taste of her sweet nectar. He pushed his body forward sending his stiff manhood deep inside her.

"Aaaahh," Heather bit down on her bottom lip arching her back exploring feelings she never had before without a drop of resistance. Amir's slow pace gradually became faster and more forceful with each stroke.

"Oh my god." Heather exhales noisily. She inched back in reverse to decrease Amir's power until her back pressed up against the headboard. Though Amir felt divine inside her the pain was becoming too much as he continuously stretched her pussy walls. She didn't dare speak the word stop because she truly didn't want it to end. She continued to try to soften the blow proceeding backward as Amir entered her sending the dresser behind the headboard up on two feet. A loud noise erupted with both stopping to see the source. A gun rested on the floor beside

Amir's clothes.

"*Amir you have a gun.*"

"*Yeah, it's nothing.*" *Amir got up grasping the weapon with his shirt handing it to Heather who quickly pulled her hand back. "No, I'm not touching that why you have it anyway. You can beat most if not all the people in school.*"

"*It's not that it's...really I just can't explain what overcame me. A guy was selling them on my way to the gym and I stopped to look just to be nosy not planning on buying anything. When I picked it up it was like whatever I was missing in my life it suddenly completed me.*"

Heather noticed a lust in Amir's eyes that she never witnessed and it turned her on even more. He walked over opening the window stating.

"*With this here at any given moment you can make someone pay for what they did to you and they not even have to know you're the one who did it. Like that man across the street, he told my father about the stolen dirt bike I was riding. Which had me confined in the house for a whole month. He didn't care about the parties or the dates with you I missed.*" *Amir stuck the firearm out easing the trigger back.*

"*No don't,*" *Heather kissed him tenderly on the lips while gripping the weapon free from his hand. She opens her eyes viewing her reflection in the dresser mirror becoming hornier. Her juices eased down her inner thigh as she stepped back to get a full observation of herself. Slowly she raised the firearm with both hands.*

"*Yo girl watch where you pointing that thing.*"

"*Now look who is scared.*" *At that moment Heather knew whatever she was going to do in life a gun was going to be a part of it.*

"*Fuck what you talking about just give me that.*" *She laid it in the shirt which he quickly tucked away. She led him back to the bed and an hour later with a pool of cum rush from her body for the third time as she passed out asleep...*

Heather shook her head returning back to the current moment remembering Amir's hot sex like it was yesterday but that look in his eyes for danger was fresher as if it was this morning and the real reason she became a homicide detective without even knowing it.

"Yeah I recall somewhat but that was a long time ago. When we were innocent now we both got blood on our hands."

"To say that you must believe I could do this to my father," Amir questioned not caring what Heather accepted as the truth he just wanted to know what she knew about him.

"I don't know what to believe. I do know you ran like a man who is guilty. Plus there are the rumors." *I don't think you want to play this mind game with me Amir I'll have you running in a circle for days. Heather thought to herself.*

"Rumors is that so?"

"Yes, and If you're not guilty, why not stay and explain whatever misunderstanding there maybe."

"Because I don't fuck with the police no matter how pretty they are. Heather you of all people know a cop never did anything good for me or my family. They locked my father up at gunpoint stating that he was breaking into his own store and a whole bunch of other fuckery."

"I understand that but I have to find your father killer. I owe him that if not more. And with you being the last person believed to be with the deceased you have to come in and be questioned. If not I have no option other than trail you anywhere you go until I get answers. Like where you were at the time of your father's death?"

"Well, I hear hell is nice this time of year."

"If you got tickets I'm down. But because we are old friends I'll give you one hour to come in. Then I'm coming to get you."

"You know what's funny is how relaxed you are from your position which you believe is as a place of authority. But in my world, where you have to hold your own I bet a dollar to a dime you wouldn't last a week."

"That's a bet you would lose but you have fifty-eight minutes left then I'm putting you in cuffs."

"Ha-ha that's the geek, these are my streets and the only way you'll find me if I want you too."

"Well if that's the case you need to get out of that taxi that should be just about..." Heather paused looking at her watch knowing most of New York like the back of her hand. She calculated everything she acquired from studying the sounds in the background. The night traffic by time and distance while computing Amir's Intelligence to always take the safe route. She continued, "Your Passing 154th street."

"Wrong I'm nowhere near there." Amir quickly covered the mouthpiece of the phone whispering, "Pull over I'll get out right here."

"But Sir this is 155th street, not 169th."

"Man just pull the fuck over." Amir tossed a hundred dollar bill and exited. He uncovered the phone, "If we meet again before I find my father's killer have your vest on."

"Likewise." The phone disconnected with them both simultaneously saying.

"Let the hunt begin!"

6

The sound of the Weeknd's song *Acquainted* played quietly in the background of the all-white mid-size bathroom. Trina sang along with her eyes closed while letting the warm shower water caressing the curves of her body.

"Baby you no good because they warn me about your type." She adored the tranquility of the wetness mixed with the heat of the steam as she left out an involuntary sigh.

"You got me touchin on your body, to say that we're in love is dangerous but girl I'm so glad we're acquainted." Trina becoming lost in the words found her freshly manicured hands traveling across her perfectly round D-cup breasts stroking her harden nipples. She massaged them gently then firmly teasing herself until she no longer could fight the sensation.

Her hands flowed as if they retained a mind of their own making their way down to her completely shaved pussy finding her own wetness. She slowly parted her plump lips pushing two fingers deep inside her than another. Emotionally satisfied she began rotating her middle finger onto her aroused clitoris whispering for Amir. The vibration inside her grew. Suddenly her phone rang, again for the tenth time. Trina tighten her closed eyes pushing the sound to the back of her head thinking,

"I'm sick of this shit people keep calling your fucking phone not wanting a fucking thing but money. That's why I stop talking to people-." Then it hit her.

"Amir!"

She jumped from the shower grabbing her phone off the back of the toilet. "God no!" She screamed seeing the text that read. **"War gang!"**

Trina with her hands shaking nervously texted back one letter *"k"* then without hesitation she slammed her phone into the floor destroying it.

She dashed for the bedroom heading straight for the walk-in closet. There she pulled back the wooden double doors and paused, letting her mind take in everything. She knew this moment would possibly come one day but the knowledge of it did nothing to help the slight fear she now felt.

"Fuck it, it's on now so bitch pull it together," Trina told herself quickly tossing the high price garments to the floor as if they were nothing.

At the rear of the closet, she stared at the white wall paneling searching for any indistinctness in its structure. Nothing, she pounded at the back of the wall continually as Amir's instructions played back in her head,

"Pay close attention Trina because what's behind here is our key out of hell if the doors were to ever close behind us." Amir pointed to the latch that held the fake panel in place that shielded the wall safe behind it."

"I would have never spotted that."

"Exactly, that's why you gotta listen." Amir began to knock on the panel...Trina stopped the moment she heard the hollow sound echo that she was told to listen for. She unlatched the hook by sliding her fingers between the two panels and pulled back hard to reveal a large safe.

"This is a code your conceited ass will remember forever." Trina quickly rotated the numbers of her date of birth left, right, then left again as the safe clicked open. She removed a large black suitcase and several stacks of money.

She quickly unfastened the case,

"Shit I knew this nigga was holding out on a bitch but damn!" At first thought, she began to pocket some of the cash when she realized she was nude.

"Damn, but a bitch had to try," Trina laughed knowing deep down inside Amir loved her whole heartily but he would murder her if she ever played with his money. Though it would be more about the disrespect then the money itself.

The mere concept sent a chill up her spine. "See bitch you be doing too much." She quickly added the money with the rest of the stacks that were neatly placed inside a slot of the suitcase while her eyes scanned over the remaining contents.

The upper right and left corners of the suitcase possessed twin nine-millimeter handguns fitted snug into the installation together with several clips of ammo. Trina removed one of the weapons carefully as Amir had demonstrated on several occasions. On instinct, she cocked it back sending one in the chamber. She felt comfortable with the way the heavy steel fit inbetween the palm of her hands but she adored the power it gave her man. A feeling that she would no longer deny herself.

On the bottom half of the suitcase, there were numerous wigs in countless styles and flavors with outfits to match. Also make-up, masks, colorful contact lenses, gloves, and a diverse collection of state identifications with Trina and Amir's photos and names she didn't recognize. Last, there were two identical black win breaker jackets.

Trina took out the things she needed immediately for her task at hand before closing the suitcase. She returned the wall structure back to the way she found it while hearing Amir say, *"Love, your mind state has to be ready for war if it ever comes to the point when I tell you to get these things. Because if they're coming after me you're going to be the first person they try to get. So we must make sure that they never find you even if you're right in front of their face."*

"Baby I listened to everything you said. Plus I got a few tricks of my own so don't worry they're about to meet a true target; I vow to you."

Trina stopped in front of the nearest mirror and began to bleach her black hair. While it dried she added a pair of thick black eyelashes and some dark mascara which in turn made her smooth caramel complexion two shades darker.

The black elbow-sleeve Armani dress that Amir selected fit Trina's frame just right though she wished it was just a little tighter. She rotated slowly in the mirror checking out her figure, "Sheesh, but nothing can hide all this ass." She laughed at her 3426-32 frame.

Trina's smile quickly vanished for she understood the seriousness of the matter from her past life as a *get-em-girl* before she met Amir.

A "get em girl" is one or a group of females that travel from one town to the next targeting the biggest player in attendance. Once marked they studied the prey finding their likes, dislikes, fantasy and most importantly their insecurities before slowly transforming themselves to become what he or she couldn't deny.

Trina applied the last touch of red lipstick that matched her Fendi handbag and dark sunglasses to complete her disguise. "Let's get it."

She cracked the door slightly, making sure the hallway was clear. Detecting nothing but the cleaning lady she paused until the woman passed then swiftly stepped out heading for the elevator.

"Boss we had movement, coming out of the apartment heading toward the elevator," whispered Detective Kim into the mic hidden in her shirt button as she dusted the wall paintings in the hallway.

"Kim, is it our suspect, his girlfriend or someone else?" Heather closed her eyes hearing a slight sigh through her earpiece knowing the answer wasn't going to be good.

"I couldn't get a positive I.D Heather because they didn't come out of the room until I passed. I'm sorry, but it is a female."

"Okay, don't let her out of your sight."

"I'm trying." Kim raced for the elevator's doors in the two sizes too small uniform she stole,

"Wait please hold the elevator."

Trina entered the stainless steel elevator with her head down to avoid the camera when she heard someone shouting. She turned around witnessing a pretty thick maid running toward her. *"She's sexy,"* Trina thought becoming aroused as her eyes trailed over Kim's body.

She paused at her c-cup breasts that seem ready to break out of the grey and white maid uniform. *"Mmm... Suck able."* Her gaze shifted to Kim's thick thighs spotting the outline of her pink panties as she ran, *"mmm...fuck able."* Her vision lowered finishing her overlook to her hairy legs then her feet seeing the black high heels shoes. *"Mmm... this bitch is a cop."* Trina pushed "L" allowing the doors to close in Kim's face.

"Shit!" Kim yelled banging on the elevator door before dashing for the stairs.

Trina grinned "You'll never get me, Copper."

Downstairs in the lobby unbeknown to Trina, several plain-clothes detectives were scattered throughout the waiting area posing as customers with her description mesmerized to thought. At the front Detectives, Billy and David were positioned in the main area seated a short distance apart facing in opposite directions. David who was pretending to read a newspaper was the first to catch a glimpse,

"Oh shit, it's her! Boss... Boss, we have a problem coming in at your three o'clock."

"Boss please let me be the one to take her in." Suez cut in hoping she didn't sound too eager. She acquired her position on this special team for her brain and nothing more. The things she could achieve with a smartphone meant no household in the state was safe. Leading one to only imagine her limitations when it came to a desk top. However, in Suez's heart, a profound fire burned for action. The only reason she enlisted in the academy in the first place. If giving the chance she vows to show everyone she could be, the best undercover detective there was.

Heather role-playing as if she was drunk sat at the bar with her back to the wall babysitting the same drink for the past two hours. She fought to hold back her laughter while listening to Detective Cohen perverted come-on lines,

"So after we put this bum behind bars for murdering his father and his bitch for aiding him. Why don't you come back to my place and let me show you how to hold a real gun with both hands if you know what I mean." Detective Cohen smoothly removed his hand from his lap revealing his swollen manhood.

"I' don't say this a lot but I'm going to past. Plus Cohen that's a little 22 you're packing, and these hands don't caress nothing less than a 9mm." Heather removed Detective Cohen's hand from her thigh letting it fall into the open air. She then without missing a beat was back with the investigation shifting from his lap staring just over her left shoulder at 3 o'clock.

"I'm searching David but I don't see anything, are you certain it's her," Heather replied into the earpiece hidden by her hair.

"Boss I'm positive, I only been looking at her face for the past few hours."

"Kim, what's our target's location?"

"I'm not really sure boss, she's was and still may be on the elevator going down and I had to take the stairs."

"And how did that happen…never mind don't tell me I'll deal with you later… Okay, team prepare to take down on David's count." Heather ordered easing off the bar stool unlatching her side arm.

Detective Cohen did the same as he whispered into Heather's ear, "Come on girl don't be so cold, it may not be a 9mm but it is at least a thirty- eight."

"Maybe a three-eighty and that's pushing it. Now can you focus, this man killed a friend of mine and hurt my assistant and now I want his ungrateful ass."

"I love a girl that knows what she wants."

"Detective!"

"Okay, I'm concentrating but you can't be mad at a brother for trying." Heather couldn't hear a word of Cohen's response or anything around her for she was now in her zone.

"Boss did you hear my request," Suez asked

"Yes, denied. Now David what's her location?"

"Wait…wait…wait, okay I got her, a visual on the target by the elevators Boss and should be walking into your 12 o'clock in three… two…one."

Heather's sights locked dead center as she hastily made her way across the black and white marble floor when about twenty feet away her target trolled into site and was quickly gripped up.

"Gun!" Yelled Detective Bill, as he rammed his forearm into the back of the woman's neck pushing down hard. The target quickly rotated her upper body halfway using his weight against him and with a harder thrust off of impulse she sent him face-first into the cold surface.

Her weapon quickly elevated like Amir showed her as Detective David went into action trained for such moments he brought the butt of his gun crossways to the woman's head with just enough presser to knock her out while simultaneously stripping the weapon free.

Heather without a drop of sweat showing reached the tip of the crowd with her weapon locked on the center of her target's cranium. "Wake her."

"What happened, where am I and why the fuck are you on me. Get your damn hands off of me."

"Bring her up." The woman was brought to her feet with Heather staring directly into her bloodshot eyes seeing a face she

wouldn't have recognized if she didn't study it so well.

"Sherry is that you?"

"Yeah, yeah it's me okay, now will you tell these two morons to get the hell off of me." Sherry spit her bloody saliva at

Heather's feet. "These mother fuckers bust my lip."   With a head nod, Bill and David released her.

"Thanks a lot, Heather," Sherry said with a hint of sarcasm while straightening out her clothes.

"I did that for you as a friend but this is business." Heather turned Sherry around pushing her face-first up against the wall and gradually patting her down asking, "Sherry, what the hell are you doing here?"

Sherry with a look of bewilderment shook her head gathering herself responding "I would guess the same as you all. I came to see if my brother was here."

Heather finding nothing turned Sherry around looking her directly in the eyes, "And if he were there what were you going to do with the weapon kill him?"

"Yes."

"Interesting she didn't blink or hesitate meaning she's not lying or afraid of death." Heather thought while continuing to interrogate, "And what did you find in the apartment?" "Nothing

I knocked a few times but no one answered."

"You never once entered the apartment tonight?"

"No, never I swear! I only found out about it today after doing some searching I found out that Amir used my credit card to have-. "

"Have packages sent here from your card on three occasions."

"Yes, how you know?"

"Believe me I know more than you think. But If not you, then who?"   Heather quickly scanned the area starting at the elevator as she whispered, "Kim give me everything you have on the description of the tar-" Heather paused in mid-sentence as she locked eyes with a woman staring into the hotel's large side window.

"Never mind Kim I think I got her," Heather said while barely moving her lips not wanting to tip the woman off that she was made. "Jake she's outside positioned at the west end of the building heading north."

"I'm on it and thanks again for still having faith in me." Jake raced to get into position."

"No problem everyone falls off their bike. It's how you ride when you get back on that counts. Look in the glove compartment there's a gift for you. The rest of the team act as if we're still looking just in case she has someone watching. Jake, she is about 163 lbs. and 5'7" with blond hair."

"Who would pick such a flamboyant color knowing we're looking for them." questioned David."

"A person that understands the mind of a detective that's who. Our brain is trained to automatically look for a person trying their best to hide, so they won't be seen…. Impressive. The touch of red lipstick coated from right to left across her mouth implicates that she is left-handed. Therefore the weapon that I'm sure she is packing is in her front left pocket fellas. Not in the Fendi handbag on the right as she would want us to believe.   Which in hand matches her dark sunglasses and gloves insinuating that she also is ready for an encounter! The black dress she is wearing suggests a time of mourning with respect to her last statement saying she will kill anyone of us given the chance."

"That's her boss but how you get all that from her appearance," Kim informed finally making it downstairs.

"Because she wanted me too this woman is deeper than she appears and I may have underestimated her and Mr. Amir altogether." Heather started staring at the malicious smirk on Trina's face knowing it was an invitation when she suddenly disappeared.

"Jake she's on the move I lost visual."

"I'm right behind her and thanks for giving me my gun back. I have a feeling I'm going to need it. But where's the other one." Jake responded, from a half a block away as he pulled the tinted undercover vehicle away from the curve at the sight of Trina's flagging down a yellow cab.

"Slow down super cop one at a time. You just make sure you debrief me every 5 minutes on your location."

"Copy, over."

A Hindu man with bad English quickly exited at the sight of Trina seeing nothing but dollars sign.

"Excuse me Ms. I'm Ali Let me help you." He reached for the suitcase and was met with the tip of a Swiss blade.

"That won't be necessary. Now, will you please just take me to this address?" Trina handed Ali a business card and a hundred dollar bill. "Can you do that?"

"Yes, yes like how you say with the quickness."

Trina paused at the threshold of the cab looking around before disappearing into the back seat.

The cab moved with the flow of the traffic as Jake whispered to himself, "That's it take me right to the son of a bitch and I'm going to make him pay for what he did to me." While staring at the scar on his eye in the rearview mirror.

"Excuse me Jake did you say something."

"Oh, no boss just promising myself something that's all."

7

A few miles away as Trina was being followed, Damon sat dressed in all black hidden behind the tint of his Audi A8. The customized license plate read **headhita** for anybody that didn't understand who they were dealing with. He pulled the powerful engine to a stop in front of the Harlem Riverside housing project under the evil gaze of many on looking hustlers.

"I got it enough said." He replied, into the car phone.

"No, it's not." Amir hastily corrected as he tightened his grip around the bruised man's neck that kneeled before him.

"But son you know we don't play these phones like that."

"Then don't say nothing this one is all on me. Right now I don't give a fuck if someone listening they can get it too. You just make sure that this one doesn't get away. I need to talk to him ASAP. I sent you his apartment number and all the info you gonna need."

"I got it don't worry. I have been wanting to show these niggas what it is anyway down here."

"Okay, but none that ego hero shit that you be doing on this one.   There's not an inch of room for that do you understand me. "

"Yeah I do but I'm your homie, not your worker."

"Then act like it nigga, what the fuck you even fix your mouth to say some shit like that for anyway? You tipping or have you forgotten that quick that your ass was just on the line and I didn't say a word! Let alone hesitate. I let my gun speak for me and right now it has a lot to say. So Nigga you either going to move like a gangster or you not, there's no in-between." Amir slowly digging his knife into his victim's armpit. "Aaaahh!"

"What was that- never mind I'm going to act like I didn't hear it. But I got your back homie. I'll get the Op's you can bank on that." Damon looked to the 45 automatic resting in his lap and grinned disconnecting the call. He turned the stereo back up moving his head to the rhythm of Future's song, "*Homicide.*"

Damon knew it was time to get busy but his thoughts were still partly occupied by Frankie's and Amir, confrontation. "*It's you, the guy with the pic-...That man lying fuck'em.*"

Damon understood that a man who was about to meet his maker would say anything to lengthen his stay on earth. However, the stare in Frankie's eyes at the sight of Amir gave him a funny gut feeling.

"I pray he was lying homie because I already had one man I respected let me down in life. I don't know what I would do if the only one I had left did the same."

Damon spoke of his father who abandoned him as an adolescent. He continued to listen to the lyrics as he got in his zone.

"*How many a ride for you, open up that fire for you. You gotta question a nigga standing next to you, cut him off. I grew up on the side you gotta make yourself a boss. Niggas'll shit on you any chance they get, Cross you out on a lick...*"

"Real talk and I been having doubts about this nigga lately but he just saved my life literally again. So even if the cross is in and I'm the one that's tagged...IT, I have no other option but to ride for him until I know for certain that he's playing me. For loyalty is not a guess it's an action... Time to work."

Damon opened the glove compartment removing the back-up berretta. He swiftly cocked it making sure it was ready in case called upon. He stuffed it into the center of his back as he collected a back-pack off the back seat and departed.

Approximately twenty feet away at the entrance of the project several men took notice to the black tinted sedan pulling to a stop as they handled they're business of selling cocaine, pills, weed, movies, PCP, heroin; you name it.

In the mist of the constant coming and going traffic two men gave their undivided attention to the automobile.

"Yo... yo son, check that piece that just parked up." Chuck said, pulling on the berry dutchie laced with crack and weed once more before passing it to Earl his right hand man. Earl took the smoke deep into his lungs then slowly exhaled becoming higher than a giraffe's ass.

"Yeah, I see it. Who that be?"

"I don't know but they must be gripping from somebody up in here heavy to be moving around in something as smooth as that shit!"

"Word son or dropping something off."

"True that... true that, copping or dropping nigga either way..." The two looked at each other saying in, "We need that." They laughed when chuck became serious.

"Now you know what you got to do so we can get this bag right."

"What you mean I'm strapped let's have at it."

"Me too but come on son don't play dumb you know we can't do nothing unless we go through your cousin Gun-smoke."

"Who Melvin? Man fuck him that nigga not like us no more ever since he started hustling and got that plug."

"Man don't even play Gun-smoke like that because he got those birds flying like they're going south for the winter. He's getting at a real dollar at the moment and I'm not mad at him. But get out of line and he'll bust anybody ass with the quickness. You know he has robbed niggas while they were robbing niggas. So still shit doesn't go down without his approval in this hood and that's on the set."

"Okay but remember you said to ask that nigga. I'm on go I don't need a nigga to tell me if I can ride."

"Yeah...Yeah just go head and walk over there and handle that and keep that noise down cause if Gun-smoke hears you talking crazy he going to bust your ass."

"Man his name is Melvin and he not letting a bullet fly no more so fuck him, he soft now," Earl whispered under his breath as he made his way through the crowd coming within ten feet of Melvin.

"Woah woah…Slow down…where do you think you're going?" asked Kenny one of Melvin's top men.

"To mind, my mother fucking business now get the fuck out the way."

"Nigga anything passed this point is my business and you know it. Keep it up and you going to make me show you better than I can tell you."

"Man I don't have time for all that shit right now I just want to see my cousin Mel real quick."

"You gotta appointment."

"Nigga you got to be fucking joking, he standing right the fuck there,"

"And he is speaking with someone that has an appointment."

"Fuck that yo cuz… hey, Mel, it's me E."

"That's it, time for you to go." Kenny with his "6.9" 310 lb. structure gripped Earl up by the neck as he blew the lace smoke into his face.

"You think that's funny well it won't be when I crush your voice box." Kenny started squeezing tightly cutting of Earl's air.

"Chill Ken we can't have the block all hot because you want to put in some action. So let him go…that's better, now what's going on?" questioned Gun-Smoke stepping between the two.

"You just saved your coke head people's life that's what's popping."

"Mines or was it yours he prolonged, pussy."

"What you say, nigga-" Kenny pulled back his fist aiming for Earl's face when the stare of confidence in the depth of Earl's glossy eyes forced him to look down noticing a gun resting at his stomach.

"Bet, I see how it is playboy. I know one thing you better let it fly when it's time."

"Don't I always?"

"No, no ken it's nothing like that I'm sure E was just messing with you right E." Gun-Smoke asked as he wrapped his arm around Earl's shoulder pulling him in the opposite direction "Fuck no I'm not jo-."

"Right E because you know Ken's family also and I don't like nobody fucking with my family, not even family, so indeed you were just playing right?"

"Right my bad Kenny."

"That's better now what brings you over here to speak with me when I know you don't like me."

"You see that nice ride that's parked up a little bit down the block."

"Yeah the Audi," Gun-Smoke looked at his Rolex, "It's been there five minutes and forty-eight seconds what about it."

"Is it one of your people if not, you already know what I'm on?" Gun-Smoke again looked at the car studying it hard, not wanting to make a mistake. Because Earl was surely to do whoever it was filthy.

"Pardon me Gun-smoke," Chuck interrupted, "Yo E peep it, he just jumped out and he had a book bag and it might got that work in it."

"Chuck you in on this too?"

"Yeah I know Smoke, I'm on hard times right now."

"Well hurry up because your meal ticket is heading for the cut leading to the buildings."

"We on it."

"I hear you, just make sure I get my cut." Gun-Smoke shook his head as he watched his cousin race off when he turned and locked eyes with the man from the car just seconds before disappearing into the cut.

"Oh shit!"

Damon pulled the hoodie down over his wool hat as he exited the vehicle now fully in his zone. He walked with the mind state of a killer another lesson taught the instant they returned from taking down his first score....

"What the fuck you smiling for Damon?"

"What you mean we did it or you don't see all that money that's in that suit case underneath that paperwork. That's why I'm fucking smiling which is the reason why you killed that man true?"

"You damn right just like it's a mother fucker out there right now waiting on his chance to tag you... IT. To sentence your ass to the earth to live, because you're eating now and their not and they possess the same hunger you did when you step to Keith to take his spot. That same hunger you possessed seconds ago before you witness that money which put that large fucking smile on your face."

Damon quickly made his teeth vanish.

"That's better, now if you want to stay getting this money you must remain with the mind state of a nigga that haven't eaten in days...remember how it feels to be starving and there you will always find the true mind state of a murderer. Walk with that before you move and you will eat forever..."

Damon grinned at the thought as he looked around in search of the two men that were staring at his car as if they haven't been fed in weeks. When he locked eyes with someone he knew.

"Gun-smoke," Damon said and from the look on his face, he knew for certain now that his name held the weight it finally deserved out in the street.

Damon loved the feeling of respect that rushed through his body at that very second thinking, *"Yeah, in a minute these streets may be all mine and I'll become too big to be tagged...IT."*

He disappeared behind the building merging with the darkness heading for the second complex. His next move was slightly different than he was taught. Instead of rotating his head away from people he passed so his identity couldn't be remembered. Damon with his new found admiration walked with his head at mid-level daring someone to look in his direction.

He reached the second building door and paused looking over his shoulder as if he sensed Earl and Chuck several feet away hiding in the same darkness from which he came. He snickered then took the stairs two at a time in search of his target's apartment.

"Yo son I think that nigga saw us following him," whispered Chuck as he gripped hold of Earl's arm who quickly try to pursue without hesitation.

"Man I don't care what he saw but I know what he is about to see, me going in his damn pockets." Earl pulled free determined as the lust for dollars danced in his vision. He rushed for the second building door not waiting to see if Chuck would follow or not.

Chuck beginning to trail his other half as normal when suddenly his ACG boots stopped in their tracks as a voice enter his head at the thought of Gun-smoke's face.

"Whenever you witness fear on a man's face and he is known to be feared be cautious because there's death on the other side of his stare," Chuck never forgot those words when he was 10 from a block gangster as they stepped into the cleaners owned by another gangster who looked shocked to see them before the gangster he was with shot the other one in his face.

"It's something up with this nigga I know it and why didn't he send Ken like the rest of the times to get his share?" Chuck shook his head to clear his own fears just as Earl slid through the door. His boots begin to sluggishly move toward the entrance then quicken until he was in an all-out race at the sound of a loud thump against the large metal frame.

Chuck slightly out of breath reached the door easing it back to observe Earl's bloody body leaning against the wall at the foot of the steps.

"Oh shit!"

Chuck rushed to his side quickly taking his own shirt off ripping it into pieces.

"Yo son where you hit at?" Chuck removing Earl's top noticing several rocks falling to the floor.

"Here, here and there." Earl's weak voice whispered. Chuck quickly applied pressure to the two bullet wounds in Earl's chest by wrapping half his shirt around his upper torso. By the position of the shot, Chuck knew in his heart that his friend would be dead within minutes.

"Don't worry you going to be straight Son, my word it's not that bad. Now tell me which way he went so I can handle this nigga." Chuck studied the other wound placed on the top of Earl's shoulder thinking it was an odd place to get hit.

"Chuck I'm getting cold man!"

"Here hit this smoke and just relax E, help is on its' way. Now tell me where this nigga at."

"No chuck just slide on this one man."

"What! This is my fault I should have come through the door when you did now I'm going to finish it."

"Then we both would be here dying, lying to each other about how bad we're hurt all because we were tricked by some rocks."

"E either way I'm going after this nigga with or without your help."

"I know ah…ah...ah," Earl coughed with blood coming out of his mouth and nose but he fought to continue to speak. "I know you would Chuck if it was only to put my name at rest but we been getting high and shit son and somewhere we lost a step or two. That kid had me falling backward before I knew what ah…ah… what was hitting m-"

Earl's eyes closed as his head fell back against the floor.

"Shit E wake up son you got to tell me which way he went so I can get this young motherfucker." Chuck removed his gun then slapped Earl across the face while continually rotating his stare. "E please tell me something."

On contact Earl's eyes reopened with his hand pointing upward. He coughed trying to clear the blood that collected in his throat as he continued to whisper something that Chuck could barely make out.

"What E, he's up there E...E is that it E..." Chuck looked up seeing nothing. "E... when-"

He stopped his inquiry witnessing his friend taking his last breathe. He closed Earl's eyes with his right hand while his left detached the weapon from his waistline. "Don't worry dog I got you."

Chuck headed for the steps when the metal door flew open behind him. On reflex, Chuck leveled his automatic off at a lady's head as she held her sleeping son close to her chest.

"This building is closed until you see two bodies come out Liz and not a moment sooner so until then you keep your mouth shut."

Chuck received a head nod before he slammed the door in her face. He looked down the hall of the first floor seeing no one in sight as if the project could smell when death was in the air. He raced for the stairs then paused as he noticed several small rock fragments lingering in the air.

"This fucking building is falling the fuck apart." On impulse, he stretched his hand out catching the falling of rocks in his palm. He redirected his vision from his hand to the floor staring at the rock lying next to Earl's dead body.

Chuck's head moved upward trailing the stream of rocks when his eyes shot open. Damon was hanging over the banister with his gun aimed in one hand while the other slowly released stones three at a time.

"Oh shy-" escape Chuck's mouth as a bullet slammed into the top of his shoulder knocking him down against the rail and out into the open.

Damon repetitively pulled the trigger placing two holes in Chuck's chest, "Clean your fucking ears out your man was telling you beware he's up there. Even I heard that."

The force of the impact sent Chuck falling back tripping over Earl's body as he fell to the floor. His gun slid down the hall to the right.

"Shit!" Chuck pushed himself up needing to win this fight to prove to himself that he wasn't a "has been" junkie before crashing back down not having the strength. His eyes open seeing the rocks rolling off of his finger tips and smiled.

"Tricked by some rocks in life and out of it, I get it now E." He whispered with his last breathe.

"You should have read the license plate," Damon stated sending a shot into both men's head. He pulled himself up from the banister as if he was doing a sit up and untied his legs from the railing one at a time. He used his upper body strength lowering himself down onto the steps.

Damon with a backpack in hand checked his watch seeing that he was now two minutes behind schedule.

"Fucking with you two clowns." He kicked Earl in the face then raced off to finish his mission.

A minute later the metal door eased open with Kenny stating, "You were right Gun-Smoke he downed them both quickly. It doesn't look like they even got a shot off."

"Okay stay with him but far in the shadow because we just want to find out what he is doing here and watch out for his partner he's slick if not the slickest."

"There is no partner he's all alone, don't worry I can handle him smoke."

"No Amir's around somewhere you can bet your life on that." Gun-smoke assumed remembering his old running mate method of cutting loose ends.

"Ok, I'll keep an eye open."

Damon reached the second floor to the sound of loud banging and people yelling "Hey open the fucking door."

"Yo who the hell got the door locked?" **Boom! Boom!**

"Peep son maybe they're raiding check the apartment and make sure they didn't cut the water off so we can't flush nothing."

Damon pulled the hoody down over his head until his face was barely visible before removing the long bicycle lock he placed on the double door handles. He pulled the door open remaining behind the larger metal sheltering himself. He studied the faces of the people who flowed passed. He remained hidden as the echoes' of screams grew in the staircase.

He listened carefully waiting on the prefect time to make his move as he relaxed like Amir instructed, *"Always stay composed for pressure is only effective to a person that fears his outcome in action. But a man who thinks in his time of danger can control any outcome...making it nothing to fear.*

"Holy god in heaven someone call the cops they're dead," yelled a woman in shock.

"It won't be you bitch because your blind and didn't see shit right. Now bring your silly ass on and let's get to the store before we're the fuck down there with them," corrected her husband as he pulled her by the arm out the door with the rest of the people acting as if there wasn't anything wrong.

"Yo who got the perc's (Percocet's) in?

"The cat in 211 got them big boy 30's but damn yo that's

Earl and his man. Somebody fucked them around," a young man stated to another.

"Word son but I don't give a fuck this nigga was holding and got caught slipping this be me, we out." The other one answered stuffing Chuck's gun into his waistline and quickly exited.

"I'm uploading this to worldstar." Someone else yelled.

Damon eased from behind the doors and merged into the large crowd that formed in the hallway. People were pushing each other to get a glimpse of the bodies to be assured that it wasn't their family. Damon examined the apartment numbers at least the ones that still remained until he came to the third one from the end, "Bingo! 238E"

Damon swiftly covered the peephole with black tape. He looked in both directions as he began picking the lock.

"Shit the masker lock on!" He placed his ear to the old dirty door listening for movement while reattaching the silencer.

He firmly knocked **Boom...Boom...Boom!**

"Wait! What was that?" asked Tonya as she paused from giving Keith oral pleasures.

"Nothing bitch you always act funny after you smoke that shit. Now get back to doing what you been doing. I'm rolling and you're blowing my shit." Keith yelled, kicking the bedroom door shut as he grabbed the back of Tonya's neck pulling her deeper into his lap.

Tonya, submitting, began running her tongue alongside Keith's stiff shaft giving chase to her preceding saliva trickling down to his balls. She slowly took them into her warm overly moistened mouth creating a slurping sound with each suction as she moved from the left ball to the right and back again. The feeling of Keith's penis stiffing to full capacity let Tonya know her job was mostly done. She gently kissed up the middle reaching the top. She forced the head of his dick into her mouth not stopping until hitting the back of her throat.

Keith pushed in deeper until Tonya gagged for air. He smiled at the split rolling from her mouth draping down her chin silently falling onto her exposed…... nipples."

Boom...Boom...Boom

"Wait! Now I know you had to hear that."

"Yeah but fuck that I'm about to bust, don't stop its right there."

"No, I got to go see who it is because it could be Brad or one of those case managers."

"That little bad ass nigga can wait out there another five minutes he probably stole something and running in here to hide out what is he like 20 now?"

"No, he's 12 and don't be so mean he is still my kid. I'll be right back you won't even miss me." Tonya threw her robe on grasping some of the cash Keith placed on the dresser leaving the rest. "Just in case you try something funny again."

"Bitch I gave you that sixty dollars though didn't I? So stop bringing that shit the fuck back up."

"Mom!" **Boom... Boom... Boom!**

"Okay...okay, I'm coming don't lose your shirt shit! If it wasn't for C.F.S (child and family services) I wouldn't even open this damn door with you banging like your crazy." Tonya made her way up the stairs looking over her shoulder making sure that

Keith didn't follow. Confident, she removed the twenty-five bags of cocaine from her pussy she stole from his pants pocket while handling her business.

Boom...Boom...Boom!

"Alright alright, I'm coming." Tonya swung the door open, "Boy why the hell is you banging on my door like that!"

"Because I forgot my key mom damn! But instead of you asking me about the door you should be telling me you have my half of the welfare check that you smoked the hell up."

"Boy, I don't want to hear that shit I said I would give it back to you and I will but here, take these 15 bags. They're the biggest out there so I don't want to hear any shit. You can get twenty for them easy but I'm only going to count it for a hundred dollars now go ahead to your room and be quiet I got company." Brad looked at the bags stamped with the gun on top and grinned saying. "You got these from Keith is he still here?"

"I didn't get them from him and stop being so damn nosey."

"Yes you did and I know they're his bags because I use to hustle for him before you stole my pack and they beat my ass then kicked me off the block for good remember?"

"Yeah smart ass I remember and what did I have to do for them to stop kicking your little smart ass. Shit, I'm still fucking doing it."

"So he is here and where is Ruby?" Brad asked speaking of his old sister

"She's outside running around somewhere with her thot ass." She lied. "Shit since you want to be in everybody's got damn business boy yeah Keith here so. What you going to do get your ass kicked again."

"No, I think I'm going to be doing the beating today," Damon said stepping out from the kitchen with his gun aimed at Tonya.

"Oh my goodness please don't kill me I'm going to pay it back I swear. I ca-."

"Sssshhhhh." Damon placed his gloved finger onto Tonya's trembling lip. "That's better…yo kid in my back pocket is the paper with a little bonus."

Brad not believing his eyes quickly recounted the five one-hundred dollar bills in his palms. Smiling he said, "Not bad for acting like I lost my key huh mom."

"Aww, you ungrateful little shit! I knew I should have swallowed your ass."

"Then where would you be sleeping, in the street like the rest of the crackheads? If it wasn't for me you wouldn't have 20 dollar rent. So I'm doing what I have too to keep myself straight and you as well. I'll be ordering dinner in an hour and don't worry he's not going to hurt you its Keith he wants." Brad walked into his room shutting the door on his mother's voice.

"Boy, what mess you have done put me in!"

The moment the door closed Damon motioned with his gun, "Lead the way."

Tonya doing as directed held her breathe with each step. She turned the knob pushing the door in slowly.

"Hurry on in here bitch you right on time I'm about to cuummm… Aaaahh!" Keith yelled as he gripped the back of Ruby's head shooting his cum into the back of her throat.

"Yo save some of that I want your mom to taste it too."

"Too late I swallowed it already," Ruby said grasping the rest of the money and cocaine from the dresser not planning on sharing.

"Damn Tonya you should give your portion of the money to Ruby she did all the fucking work for-" Keith's words got stuck in his throat at the sight of the weapon resting on Tonya's shoulder aimed at his face. He was insightful that this moment would one day come for he had been doing people grimy since he was born.

Keith studied the mask man's facial structure knowing that it could possibly be anyone. The Jamaicans, Russians, the Mob, Jews and so on. He took a deep breath as his eyes shifted to his pistol lying in the middle of the dresser. He quickly distinguished it would be impossible to reach and survive.

"But what if this man is not the real deal?"

Ruby sensing the sudden tension in the air lifted her head from the lines of cocaine asking, "Baby what's wrong? You ready to go again."

"No, it's you that will be going… now get your clothes and get out…me and Keith here have somewhere to be." Damon demanded.

"I know that voice from somewhere." Keith thought to himself as he watched Ruby quickly gather her things.

"Get the hell on you unappreciative bitch."

"What the fuck ever Keith, this man got a gun what I'm supposed to do die for you because you got big bags nigga bye period." Ruby rose from her knees rushing behind her mother toward the exit.

Keith kicked her hard in the back sending her flying off balance in Damon's direction. Ruby still high from the cocaine couldn't keep upright and crashed into Damon knocking him back into the dresser. On impulse, he pulled the trigger distributing several shots in the direction of Keith's weapon. The force of the kickback slid him across the dresser top up against the wall. He pushed Ruby to the floor just as Keith raced passed ducking. Damon knew what he was ordered to do but at this point, he could care less whether Keith lived or died as he took aim and fired.

Keith headed up the L shape stairs feeling the power of bullets flying pass his head slamming into the banister. He turned left lowering himself while taking the last section of steps three at a time. His mind raced at hundred miles per hour searching for a plot to stay alive.

Keith made it to the top of the stairs listening for footsteps pursuing him. Hearing none he dashed for the front door when several shots came exploding through the thin drywall.

"Aaaahh!" Keith yelled, in agony as he fell to the floor. He stared at the blood running out the quarter size hole in his side.

"*Damn I'm fucked up-*," Keith whispered when the sound of footsteps slowly approaching stopped him in mid thought. He took in a deep breath before struggling to return to his feet refusing to die on the floor of a crackhead's apartment.

He stood up right to be met by the barrel of a weapon place to the back of his head. "Enough of the playing around you know what this is." "Young boah?"

Damon didn't response instead he swung his weapon several times into Keith's head until he went out cold.

"You still didn't bust your gun pussy."

Damon stuck his head out into the hallway looking before stepping out with Keith draped over his shoulder.

"Ah, he just had a little too much to drink." He stated to no one in particular but to diminish any curiosity as he walked through the small crowd. If Keith's feet weren't in the way Damon would have seen Kenny standing in the mist of the crowd watching him with deep hatred in his eyes that he couldn't hide.

Kenny moved away from the elderly woman in the yellow dress to follow his own orders as he stepped away from the crowd placing another call.

"Yo Gun-Smoke our boy is putting some serious work in on home turf now he just kidnapped Keith."

"What! Where? Out his own dope house? What lil Moss, kill Mo and them niggas do."

"Nothing because who ever gave the paper work up on him really did their homework. They caught him lunching at the young girl's spot they say he be fucking on the second floor."

"Damn Keith them hoes will play you out every time shit! Now Ken where you at?"

"I'm following him now coming down the back staircase."

"Man hold up, whatever is going down got to be deep and I don't think we want to be a part of it. I know Amir is around some where I can feel it in my soul."

"Kopi but that nigga can't be in motion on this one or I would have spotted him already. Plus Keith owes us. I think it's like 30 G's left on his tab so if we let him go we're saying bye to our cash and I'm not having that." Kenny said peeping out the exit door spotting Damon heading back toward his car.

"Excuse me, dear, can I get out." Asked an old lady coming down the stairs.

"Just one second grandma." Kenny said as he continued listening to his partner's reasoning, "I understand all that but on this one, we should just get what we can from his young bulls and call it a day.'

"You know that's not happening without his word."

Gun- Smoke let out a deep sigh trusting that his best friend was right before the words departed from his lips. "Okay go get him but be safe and quiet because in no way can this be lead back to us or we'll have a war to remember."

"Kopi-"

"Excuse me, son, I really have to be somewhere soon, can I please be on my way?" The old lady interrupted, now standing right beside Kenny. He turned facing the elderly woman as his eyes roamed over her filthy appearance. The large hat which had seen to many Sunday services was pulled down low over her face.

"I guess she's trying to hide her shame." Kenny assumed while still observing her. The antique wooden cane her shaken gloved hands held tightly to keep from falling rested at her side.

He paused at the cheap yellow dress that shelter her tall frame from the naked eye and shook his head. All things considered, Kenny deep down inside felt sorry for her being alone in this rough project like his mama when he went to jail.

"Yes come on you can go." He stepped aside holding the door open.

"Yo Kenny who you talking to."

"Nobody just some old lady but don't trip he's not getting away, I'm just letting her pass so I don't come out right behind him and he gets hip to me following him."

"Wait, some lady, then that means he doesn't know her not in our hood. We know everybody something doesn't sound right." Gun-smoke thought to himself when it hit him. "Oh shit…. No
Ken don'ttt!"

Kenny with the phone to his side extended his hand to aid the elderly lady just as she spun the cane around pushing a button on the side of it. A sharp double edge blade projected out of the end.

"What the fuck-" escaped Kenny's mouth as the blade sliced through his neck.

Amir knew he was dead before his body hit the floor but that didn't stop him from stabbing him in the face twice. He quickly removed the wig, make up and old lady outfit. He unrolled the pant legs to the jumpsuit he wore underneath. All together Amir pried the phone from Kenny's fingers.

"Gun-smoke is that you nigga?" Amir grilled stepping through the metal door out into the night air.

Gun-Smoke shocked to hear his name smirked as he removed the nervousness that overcame his body as he thought of his next move. He quickly muted the phone shouting, "Yo everyone get the fuck on point now! The ops are here."

"What is it 12, you want me to put the coke up."

"Fuck the cops this nigger is the worst." Gun-smoke was well acquainted with Amir's reputation in the street and knew he wasn't a sucker by far. When it came to killing a man he never second guessed his orders and depending on what they did was how he made the decisions on how bad he would do them. Over time he was labeled one of the best head hitters in the game.

Gun- Smoke decided not to follow his first instinct, to hang up and denying he knew anything of Kenny's plans. This would only lead to a dishonorable war and Gun Smoke was far from a coward himself. But he knew the only way he would get revenge for Kenny was to remain calm and sharp as a razor and to do that he had to remove all emotions of his best friend. Who he knew now was dead; but how bad was now the question.

"Yeah, it's me, Amir, what's good?"

"Nothing."

"I'm sorry to hear that, so I guess this means there can't be a good reason you're in my hood."

"I'm here because my father was murdered making every hood now my hood until I find his killer and murder everything he or she knows and loves. Therefore whoever gets in my way of doing that will get the same. Do you have a problem with that main man?"

"Point noted and Kenny's condition?"

"A closed casket."

"Dammit."

"Shit it could have been worst and you know it." Amir tossed the phone out into oncoming traffic watching it being smashed into several pieces before racing off to join Damon.

8

1:00 am on the second floor of the homicide special division Building, Heather and several detectives were hard at work prying through Amir's life. They pieced it apart from separate perspectives trying to understand who Amir had actually become since Heather knew him several years prior. Their main objective was to make a distinction as to why he would kill his father and what his exit plan was now that he was on the run.

Heather who was never unpunctual to a team meeting for she led by example based on the method spoken by Eleanor Roosevelt, *"It is not fair to ask of others what you are unwilling to do yourself."* But, today Heather was actually a half an hour behind schedule in addressing her team on the main floor.

She sipped on her tenth cup of coffee with her eyes fastened to the computer screen as she read over Amir's life and criminal history for the twentieth time.

Amir commenced in a life of crime on record merely at the age of 13. He was found in the possession of a loaded firearm shortly after the death of his mother. The officers in charge believed the weapon was recently fired in a robbery nearby but with no witnesses and Amir refusing to say where he got it from, he was sentenced to six months in a juvenile detention center.

Amir escaped three weeks later in which a security guard's arm was fractured. He was apprehended seven months later in Philadelphia during a routine traffic stop where he was badly beaten before being sent back to New York to face his charges. The two police man who was believed to have harmed him was murdered the following day. Amir's Uncle Robert was charged will the assassinations with his own trial ending in a not guilty verdict. The astonishing thing to Heather was after the verdict he yelled. "This will happen again in a heartbeat to anyone of you that touches my blood for nothing happen to my family without repercussions."

Heather shook her head as she completed the rest of the twenty two pages. She memorized Amir's past word for word still not believing her eyes.

"This man will do anything not to be put in a cage. He may even kill again. I have to stop him now weather I like it or not. Now, where is it? I have to be missing something but it's here I know it! I can feel it in my bones. Every murderer leaves a trail of his or her motives in their past for their killings in the present, but what's his?" She shouted slamming her fist hard into the desk top frustrated.

Heather took a deep breath pausing to let her brain rest devoting several minutes to Barbara's case. She then started back from the top with Amir's when Alex tapped her on the shoulder.

"Hey hey, lighten up pretty girl maybe you should go home and get some shut eye for a few hours and I'll handle everything here until you get back."

"Come on you know I could never do that. This means too much to me, plus you know we only have a two day window to find him. After that our chances are slim to none."

"I understand the value you have in all this. But this is not like you. You're running late to command your crew, you look like shit. All in all, I think your just being too hard on yourself.
We just got to gather up this sick son of the bitch and I'll make him talk. Then you'll put him away right Heather?" Alex's words were more like a demand than a question.

"Yes but we only have the knowledge of what Sherry said and she didn't witness the murder. The DA won't take the case at all at this moment with only circumstantial evidence. We need more information before I put him away for the rest of his life.
That is if he doesn't talk."

"What is there for the DA to have doubt about this time? The father said he was there and 20 minutes later he was dead and to top it off the man that we found dead next to the victim, just happens to be a longtime acquaintance of Amir's. Shit, we have people on death row for less."

"I understand and you're right but something is missing. I read over Amir's record again and again and his father had never let him down not once that I can find. He always paid the top lawyers when he was in trouble. I talked to a few of them today and they all said the same that Mr. Patrick paid on time biweekly.

That's why Amir never had a conviction stay on his recorded. His father never missed a court appearance or showed a lack of support that I can see."

"That's all fine and dandy but maybe the reason is there and you don't want to see it and that's why you can't find it."

"And what the hell is that supposed to mean?"

"Heather you can't bull shit a bull shitter I saw the look in your eyes the moment he stepped into the store."

"And what look was that Alex if you don't mine me asking?"

"The   look   of   lust."

Smack!

Heather's hand connected hard with Alex's face as she jumped up from behind her desk, "Don't you dare stand there questioning my integrity when it comes to my work ever! Do you understand me? I give a hundred and ten percent from the moment I get up to the minute my eyes collapse."

"I can't question it but you can?" Alex inquired turning Heather's hand over onto its bruised side, "The desk never hurt anyone but yet I find you here hurting yourself. It sure seems like doubt to me."

"Point taken but if I'm not missing it then it's not there."

"Oh, it's there because this son of a bitch is a cold hearted killer. Do you know in some parts of New York they call him the Wolf of All Streets? Oh, you didn't think I read his file? Well, I did and there's nothing in it but violence. Then I hit the streets to see what they had to say about him and believe me this guy put down more men than a two dollar hoe in Mexico. So we have to get him off the street before he gets away with another murder. Now show me once more why they call you the best detective in

New York because you don't miss anything."

"Your right Alex I don't miss…I take shit down." Heather's eyelids reconnected visualizing the crime scene, first the victim's home followed by Amir's apartment. She rearranged things around in her head at each section like chess pieces in a game being played against different players each on a level higher than the previous.

After forty-five games going into the forty-six Heather's eyes shot open.

"Checkmate, I can't believe I didn't think of it sooner." She kissed Alex on the cheek "The reason for the killing wasn't missed we just wasn't looking for it in the right place. Get your coat while I address the team."

"That's my girl I'll meet you out front in 5 minutes."

"Oh and Alex,"

"Yes."

"Is Sherry still down stairs being interviewed?"

"Yes but she'll be cleared in about a half an hour or so. They're just waiting for the paperwork on the gun she had to come back but it's clean I ran the numbers personally."

"Well see that it gets lost for a few hours."

"I will try but as you know her father was a powerful man in the community and there have been a lot of calls to make sure she is getting the proper treatment mostly from some firm out of

Philadelphia."

"Which one in particular?"

"They didn't say I'll have the calls track down."

"You do that."

Heather stepped into the center of the room with it instantly becoming silent. Her look of determination and accomplishments demanded such respect and every law enforcement agent knew this without it needing to be said. She waited a few seconds in the quietness to let the enthusiasm of being in her presence past. She knew many detectives young and old had fought for years to work with her even though she really didn't know why since her life was a living hell. Whatever the case after all their hard work they had finally made it.

Heather didn't only prefer the best team on paper to put away the worst murderers in New York. That was just the tip of the iceberg. She researched detectives time sheets, dating routines and actual phase in their field history to elect her team by the premier scorer and most dedicated.

She scanned the room making sure every eye still possess the same hunger as she once did, before speaking,

"I know a lot of you are tired and want to go home and get some sleep but a man is dead. It's our job to make sure that the people or person that did this appalling crime is brought to justice. This will happen over and over again until there is not a killer left in New York City with or without you. Consequently for whatever reason if you're not willing to give a hundred and ten percent raise your hand and you can go there's the door…

thank you Mr. Jordan have a nice night."

"What! I didn't raise my hand."

"Yes, but your eyes did and tell her whomever she maybe that I said hello. Now please shut the door behind you when you leave we still have a lot of work to do. Which starts by being focus."

"Fuck!" Detective Jordan yelled while exiting as he thought, *"Damn she's good. I got to remember to dump my side chick while my wife and I are on vacation."*

Heather continued, "As for the rest of you I apologize for my delay and it won't happen again I promise. However, something very important to our case has just come across my

114

desk that may possibly break this case wide open. So I'll need to be debriefed with every drop of information you have established."

Heather's eyes shifted to the right side of the room stopping on a slim pretty woman with a rich caramel complexion. The shoulder length ponytail and new but traditional black office glasses she wore assumed the beauty of her green eyes and nice figure.

Heather cleared her throat so her words wouldn't be mistaken thinking; *"I understand your afraid of being who you are hopefully this will break you out of that...*Suez will you please come up front. This is Suez for those of you who don't know. She is our technology field specialist and one of the best I must add or she wouldn't be in this room. You all will be debriefing through her and she will relay it to me in order of its significance.

Suez don't let me down."

"Never."

"That's good to hear." Heather smiled leaning into Suez's ear whispering. "Fuck words they mean nothing from this point on, look around you... without moving your head dammit! Just your eyes and keep on smiling. You see there's only one other female in this room and that's Kim and she would be up here in your place but she fucked up by letting our target get away.

Which in turn told me she isn't ready for the position. So there will be no support on her behalf because she will have her own shit to deal with mentally and physically. But these men from this moment on are going to do anything in their power to prove you don't deserve this position. A position of authority over them which makes you a threat. So show me what you can do and save the small talk."

"If you knew this would happen then why do this to me?" Suez's uttered without moving her lips.

"Because it was done to me, and I still can't thank that person enough for showing me not to be afraid of who I am, rather than embracing it. Now pull your skirt down and your chin up or you're going to be fucked." Heather spoke the rest of her statement out loud, "I will be prepared to give you and the team my full attention in about ten no make it twenty minutes because

I need to freshen up."

"You look fine to me.?"

"Flattery will get you nowhere-."

"Excuse me, Boss, this just came in and I think you should see it," yelled Kim ripping a sheet of paper from the printer racing from the back of the room to Heather's side.

"Okay, what does it say?"

"It seems that Amir is back at it already. A few hours ago two men were found dead in a Brooklyn home with three gunshot wounds lodged in the back of each cranium. They were shot executional style but only after being tortured for hours according to the coroner's report. The men were stabbed over forty-five times. In the hands, feet, and armpits. He slowly let them bleed out until finally putting them out of their misery.

"And what makes you believe it was him?"

"Because one of the men happens to be Shane Peterson. The same Shane Peterson yo-."

"I placed the A.P.B on." Heather finished the statement.

"Yes, and his cousin Tommy Harrell who, Intel believes was at the wrong place at the wrong time." Kim handed Heather the photos of the dead bodies.

Heather skimmed over the images searching for any mistake that Amir may have made. Her eyes zeroed in on the victim's puncture wounds. "I'll be damned Alex's was right."

"What is it?" Kim probed eager to know what she missed.

"Whoever did this is an assassin by heart. The way they were killed was not a random act. Look at the wounds, they all are half an inch apart never hitting the main artery. Some spots have been hit harder than others. Pay close attention to where the muscle became thicker. He makes a slightly deeper incision. The killer wanted answers and I think I know of whom. Find Keith Johnson immediately because by the looks of it he will be dead sooner than later."

"I'm on it boss."

Heather now dressed in a change of clothing listened to Suez through her Bluetooth from the passenger seat of Alex's Corvette. She listened meticulously to every word as her hands quickly moved over the keys of her laptop validating the most significant info.

"Boss the footage from a surveillance camera within the six block ratio come back with something. It showed two men wearing all black who tried to stay hidden in the darkness and they were doing a fine job at it, if I may add.

"Suez what side are you on."

"Surely the side of the law boss but that doesn't mean I can't appreciate all acts of genius and these guys were like ghosts. Until one little slip up three blocks from the crime scene as they loaded several cardboard boxes into a van."

"From this error could Intel pick up any shape or sizes sticking out from the boxes to give some kind of inkling as to what was in it?"

"Not one boss these guys are the real deal and if it wasn't for the dome light inside the back of the van we would have nothing. It happened to capture the facial outline from behind their mask. After that point, we followed them into the Lincoln tunnel where they must've had a vehicle waiting."

"Suez you say that as if you're not sure, what did they do just fucking disappear?"

"You can say that the assailants gave us the slip but we're running a check on every vehicle that left after the van entered to see which one seemed lower to the ground. The getaway van was abandoned and had some kind of explosive set to a 2 minute timer and it had already gone up in flames and burned to a crisp before the first response team made it on scene. We were able to gather their height and six points of their facial.

Which you know we only need 4 points for a conviction. I'm running them through I.N.C at this very moment hopefully we get a match soon. But we do know one is 6 foot the same height as

Amir."

"Great and now we know it was three people like the bum said... the question is why did they leave him alive?"

"I don't know."

"Well, you need to find out, have him picked back up. It's just pass two in the morning so you'll find him on 123rd street in

Harlem at the neighborhood speak-easy called Cutty's."

"Speak-easy."

"Suez you sound puzzled like you never heard of that kind of place before?"

"Aaaahh."

"I'll take that as a no. Well, missy you better get hip and I mean soon. It's in the back of the building on the corner and wait

until quarter to three then he'll be nice and drunk."

"How do you know all this....Oh, I get it this was your tactic all the while. You knew you were going to pick him back up again the whole time."

"Suez you have to decide in life what will make a person drop their guard within the first 60 seconds of meeting them in this case its beer but it could be women, drugs, art, whatever; it's our job to find it and quick."

"Noted, I have Jake on the other line do you want to speak with him?'"

"Yes Patch him through...Jake, what's going on?"

"Boss I'm here on 119th street parked on a small side street where I have a perfect view of the third floor apartment where I shadowed the target to. I couldn't see much because she shut the door quickly behind her but I did notice at least one person in the background a female I think. The suspect has been up there since twelve o'clock. Prior to that she only made a few stops. First was the market on 63th street, stayed approximately ten to fifteen minutes. Then she stopped by Sam's pizzeria and got a roast beef sandwich."

"Not Sam's pizzeria next to precinct 11 where I use to work."

"Yeah, that's the one."

"I wonder why she stopped there out of all places," Heather questioned aloud however she was speaking to herself as her brain quickly searched for an answer.

"Yes because she had to know it would be full of cops, yet she didn't care." Suez cut in, "Maybe she had a reason that we're just not seeing."

"I was thinking the same thing," Heather added

"Right now I'm running the background history on the address of the place she at now. Oh and before I forget to tell you Sherry will be release sooner than later so put a move on whatever you have in mind. I hear it some big wig lawyer down stairs making a stir for her."

"Ok Suez but keep searching there's something more to this. What you think Jake?"

"I think I-."

"Fuck what you're thinking. You better get the fuck from around here before something bad happens to you," a man yelled from beside the car, "They been killing your kind all week and nigga you can be next"

"Word you fucking pig." **Boom!** The man's friend added tossing something at the car.

"Jake, what was that sound?" Heather questioned trying hard to hear more of the disturbance.

"Nothing just some fucking kids throwing eggs at my car, they somehow made me."

"Are you definite they made you?"

"Positive the last time I checked a pig was still a cop."

"If they made you who's to say that our suspect hasn't. Jake go and get her now, we need to get him off the street and she's the answer." Heather demanded.

"Copy 7 exiting the vehicle."

Jake spotted a woman in an orange dress approaching the lobby door and quickly jumped from his vehicle. He dashed across the streets looking in both directions.

"Hey...hey, Ms., hold that door please!" The woman hesitated to glance in the direction of the sound where she noticed Jake and smiled.

His run slowed to a lite walk as he shorten the distance between them. She observed the police badge on his hip with her smile swiftly vanishing as she pulled the door shut behind her.

"Black lives matter also you piece of shit."

"I guess we aren't liked around here as of lately." Jake banged on the bulletproof glass door locking eyes with the lobby hall monitor. "Sir, will you buzz me in I'm here on very important police business."

"And like I told you a few hours ago if you don't have a warrant I'm not letting you in it's against the law. You know how I know that. I was going to be a policeman also but I got this bad knee-."

"Yeah...yeah, I'm sorry to hear that but this is different. I'm responding to a call from dispatch about a person in apartment 336B is in need of assistance."

"Good try if a call would have gone out to this building I would have heard it come over this." The hall monitor held up a scanner.

"Jake do you have her......I repeat Jake do you have the suspect in custody copy?"

"Not as of yet boss I'm having a little bit of a problem," Jake whispered into his receiver

"Jake stop the fucking soft shit already. There's no time for it out on these streets, now go get that girl and bring her in for questioning and I don't care what you have to do to get her there copy."

"Copy over."

Jake stared around puzzled not spotting anyone coming or going as he deliberated on his next move. He was mindful that disappointing Heather again was not an option or he would never be permitted back out in the field.

He pounded on the bulletproof glass yet again to get the attention of the hall monitor who quickly looked away.

"Fucking wannabe cop." Jake shouted detaching his weapon saying to himself, *"I deserve to be out here,"* He aimed at the metal door handle and fired. The door swiftly open.

"Hey… hey, what the hell do you think you're doing?" The monitor rushed into the pathway of the door

"My job and if you don't step aside you're going to get more holes in you than that door frame."

"Your bluffing you're a police officer you can't do that."

Jake paused having his card pulled for there was no way he was shooting an innocence man. He looked at the floor then back. "You got me there, but I will kick your ass," Jake yelled hitting the man upside the head with the butt of the gun.

"Worldstar bitch."

Jake rushed passed the man and headed for the stairway daring him to follow. He took the steps two at a time until he reached the third floor. There he slowly eased the door back with his left hand as his right raised the police issued automatic to his waist. Shaking, Jack tried to calm his trembling arm as his hand began to sweat from the feeling of the cold metal nestling in his palm. A sensation he has yet to get used to but understood it was undeniably necessary.

Jack desired to use his brain the same way he moved up in position, by exposing the weaknesses in others, no matter how deep he had to dig to find it. He took in a deep breath sensing death in the air. An insight he learned as a child that he could never get rid of. He silently prayed that it wouldn't be him.

He pushed the nervousness into the back of his mind and slid out into the hallway. "It's all or nothing." He reminded himself while approaching the target's apartment with caution. He posted on the side of the threshold slamming the butt of his gun against the metal.

Boom! Boom! Boom!

"Police search warrant, open up you're surrounded!"

The door squeaked as it eased open under the strength of the blow. Jake without missing a beat moved right along with it. He rotated his weapon from side to side while moving forward as the academy instructed. He entered the living room surprised to him to find it perfectly spotless.

"There goes the chance of getting any finger prints."

He moved into the dining room where he became astonished at what he witnessed.

The room was equally clean as the other looking as if no one had lived there in years. Jake noticed the chair positioned in front of the window that he had been surveilling moved. He raised his weapon locking on the back of his target's head demanding,

"Lady I'm homicide detective Jake and I need you to put your hands above your head where I can see them and everything will be just fine."

Trina without responding continued to rock back and forth in the comforter. Jake inched closer with his unsteady trigger finger shaking more and more with each step.

"I said let me see your hands." The chair moved again startling Jake who out of fear pulled the trigger several times.

"Die bitch die, now see what you went and made me do. And I don't want to hear that black lives matter bull crap either. Because you surely did this."

His aim was off more than a little as bullets flew in every direction hitting his suspect in the back, head and neck slumping her down in the seat.

Jake spun the chair around finding a manikin dressed in Trina's clothes with a note penned to its chest.

"Shit Heather is going to kill me for this, but she... I mean it looks so real." Jake ran his fingertips along the jawline filling the texture of the makeup astonished by how genuine the replica looked. He removed the note and began to read when the chair moved again.

Jake jumped drawing the trigger inward until his weapon kicked back empty. He stared at the shredded frame and holey floor convinced that he was now safe. He wiped the sweat from his brow as he inspected the chair seeing a rope tied to its leg.

"What the hell." Jake trailed the rope under the only bedroom door. He quickly reloaded and set his aim pushing the door open.

A tan tricolored massive Pitbull instantly showed its teeth growling like it hadn't eaten in weeks. The white and tan hairs on its back stood up when it rapidly charged Jake. He fired and missed as the pit jumped in the air aiming for his face. Jake quickly slammed the door shut just in time.

"Damn that was close." He removed his phone looking to the note now on the floor, "Suez connect me with Heather again please."

"I'll try, she hasn't been picking up. But Jake did you get the target?"

"No she gave me the slip but she left a message behind that Heather should hear ASAP!"

9

Heather ignored her phone once again as she steadied her hand picking the locked to the back door of Mr. Patrick's Brooklyn four bedroom two bathroom brownstone. Alex's head moved back and forth nervously as he stood on lookout. He has done this numerous times in his career but it was something about this house that didn't feel right in the pit of his belly. Which has yet to be wrong.

"Come on Heather I think someone is on to us."

"And! What they going to do, call the police."

"Ha... Ha... real funny but you and I both got dirt under our fingernails, maybe you more than others but we can't be seen entering this house without a warrant or the captain will have our badges for sure and that's, to say the least."

"We agreed to never speak of that again."

"That doesn't mean it just goes away."

"Alright just stop your fucking crying you big baby and do something like checking the trash. I can't hear the click with all your sobbing."

"What I tell you about that big baby crap."

"Yeah like I really listen to you, but if it makes you feel any better Alex you're always going to be my big baby...Come on we're in."

Heather stepped into the lavish kitchen scanning for the paper-towels as she counted down from ten.

"Eight...seven....six." She grasped a cloth from off the dish rack.

"Heather what are you doing you said we weren't going to touch anything,"

"Three... two... one."

Ring....Ring

"Hello."

"Hello ma'am I'm Steve from Top home security I just received a silent alarm from your residence is everything okay there."

"Oh yes, I just came home and thought I disarmed it I'm sorry for troubling you."

"No problem ma'am just give me the password and I'll handle that for you right away."

Heather's brain promptly went over everything she knew about Mr. Patrick then subtracted the negative before adding what people stated about his likes and dislikes.

"Hello ma'am the security code now please or I'll be forced to alert the authorities."

"Uummm..."

"Dammit Heather hang up already and let's get the hell out of here." Whispered Alex

"Ma'am I'm notifying the police now."

"King! The password is king."

"Thank you, ma'am, please enjoy the rest of your night."

"You too."

Alex held off until the phone reconnected with its cradle, "How the hell did you know the password?"

"Easy, the name Amir is of Hebrew and Arabic origin and the meaning is treetop but it is also of Persian origin with the meaning coming from King Emir now which one you would've picked if your son was the closest thing to your heart?"

"You mean to tell me you put our careers on the line with a guess."

"It's a hypothesis and mister you were just staring at the wall from your desk and still would be there if it wasn't for me."

"Well, what are you waiting for let's get started so we can get the hell out of here." Alex walked around taking in the allwhite traditional u-shaped open kitchen with the costly stainless steel appliances hanging from the ceiling rack.

"Nice." His gloved finger trailed over the white and black marble countertop to the white shaker cabinets. He stopped at the metallic under mount sink. "Beautiful."

"Knock it off Alex. I know you, so don't beat around the bush if you got something to say fucking say it."

"Maybe this house is a little too gorgeous for a corner store owner's salary don't you think?"

"No, I don't and let's get one thing straight Mr. Patrick was one of the good guys that helped my family when he didn't have too. So let's not make him a bad guy without good reason."

"Okay but this is very expensive I'm just saying."

"Well, you said it."

They began searching through the large home with a fine tooth comb both having separate agendas. Heather was there to find the reason Amir killed his father and anything that could possibly lead them to his location.

Alex, on the other hand, wanted nothing more than to demonstrate just the opposite, that Amir and his father were identical up until a few days ago when Amir wanted to be more than just a partner; he wanted it all.

Meanwhile back at the station a handsome Jewish man a bit taller than average with a full traditional salt and pepper beard glanced at his leather Cartier watch.

"Times up…Excuse me please."

He stated to the young lady seated beside him playing on her phone. She was sitting too close for his comfort in the packed waiting room that smelled of cheap perfume and sweat. He stood from the hard metal chair where he had been waiting for the pass 20 minutes irritably.

The wrinkles in his skin and the dark bags under his eyes, hidden behind his transparent reading glasses told a tale of a man that possessed wisdom. That had witnessed many trying moments throughout his 67 years of age.

He approached the clerk's desk with a stride that screamed self-assured with each step. He smoothed out the tailor made double-breasted suit he wore until there wasn't a crinkle perceptible. The light crease at the tip of his slacks was as piercing as the man's brain who owned them.

"Excuse me, officer Dickerson am I right?"

"No shit big shot lawyer you can read. Now, what can I do for you I don't have all day I gotta lot of paperwork here to attend too?"

"It's Goldstein... Joshua Goldstein Esquire the same as it was a half an hour ago when I spoke to you about my client Sherry
Patrick and I would like to know why she hasn't been released as of yet."

"They're still working on it, pal."

"It's Goldstein." Joshua corrected through tighten teeth.

"Well, Mr. Goldstein why don't you go have a seat over there in the waiting area for about-".

"About twenty minutes and I'll make sure she'll be right out being that she been through so much today." They finished the last half of the sentence simultaneously.

"How you know I was going to say that?"

"Because you sold me that bull crap for free twenty minutes ago you no good out of shape disgrace of a lawman."

"Wait one got damn second you can't speak to me like that I'm a police officer and I'll have your high price ass tossed in the box right with your client if you don't mind your lip. Do you understand me, Goldstein?"

"On no account, what I do comprehend is that you will do no such thing. How's that little gambling problem you have that you think no one knows about? Which in fact landed you here on desk duty."

"Listen, wise ass I'm here because of a misunderstanding with a motorist that complained that I roughed his scumbag ass up a bit too much which is a lie and I will be cleared of any wrong doing by the I.N.A shortly. You can bet your ass on it."

"You're lying and you stated that with a straight face." Joshua shook his head. "You cops are becoming better than the criminals you know that, but not to me I see straight through you. The scumbag was Fred Jameson oddly you and Fred have the same bookie and you both owe money and you were paid to rough him up for mob boss-."

"Hey... hey, fella keep your voice down-"

"It's Goldstein."

"Mr. Goldstein will you please keep your voice down saying something like that even though it's not true people will tend to believe what they hear."

"What about what they read?"

"You wouldn't dare!"

"Oh how New York has gotten soft. Back in the day, we had no problem putting a dirty cop's clothes out to dry and at the moment I feel it may be time to do some laundry. Now if my client is not out here in exactly two minutes you will be in the New York Times by morning." Joshua removed his phone.

"Ok don't do nothing crazy, give me five and she'll be right out I promise." Four minutes and thirty-six seconds later Sherry appeared from behind the rusted metal doors yelling and kicking.

"I don't give a shit about no mishap ya'll kept me back there handcuffed to a fucking wall like some kind of criminal yet my brother who killed my fucking father is still out there on the loose. But don't worry if you don't want to bring him in, me neither. I will get justice my own way-."

"No...no...she didn't mean that." Joshua slid in between Sherry and the policeman who was escorting her, taking her by the arm he lead her towards the door.

"Ms. Pender don't say another word for it can incriminate you in the near future."

"I don't care my father is dead and his soul can't rest until he is given retribution and get your hands off me. Who the hell are you anyway a retired cop bitch."

Joshua smiled removing his hands, "No I'm here to help but Spoken like a true Patrick.... Hello, Sherry, I'm Joshua your lawyer nice to see you again and I must say you have grown up into a beautiful woman. Just like your mother said you would."

Sherry just stared at him not knowing whether to believe the man or walk away as her vision journeyed up his body she thought, *"This man can't be over forty-five years of age by the strength in his physique but the pain she sensed from his body had to be real meaning he is much older."* When she demanded "Remove your glasses."

"Pardon me."

"Your glasses take them off I need to see your eyes because my father always said a man can't h-"

"Hide his Skelton from his own soul, therefore, look within his eyes it's the threshold to his ambiance." Joshua cut in finishing the statement.

"Ok... You got me you know my father but how do you know my mother she died when I was a kid?"

"Deceased, don't you mean mur-?"

"Mean what Mr. Joshua?" Sherry probed cutting Joshua off eager to know any information she could acquire about her mother's for her father spoke so little on the subject. She knew the basic like any other little girl that longed for an absent mother. That she was beautiful, and a good mom that loved her sincerely. But when Sherry would continue with her curiosity she could witness the deep pain in the depth of her father's eyes at the mere mention of the love of his life name. She knew the emptiness in her heart hurt extremely. So she couldn't begin to imagine what her father must be enduring.

One day at the age of 16 a single tear fell onto Sherry's forehead as she sat listening to her father once again attempted insight?

to answer her query about her mother. It was at that moment seeing the man she loved over all cry. Sherry vowed to never probe again.

Joshua studied Sherry thinking before answering *I can't believe she doesn't have a clue but certainly now is not the time to tell her.* "Because your father was not only my client he was my friend," he slowly removed his glasses looking Sherry dead in the eyes. "And his words were right, but not only for your first date. They work now more than ever. Because you can't trust anyone at this moment for reason unknown to you. So please allow me to accompany you home so that I know that you're safe. I owe your father at least that. My driver is right out front."

"I guess I can put some hope in you. Plus anything beats taking the subway. My car is still back at the hotel if they didn't tow it."

"Don't worry I'll have someone see to it that your vehicle is returned to your home. Now come on you need to get some rest. I can't envision how you must be feeling at the moment."

Joshua glanced out the first set of double doors and couldn't believe his eyes as over twenty reporters crowded the steps.

"That damn cop." *Today will be his last day on duty.*

"What's wrong?" Sherry questioned perceiving the sudden change in Joshua's facial expression.

"Nothing I can't handle come on." Joshua turned on the heels of his brown leather shoes and hastily walked back to the front desk where officer Dickerson spoke on the phone. "Yes, captain I'll get right-"

Joshua placed his finger over the receiver. "Hey that was my superior"

"In five seconds you won't have a job if you don't tell exactly what you did the moment I walked away."

"Nothing."

"3...2"

"Okay...okay but I didn't mean for anything to happen for you to become so upset, I swear. I called an old contact at the Post and gave him your name. You know, to see if you had the juice to back up your threats. That's all!" Officer Dickerson explained nervously, "At the sound of it he became apprehensive saying indeed you were very connected having gotten three Mob bosses off on R.I.C.O (racketeer influenced and corrupt organization) charges more than once. Then shortly after the last trial you just up and left. Until you resurfaced in Philadelphia some years back. Becoming a private attorney for only one person and from what I hear he is the second most feared man in that city. He ended stating that something had to be very important if you're
involved. That's all I swear."

"What's his name?" Joshua questioned while texting his driver having a plan in mind.

"Eugene Freeman but if it means anything to you Mr. Goldstein it was as if he was waiting on the call."

"So that's where the bastard landed."

"You know him?"

"Yes, I got him off for killing his wife. Now, where's the back door?"

Joshua gripped Sherry's hand. He led her into the back toward the wood and glass door that read *"Police only."*

"Wait...wait, you can't go back there!" Joshua ignored the request as the shadow of their frames disappeared behind the pinhead frosted glass. He led the way as they quickly walked passed the officers' cubicles'

"Hey, you cannot be in here."

"Don't worry we're leaving...this way" Joshua made a quick right down into a stairway past the waiting room and out through the locker room doors. Sherry smiled seeing the exit stating, "Something tells me you did this before."

"A few times but don't worry no one will know you were ever here." He interlocked his arm with Sherry's whispering. "You're safe with me."

"From what?" Sherry questioned confused but her misconception was shortly lived as Joshua's hand pressed on the emergency exit. The sound of a camera clicking with the flash of the light temporarily blinding her.

Outside a reporter and a cameraman stood taking pictures to get a glance at the reason that the ever so famous Joshua Goldstein was back in town.

"Ms. Patrick hi I'm Roy Townson for Sunrise newspaper is it true that the gun you got caught with was the actual weapon that killed your father."

Roy was a small time reporter who was quickly building a name for himself as a solid reporter. One that would go to no end to find the truth in a story no matter who it hurt.

"That's absurd I would never do anything-"

"Ms. Pender has no comment at this time boys now will you excuse us," Joshua said which sounded more so like an order than a statement. He pulled Sherry into his arms as if he was shielding her from some kind of disease. He whispered feeling the nervousness from her shaking figure,

"Pretend as if they're wearing thongs and it will go away, I promise."

Sherry smiled doing exactly as instructed.

Joshua could feel the tension in her body relax as they made their way down the steps to his awaiting Maybach.

"Come on Mr. Goldstein I know you want to get your side of the story out or read the tomorrow headline, **"Sherry Pender points finger at brother but she may be the actual killer of their father."**

"Cute everything he said is factual and using the word maybe made it legal to point the finger at Sherry by her being held at the station, one could contemplate that so I can't even sue him... he's good but how good." Joshua thought while

remaining silent having encountered many too smart for their own good reporters.

He saw to it that Sherry was safely in between the plush leather peanut butter interior. He gave a short head nod to his driver, "Get her home safely."

"No problem boss." With a push of a button, Sherry disappeared behind the curtains as the spotless automobile pulled away.

Joshua slowly turned giving the reporter his full attention, "Ok Roy I may have something for you if you promise to leave Sherry out of this, in anticipation of you having hard facts to support what you're declaring." Joshua's voice slightly began to rise, "Other than the element of her losing her fucking father."

"I'm sorry if I hurt your feelings Mr. Goldstein but its rough out here in these streets. When you're forced to deal with criminals who murder, steal and lie day in and day out all under the bander of being a journalist. So yes I may have lost some of my sensitivity when it comes to peoples' emotions but one thing I do know is that if you were to shake anyone of us long enough a skeleton will fall out. So I'll watch who you raise your tongue at."

Joshua smiled, "Now I remember why I miss New York so much. There is always someone throwing a stone at a tall building wishing that it would come down but yet the Empire State still remains standing strong."

"Yes, but what about the other two that thought they were built just the same."

"Hey... Hey... now you're going too damn far." Joshua's fist quickly tighten.

"Your right I'm sorry there goes my sensitivity again but the facts remain."

The cameraman transcribed this small battle of the minds just as Roy had planned to have the moment he heard Joshua was back in town.

"I get it now... you enjoy playing with words." Joshua paused looking up into the unruffled night air as if he was thinking, "Well how about this if you leave Sherry be until you have justifiable means to do otherwise I'll let you pick my brain if you can handle what you get out of it."

Roy grinned "Just say when"

"No time is better than the present." Joshua now wearing a smirk of his own, stating the rest of the deal. "We'll each get three questions that have to be answered truthfully and at any time if one finds out that the other has lied the consequences may be very severe..." Joshua paused to let the weight of his words set in. "Being that we are both forced to deal with murderers, thieves, and liars. I know you have someone to call."

"Okay, you first."

"I'll take that as a yes. Now, why did you pick this door when there are four other exits I could have come through, that would have left you standing here with your dick in your hand?" Joshua asked thinking *"Ask your question in reverse too mislead people from the direction where you're heading so their brain has no time to prepare."*

"The front door would have been great if you wanted free press. But to protect an old army friend's child a person would do anything like break the rules to make sure their safe from people like me. Plus who would had followed you into a cop locker room anyway."

"Noted."

"My go... how long have you and Mr. Patrick Pender been friends?" *He will never see this coming*

"Ever since we were in grade school. We got into this little fight over a girl and neither one of us was willing to lose in front of her. In the end, both of us were too exhausted to keep going so we stopped and became friends."

"What happened with the girl?"

"He married her but I'm certain it is my turn? How did you know I was in town, Eugene Freeman send you?"

"No, it's more like I send him. How else would I have gotten you to think of the last possible exit?" Roy detailed.

"Is that so?" Joshua thought of officer Dickson's words, *"Mr. Goldstein if it means anything to you it was as if he was waiting on the call. I guess he needed to confirm a two bit reporter's word."* Joshua continued, "But that still doesn't answer my question."

"I believe it was on YouTube, or T.M.Z you know one of them sites where people can post their personal videos. I check them randomly every hour on the hour and low and behold I see you. The young lady who posted it had no clue of who you were. I think the caption read *Man puts cop in place,* hashtag black lives matter."

"But yo-."

"I trust it's my go."

"Certainly but make it good because it's your last," Joshua said with his trademark wicked grin knowing that he had out slicked another can of oil.

"Somehow you must have lost count because I have two questions left not one."

"Definitely not I remember clearly it was the one about my friendship and another about a female."

"You got to be kidding me. You took that as a question."
"Absolutely you're the one who asked and I believe that there makes us even." Joshua elevated his hand with a taxi pulling to
a stop in front of him.

"Dammit, I can't believe I did it the fuck again," Roy yelled.

"Come on kid don't be too hard on yourself you're a reporter all you do is ask questions ha, ha…" Joshua laughed sliding into the back seat. The cab pulled from the curb then stopped as the rear window lowered, "I'll call you when I'm ready to ask my other two questions"

"Oh I get it, now I work for you and if there's a question I don't have the answer to I better go get it or you'll have your friends pay me a visit."

"A deal is a deal,"

"Fuck you," Roy yelled as he watched the taxi disappear wondering what he had gotten himself into. Then his reporter instinct kicked in giving him one thing he was certain of. That he was going to find out the truth in all of this because something surely wasn't right if Joshua would to this length to derail him.

10

"Thank you and please tell Mr. Goldstein I will speak with him again soon. I'm just not up to it at this moment." Sherry shut the car door as she slowly turned to stare at her home. A sight that once held an abundance of love, promise, and life to her now seemed of nothing but loneliness and heartache. She felt as if the weight of the world was now upon her shoulders knowing her father wouldn't rest fully until his killer was in the ground also.

Sherry took a deep breath before heading up the ample drive way. She hesitated midway sensing that someone was watching her. Her eyes promptly shifted left to right keying in on her environment the way her father instructed yet noticing nothing. She continued to the glass and wood framed door opening it she still was unable to believe that her father wouldn't be on the other end to greet her. Her mind wondered,

"He will never ask how my day went again. Lay eyes on my first born. Give me away at my wedding." The feeling of anger again overcame the flow of her blood as tears began to fall from the raw reality until they sheltered her face as a mask carved of her own skin. Her legs weaken as she closed her eyes envisioning her father's warm embrace for the last time coming to terms that he was gone from her life physically forever. She understood from that moment on there wouldn't be another second wasted on being frail, ever.

"A...A...Look at this bitch ready to pass out and shit. And yet I thought this family was all tough hearted and shit!" whispered a masked man from the driver's seat of a stolen captain's van as he studied Sherry's actions from across the street.

"Take it is easy-z on her man it looks like she had a hard day." The other masked man interjected.

"Well pray that she doesn't have an even harder night because if things don't go as planned I assure you she will." Sherry stood up straight wiping away the wetness from her skin until it was bone dry as her father's scent exited her soul. She kissed him on the cheek, "Daddy I will always love you and your soul will rest soon I guarantee It." she uttered into the night.

Inside she paused pondering if she heard voices. Her eyes scanned the room knowing something was off. She rushed to the large flower vase in the corner of the living room retrieving one of Amir's back up weapons that he thought no one knew about.

"If someone is here I better not find you," she yelled moving with a new found desire.

A few steps away Heather and Alex stood at the bottom of the stairs in a heated debate. After functioning as a wellrounded team on a mission that started from the Attic and worked its way downward through the house observing nothing out of place. The fact alone made Alex more than disenchanted. He paused at the bottom of the stairs uttering,

"Let's search the basement now and do the living room last. I got a feeling it's something down there to prove these bastards are guilty."

"Bastards."

"Come on Heather you know what I meant something to put Amir's ass away.

"Yeah right and now you got a feeling, was it the same feeling you had in Amir's room or Mr. Patrick's no... I got it. This is the same feeling you had the moment you arrived at the store and found out that the man who saved me and my family in our time of hardship was black."

"Heather you know it makes no difference to me what color people are hell I'm black-."

"Save that shit Alex I saw the surveillance tape of the first team and if you're going to hate people for the color of their skin at least have the balls to say it. If not next time cover ya fucking lips. Don't get me wrong you're a worthy cop but when you start letting your emotions effect the way you do your job that's when we have a fucking problem do I make myself clear."

"Way clear," Alex said as he thought back to the crime scene when he lifted the yellow tape and walked into the store with his badge in the air.

"May I have your attention please my name is detective Alex from the special homicide division. I will be in charge until my boss gets here. This man was very important and dear to her so treat him like he's one of ours. I don't want anything overlooked."

Alex removed his eyes from Sherry's beauty to the body and whispered unconsciously. "Shit it's a nigger!"

Alex shook his head at the thought of people knowing the secret that he fought so hard not to let win him over. "Heather you of all people know I wouldn't fee- wait did you hear that,"

Alex said speaking of Sherry's footsteps that were quickly approaching.

"I didn't hear anything now come on." Heather proceeded down into the basement. Alex remained listening for the sound to repeat.

"Let's go, Alex, we don't have much time!" Hearing nothing due to Heather's voice Alex followed closing the door behind him just as Sherry entered the kitchen.

Sherry looked to the basement door raising the weapon. Her heart beat reduced with each step as she slowly approached. Her nervousness calmed to a standstill a lesson learned from her father... *"Sherry settle yourself, dear a gun is not your enemy it's your friend. One day it may save your life if I'm not here too." Mr. Patrick said swallowing his anger to keep his composure as he again watched his daughter pull the trigger instantly dropping the weapon from her palm's missing her target by far.*

"Ah-ha she scared to hold a gun but not me dad, look."
Laughed, a ten year old Amir who repeatedly squeezed the
trigger aggressively on a military Beretta six times just missing
the center of his target by inches.

"Smack!"

Mr. Patrick's hand connected to the back of Amir's head
"Shut up boy! What I tell you about making fun of your sister?"

"Don't."

"Alright then."

Mr. Patrick picked the weapon up from the dirt floor
wrapping his arms around Sherry placing it back into her hand.

"Dear there is no reason to be afraid, I see that you don't like
the power of the kick back."

Sherry nodded her head. "Yeah, it hurts sometime."

"That was only once dear you have to let go of the past
but if you hold it tight like this." *Mr. Patrick spread his finger*
wide over Sherry's showing her the correct way to grip a
weapon.

"But dad this is how I was doing it."

"I know dear now relax your body and tighten your
arms." *"Like you taught me in baseball and I got to second*
base?"

"Exactly and you will control it as you did the bat and it
will never hurt again."

"You promise?"

"I promise." *Sherry trusting her father as always pulled*
the trigger relishing the vibrations that ran through her body...
Sherry's hand slowly turned the knob to the basement as a cold
wind brushed against her cheek. "That's odd dad hated it to be
cold." She altered her glance trailing the source of the breeze to
find the back door slightly ajar.

She turned with her weapon positioned in front of her
while inspecting the door frame. She perceived no damage but
with the need to be certain she crept into the back yard. Her eyes
were forced to adjust to the darkness due to several unscrewed

lights. She examined the area as if it seeing it for the first time. When the shadow of a figure appeared in her peripheral vision to the left.

She pointed the weapon in the direction and it was gone. "I got to get some sleep I'm seeing shit." Sherry heading back to the house then hesitated. "But daddy always said you have to be sure." She walked a few feet trailing her vison coming face to face with a masked man.

On impulse, she squeezed the trigger but the masked man's reaction was quicker gripping the gun from her hand leaving her flickering the air.

"heeeel-" Sherry attempted to scream when the back of the man's hand came down hard across the side of her face.

"Smack!"

He placed his finger over his lips and blew. Ssshhh...

"But I h-"

"Smack!"

The man's action repeated but this time harder. The capacity behind his blow sent Sherry's head back as the taste of blood filled the inside of her mouth. Slightly dazed and in disbelieve she slowly brought her trembling hand to her face. The sight of her fingers coated in blood made her lose it. She spit the red saliva in the masked man's eye.

"I see nothing but pure rage," Sherry yelled hearing her father... "*After any action, there will be a reaction. It's when you can dictate the reaction of your enemy is when you will control your own fate.*"

"*And how are we to do that dad.*" Sherry and Amir questioned in sync as they hung off on their father's every word.

"*By making your enemy do the same thing twice without them knowing you're the one who is making them do it. On the third and there will be a third because by now their mind is on automatic...*"

Sherry ducked moving to the side as the man's fist flew pass. She waited until it crossed his body then quickly stepped inward throwing several punches to his unprotected face.

She took another step to the left using his mask against him knowing he could only see so far. She bit down on her busted lip kicking as hard as she could into the side of his kneecap forcing him down onto one knee.

"Aaaahh you bitch!"

Sherry thinking for the kill on instinct took the gun from the man's mitt when his voice hit her. "Damon?" was all she could get out when everything went black as the butt of the second masked man's gun connected to the back of her head. "Man stop fucking around and get her in the van so we can finish what we came to do."

"What you trying to clown me? I had it under wraps I just wasn't trying to hurt her because she like family." Damon explained.

"No, she's you and your people's family not mine and remember that. Now let's get busy we got work to do." The other masked man said acting as if he didn't hear the anger in Damon's voice.

A few feet away Heather and Alex searched the basement twice which was converted into a personal home theater ending with the same outcome. On the way back upstairs Heather paused, "Hey did you hear that?"

"Real funny Heather I get it, we didn't find anything you don't have to rub it in."

"No, really I think I heard someone scream." Heather shut the basement door behind her.

"Well I didn't hear anything, so can we just finish this last room and get the hell out of here." Alex insisted without waiting for an answer, he headed for the front room. Heather glanced at the back door with her suspicion getting the best of her. She started toward it.

"Heather!"

"Ok, I'm coming dammit and keep your voice down before you go and wake the whole community. God! This man making me so crazy I'm getting just as bad as him."

They entered the well-furnished living room with their feet sinking into the plush black wall to wall carpet. Heather unzipping the cushions from the two chairs and sectional couch checking them inside and out before placing them back in their original position. She moved to several magazines positioned nicely on the coffee table going through them page by page.

She paused on the pages that were indented the most by finger prints and quickly read over the article memorizing them to thought, attempting to get an understanding of Mr. Patrick's state of mind before he was murdered.

Alex roamed on the other end of the room dusting for prints alongside one of the three large paintings hanging throughout the room when a section of the wall clinked as it sunk in.

"Did you hear that?"

"Yeah what was it."

"This." Alex pushed in deeper with a door sliding open at the end of the wall.

"I guess we found what we were looking for?" He laughed with a big smile as he unfastened his holster.

Heather doing the same parted two fingers pointing to her eyes than to the door giving Alex the sign that she had his back. Alex with a slight head nod placing three fingers in the air as he began to count down slowly approaching the door's threshold.

His cell phone light guided the flow of his weapon as he stepped into the pitch black room with Heather hot on his heels. He felt wetness beneath his feet and raised a fist in the air that instantly paused Heather. He bent down touching it with his index rubbing it against his thumb. "What is it, Alex?"

"Blood." He followed the trail disregarding Heather's objection, "Wait; let's find the light switch first before we go any farther."

Alex with his mind determined continued. He rotated his weapon throughout the massive room when abruptly something moved to his right. He injudiciously fired twice with the light trailing behind.

"Alex Nooo," Heather screamed then on compulsion she went into action backing her partner up with the hopes that it was a stray cat or another animal that startled him.

A large thump echoed in the center of the room erased Heather's hopes. Her hands hastily searched the wall turning on the light. She discovered Alex kneeling next to a badly beaten man strapped to a chair. A large portion of duct tape enclosed his mouth and wrist.

Alex with his knife in hand cut away the man's restraints laying him flat on the floor. He ripped open the man's off his shirt applying pressure to the gunshot wound in his chest.

"Heather call for help this man is bleeding badly."

"Okay."

"You shot me…" The man stated as he gasps for air. Heather who was now standing over top of the two wasn't shocked to find that she knew the victim.

"Keith who did this to you."

"Bitch you just did wait… Heather is that you from Mr. Brown's English class?" Keith asked with his weakening voice.

"Yes, it's me."

"Bitch y…ou 12? A no good ass cop."

"It doesn't matter who I've come to be. I'm here to help you, Keith, you must believe me."

"Really you're here to help me or your damn sel-?" Keith spit to the side trying not to choke on his own fluids. He then with the help of Alex sat up looking Heather straight in the eyes and continued, "For the record, I don't fuck with you pigs and I would never hurt Mr. Pa-trick as they believe." Keith's voice cracked as it got low to just above a whisper.

Heather struggling to hear him for he was losing his strength quickly.

"It's okay dear just relax help will be here soon. Now you were saying."

"Amir is going crazy out here he did this to me because I to-told people he robbed his father and had him killed."

"See I told you the piece of shit did it."

"Shut up Alex! Keith did he, I know it was your cousin and two other men who did it. Was Amir one of them?"

"I'm not sure."

"But you just said you told people he did it."

"Yeah he could have because he is a sick son of a bitch but I-I was just hating that's all, you know popping shit and got my ass kicked for it. Amir is too smart to have a slow leak in anything he does. The man cuts off their head before their lips speak. If there's a leak he poked the hole. But from the way he's acting, I doubt if he did. Whatever the case you have to stop this madness, it's getting out of hand. The man got no picks so watch your back and Drew Shearson's, especially because everything isn't what it seems he's...he ku." Keith began coughing up more blood.

"Keith finish what you were saying please he is what?" Heather insisted while lowering her ear until it practically touched Keith's lips to hear his now frail voice. "He's on Drew's head."

"And by *He,* you do mean Amir right?" Heather quickly quizzed knowing that Keith would be dead soon by the way he kept sucking on his lips. Which could only mean that the taste of lead had begun to sit into his mouth. A sign that death was within walking distance.

Keith shook his head feeling the need for water.

"And why is he after him."

Keith swallowing his own spit mixed with blood attempted to answer. "Drew is a fly young cat who quickly moving up in rank on the street trying to make a name for himself he's smart and they said he was in the store moments before Mr.

Patrick died and is a major part of what happened to him."

"Okay I will, but how is he a part of this and where can I find him?"

"The club in Harrah's after the fight in Atlantic City tomorrow night, the after party. He will be wearing black and white dress to the tee."

"How can you be so certain?"

"Because he never misses a chance to show off it's the Harlem way."

"Keith, is he the reason Mr. Patrick is dead?'

"Ha-ha, you're a pig and you still lost like shit. No Mr. Patrick is dead because of you. Ha... ha kuku." He coughed

"What! You have to be mistaking Mr. Patrick can't be dead because of me. I haven't seen him in ages...Keith why is he dead Keith...Keith?"

"Heather the man is gone. Now what the fuck are we going to do, we're not even supposed to be he--?"

"Shut the hell up, will you! What is done is done. The only way to find out how to get out of this mess is to find out how we got into it in the first place. So search him, he may have a clue to how he got here and where he came from."

Alex doing as instructed removed Keith's shoes and socks before patting down his body seizing a bank roll of cash, two condoms, and a cell phone.

"Is that all."

"Yes."

"Ok bag the phone so we can find out who was the last person he called."

"Heather I didn't think we were going to have to do that."

"Why not."

"Because their still on it."

"What?"

Alex placed one finger in the air for silence then held up the home screen for Heather to see. The phone was face timing with the other phone's camera placed in front of an old picture of Heather fresh out the police academy.

Heather seeing that the call was going on for the past hour and ten minutes knew whoever was on the other end heard everything that was said and done.

"Give me that." She could hear the sound of breathing on the other end, "Who the hell is this?"

"Your worst nightmare." a deep voice responded.

From the tone, Heather could tell that the person was using some kind of device to alter the pitch of their voice. The call disconnected.

Heather instantly cast an eye over the room taking it in for the first time. She knew now that whoever did this was attempting to send her up the river without a paddle.

"Damn it I get it! And I made it easy for them by coming here just like they wanted me to… but why?"

"Heather you think this is some kind of a set up."

"I don't think I know. There's no other explanation for the man we were searching for body to be here fastened to the fucking floor waiting to be shot. And the person who put him there was just here moments before we arrived." Heather elevated her weapon. "If there not still here."

"How can you tell?"

"The phone, the time of the call. He couldn't have answered it and place it in his top pocket with his hand tied. Plus it's the new one with night vision."

"Shit! They were waiting on us but don't be too hard on yourself Heather you did what any good detective would do and checked the home of the victim."

"That's just it, I should have seen this coming but me being too apprehensive about our offence I never consider any defense."

"And why the fuck should you? We're cops we didn't break the law this piece of shit did."

"And this piece of shit is in combat for his life. I should have known he wasn't going out without a fight he never does." Heather bent down picking up the loosened screws with a napkin placing them into a zip lock bag from her purse.

"Search the room because somehow their keeping tags on us and I want to know how." She swiftly searched the dead body again before sending two more shots into his frame declaring all bets were now off.

"Now we both killed him."

Alex knew from the look in Heather's eye as she tucked her weapon away that whatever love she held in her heat for Amir was gone and the war had officially begun.

Heather's Bluetooth vibrated. "Yes, Suez."

"Boss please tell me you are not still at Mr. Patrick's house."

"And if I was."

"That would be really bad because an APB (all-points bulletin) was sent out to that location one minute ago with the report of shots fired and a possible 187. (Murder) Boss is everything ok?"

"I'm fine but I'm going to need you to call-" Heather began when it suddenly hit her, "That's it! Suez what kind of sandwich did Jake say his target ordered?"

"A roast beef on rye."

"I'll be damn we're the three little pigs." Heather thought back to Jake and Keith's words, *"That last I remember a pig was still a cop… And For the record, I don't fuck with you piggy."*

"Boss I'm not too familiar with the tale, but I think it goes, this little piggy went to the market, one stayed home, this little piggy had roast beef, this little pig had none, and this little piggy went wee… wee, wee all the way home… I get it Jake had the sandwich. I stayed and now you're at their home I imagine. But what does it all mean."

"That someone has been victimized as a kid and now it's time for payback for everyone and we're up against the big bad wolf."

"Boom, Boom."

A loud noise followed by a crashing sound could be heard echoing in the distance.

"Boss, what was that?"

"I presume that our guess has arrived so I need you to just follow by lead." "Always."

Heather removed her walkie talkie taking in a deep breath yelling, "64.com this is detective Heather I'm at the Patrick residence in pursuit of a black male dressed in all black on the far left side of the home in need of back up do you copy over."

Suez appreciative of where this was leading let her hand do magic as she began to hack into the local dispatch giving the order. "All officers' report to the left side of the house, a detective is in need of assistance." Suez whispered into the Bluetooth, "I hope that buys you enough time to get out of there."

"More than enough...oh and Suez."

"Yes."

"Give me everything you have on a Drew Shearson."

"I'm doing it now."

"And one more thing I hope you like to gamble because you're coming to A.C with me. You just earned your moment in the field for saving my ass." Heather said while thinking. "*Amir will pay for this...*"

11

The next evening at 11:43pm inside the Harrah hotel and casino in Atlantic City. Amir stood in his deluxe suite on the third floor from the top with his hair dyed a salt and pepper gray brushed to the back. The added dark makeup gave the impression that he was ten-fifteen years older. A fake tattoo of an eagle's head peaked out from the cuff of his silk shirt just enough to catch someone's attention. Though slightly sufficient to remember on second thought if questioned.

Amir knew the ways of living as a man on the run like the back of his hand. Being a stick up kid he had no choice though it was nothing comparable to the childhood version of cops and robbers. The outcome for a real hustler/robber was a twenty four hour a day contact sport. That came with nothing less than his demise if he was ever caught slipping. Still, some of the childhood rules applied. In both versions, you had to be tagged IT. However in the street, if you got tagged they hit you with bullets instead of a hand and the tag went on your toe and not your name.

Amir smiled as he stood in front of the gold frame mirror looking at the appearance of him as an elderly gentleman. He was dressed in an impressive tailor made double breasted black suit, white silk shirt, and black Salvatore Ferragamo shoes. He altered the thick black and cream pin stripe tie around his neck until it laid evenly on both sides of his collar. He began to tie a prefect Windsor knot the way his father had shown him. The very first lesson his father gave him in being a man just minutes before his mother's funeral...

"Son I know you're hurting and you miss her as we all do but you mustn't cry. That pain you feel now can only make you a man. That is if you learn how to control it and not let it control you. I wish I could promise that this would be the last time you feel it. But I would be lying, hard times will always

*repeat as long as there's air in your lungs. But as your father it
is my job to show you how to prepare for them.*

*Its hardships that make you a man but how you deal
with them defines what kind of man you are. Now watch my
hands carefully because in every true tough time you experience
in life someone is usually going to be forced to wear a tie. So
you will have to know how to tie one...*

"You were right dad and if I don't get the answers I
want tonight a lot of niggas are going to be forced to wear a tie."
Amir set his smartwatch giving himself one last glance, "I'm
open casket sharp, the sad thing I'm not going to be the one in
it." He chuckled heading for the back room. He lightly tapped
on the door then entered without waiting for a respond.

Inside he stared at his dearest love sleeping peacefully in
the center of the king size bed. He half heartily didn't want to
disturb her but this was war and she couldn't rest until his father
could. He eased onto the bed beside her envious to the
tranquility she must be receiving. He thought that maybe one
day his dreams wouldn't be haunted by others and he too could
rest freely. He pushed his personal sensitivity to the side as
always and casually shook her arm.

Sherry's eyelid flickered as she observed the room as if in
some kind of a daze when she saw Amir. A sigh of relief leaked
out no matter how hard she tried to portray she was strong Amir
was her true back bone.

"Amir you look handsome."

"Thank you."

"Get over yourself. But you won't believe the awful
dream that I had. Damon done lost his damn mind and tried to
break into our house and I was about to shoot him when I got hit
in the back of the head- Aaaahh!" Sherry screamed rubbing her
skull. "Oh shit! It's all true and you killed daddy." She jumped
up to find her ankle cuffed to the bed post. She swung several
wild punches aiming for Amir's face which he easily blocked.

"Come on that's enough of that." Amir stood removing
his gun from his waistline.

151

"Oh now, you going to shoot me?"

"Why not you already told the police I'm a killer and I wouldn't want my sister to be of all things a liar."

"But it's all good to make me a fucking orphan?"

"Are you listening to how stupid you sound? We're talking about the man that put food on my plate every day until I became a man and you think I would have him put in the ground."

"Shit you're a man now and what about Rich, Tyson, and even Keith? Weren't they your friends that you ate off the same plate with? Oh, don't look so fucking surprised. I'm still from the street just because I don't act like a thug or look like one I'm still connected and I hear things. Like Keith getting grabbed from his projects the other day. That was you wasn't it?"

Sherry stared her brother dead in the eyes waiting on the words to confirm the answer she already knew. For years she couldn't get a date due to the weight his name held in the street.

"Fuck them and anything I do I can stand on it. Meaning why the fuck would I have to lie to you, about killing Daddy when you already told homicide; you fucking pig. And if you from the street so much then you know what happens to people with slow leaks they get plugged."

Sherry heard the words but was more frightened by the sight of Amir's veins bulging out the side of his neck and hands. She had never seen him this way. The rage suddenly brought her to understand the fears of many. In her mind, she replayed the last words her father would ever say to her because no one should be this mad for something they did or am I scared also?

"I hear you dear but wait… I think I see him coming now I'll call you back. I think I see him coming… I think."

"Oh shit!" Sherry began to second guess her thoughts but the love her heart held for her father mixed with his blood that raced through her veins wouldn't allow her to turn back an inch.

"I swear if you had anything to do with daddy's death you will no longer have the option. You'll be forced to kill me or die." Sherry spit at Amir aiming at his new suit.

He effortlessly dipped the soaring saliva and smiled. When Sherry hastily spit again hitting him in his face and cheek. Amir's smirk removing the hot wet texture.

"I like that, a small but effective diversion, at least you didn't forget. A little wetter than I like but I needed to know you still cared. On the other hand, some shit even love can't heal," Amir swung with half might aiming for Sherry's presser point slamming the butt of his gun up against the tip of her temple knocking her unconscious.

He applied duct tape firmly across her mouth cuffing the rest of her limbs to each corner of the bed. He gave her one last glance hoping that one day he wouldn't have the thought of killing her on sight, before heading for the main door speaking into his smartwatch. "Text D. ... I'm on the move. ."

"Your message has been sent."

Damon was down stairs in the parking lot disguised as a parking attendant. He blended in acceptably well with the several other attendants as he moved in-between cars meeting and greeting the fine dressed hotel and party patrons. His vision inspected the lot for Drew when it again locked onto the red and white balloon van parked several feet away. He studied it placing his hand on the butt of his gun under his jacket. "There's something odd about that."

Damon inched closer to get a peek through the van's tinted windows when a man exited with an abundant of twisting heart balloons that satisfied his doubts. *"His fat ass could never be a cop."*

Damon's attention shifted to the five females exiting a black BMW wearing almost nothing "Bingo!" He smoothly touched the brim of his hat playing it off as his watch vibrated reading the text.

"Game on." He uttered as he rushed for the employee locker room to change.

"Hey hey, Sam where the hell do you think you're going these cars need to be tagged."

"Then tag them, nigga, I quit," Damon responded without missing a step in his stride.

Inside the locker room, he instantly checked each stall and shower to be certain that he was alone. He locked the door dialing Amir who picked up on the second ring as he stepped off the elevator into the main lobby, "What's the situation."

"It's on, the target has landed in a snow white S550 Benz I'm texting you the plate number now. He is dressed, in a black suit, white silk shirt, tie, and black shoes as you stated he would be.
He's heading for the lobby trailing five beautiful hoes you can't miss him."

"Or them for that matter," Amir added sliding his phone into his pocket.

"Hey handsome your looking fine." One of the five ladies flirted as she ran the tip of her tongue slowly over her gloss covered lips.

"Yes, he is, drinks on you tonight sexy." Another lady added.

"Don't pay that bum ass bitch no mind. We don't need anybody to buy the drinks we got money. Shit well I know I do." Another replied

"I'm pretty sure you all are very independent but I must insist, as they say, anything for a pretty face," Amir replied with his trade mark smile thinking fast on his feet. He slid into the middle of the group while from the corner of his eye he watched Drew who just walked through the sliding double doors as if he owned the place.

"He's tagged." Amir texted.

"Ok, I'm on to stage two," Damon responded quickly changing into an all-black suit.

"I'm doing the same." Amir stopped at the front desk ordering five dozen white roses. "Yes, have these charged to my room, please...Richard" Amir said reading the man's name tag.

"Will do Mr. Durst."

"No please call me Tom and give yourself a thirty percent tip you deserve it...oh and before I forget will you please take this," Amir removed a white envelope from the inside of his jacket pocket. "A beautiful lady will be by here in a little while to receive it."

"No problem and how will I know her."

"Believe me a girl this pretty you'll know her when you see her."

"Very well Mr. Tom."

"Can we call you Tom also?" One of the ladies inquired

"No, you can call me Dicky... now can we go."

"Oh, you nasty but yes fuck it let's turn up!"

"Or turn someone all the way off." Amir grinned locking his stare on Drew as he passed several feet ahead of them.

Richard waited until Amir was out of ease dropping range and said into the two-way receiver/camera stitched into his uniform camouflaged as a button.

"Boss I think that was him but I'm not a hundred percent positive more like eighty percent even though he looked way older. Also, that other guy looked like him earlier. Check him out he's heading for the ball room right now."

Heather remained silent as she stared at Amir's face flashing across the 13 inch screen with the words, *"Alert* **man known to be armed and dangerous,"** beneath it.

"Yes, Intel has just confirmed a facial match detective. I'm shadowing him as we speak. I want you to email a copy of his registration to the team's point man now." Heather replied adjusting her headphone from the inside of the mobile command unit concealed as a party balloons van located in the middle of the parking lot. Her eyes were pasted on four of the seven monitors patched into the hotel security and the local police surveillance database.

She sprung the mouse in her right hand quickly rotating it trailing Amir's every move as he intermingled with the females.

"Look at him, it's as if being a criminal has become his first nature. The way he keeps his head tilted so his face won't be capture by the cameras. Yet it's not too low for anyone to become suspicious. The nerve of him laughing with such confidence like he's not wanted for murder? I'm going to get this sick son of a bitch tonight. I promise you that. " Heather declared without concealing a drop of anger, fed up with Amir's lack of respect for law enforcement.

"Now you're talking," uttered Alex who sat on the opposite side controlling the other half of their surveillance. He used one screen with a still motion tracker that followed Drew's whereabouts second by second since he was spotted by a toll booth camera a few hours ago. The other two screens were doing spot checks in all areas searching for Trina.

"We have one half of the duo but if he's here I know that bitch isn't too far behind, so find her. I need to know what the real reason for that letter. Plus the moment we nail Amir's ass I want to have her in cuffs right beside him for aiding and abetting and whatever else we find. Because something big is going down with this guy I can feel it and she will be needed as leverage if we have any chance of getting a confession out of him. Did everyone get that at this very moment that's what the fuck is necessary to put this son of a bitch away? So tighten the fuck up!"

"Copy boss." Detective Kim mumbled into the cufflink of her waitress ensemble from the ballroom floor as she headed for the V.I.P to deliver more drinks.

"Copy that." Det. Jake said into his Bluetooth after reading his email. He stepped on the elevator heading up to Amir's room.

"Yes, boss." Det. David smoothly responded placing his hand over his mouth pretending to cough just seconds before opening the ballroom door for Amir.

"Thank you, sir, thank you." He bowed his hat giving his best jigga-boo impersonation receiving a twenty dollar bill. He waited until the door shut firmly,

"Boss the eagle is in the nest. I repeat the eagle is in the nest." Det. David strode off dropping his hat in the trash while quickly unbuttoning his jacket moving onto his next assignment.

"I copy," Det. Cohen responded, "But I still don't know why I had to be the one in the kitchen." He plunged another pot into the hot dish water.

"Because maybe there you'll stay focused on your job and less on my breast."

"Damn boss you can't be mad about a man showing you a little affection."

"You got the little part right but mad certainly not or you wouldn't be here. Now if we're done stroking your ego, has everyone checked in?" Heather questioned as she eyed Amir entering the V.I.P section.

"Yes everyone except Suez," Alex interjected.

"Suez report, are you in position copy?"

Suez with her dress hiked up on both sides stayed close to the wall to avoid the camera as she passed hastily making her way from the 16th floor down to the first through the staircase. Midway Heather's voice echoing through her earpiece demanding a report.

"Shit! Not now." She picked up her speed ignoring the order. She progressed as fast as she could in heels determined to make it to the bottom level. She paused on the second step from the bottom staring at that still camera just above the exit.

"Suez come in, are you in position at the rear of the hotel... report. Dammit! I need to know I have an eye at the back of the building." Heather yelled becoming distraught.

"I knew that girl was too smart for her own good," added Alex when suddenly screen two went black.

"What in the world." He turned to tap Heather's arm. "Look we have a problem."

Heather spun around. "What I don't see anything."

Alex looked back at the screen seeing that everything was normal, "*How in the hell.*" He thought when Suez's voice interrupted,

"Boss I'm in position at the rear of the building copy" She lied.

"Well, it's about time, what took you so long?"

"Nothing I couldn't handle," Suez said looking up at the camera she stood underneath on the first floor while returning her iPhone to her hand bag.

Inside the ballroom, Trina stood in a skin tight dress against the wall inspecting the whole scenery intensely. She was prepared for anything knowing her past and the way Amir remained unpredictable. She still couldn't put her hands on why he insisted on meeting here. She looked at her watch again annoyed.

"Shit its 12:22 and this nigga said he'll be here at 12 sharp...hell well I'm not going to keep holding up this wall." Trina grasps a drink from a waitress's tray as she passed taking it straight back.

"Hey, that's not yours."

"Bitch please I can't believe you fixed your face to say something about this weak ass drink." Trina slammed the glass back down taking another while tossing a credit card onto the tray.

"Give yourself a forty dollar tip you look thirsty." She swallowed loving the way the hot liquid burned on its way down.

"Mmm, now I'm nice." Trina licked her lips heading for the dance floor letting the loud music of her favorite song consume her body. There she closed her eyes to words of The Weekend.

"And I know she'll be the death of me, least we both be numb. She always gets the best of me the worst is yet to come."

Trina slowly began moving her hips from side to side in a seductive manner as her hands freely roamed over her body stopping only to caress her breast. Her eyes shot open alarmed at the touch of a large hand palming her right ass cheek aggressively.

On instinct, her hand connected violently across the tall handsome man's face standing before her.

"Ooooh…yeah! I like it when it's rough." The man said squeezing harder.

Trina couldn't deny that the man's actions did turn her on a bit as her inner thighs moisten. She swiftly scanned the overcrowded room yet again for Amir but not in fear of jealousy due to insecurities. He was tremendously confident in himself and didn't have any issue with her having some fun on the side and if the person was right meaning female he would sometime join in.

The actual reason for Trina's exploration was that she truly missed him whole heartily. She hasn't seen Amir in over twenty-four hours and her body cried for his' touch. After following her orders to mislead Jake to get his message across. She was informed of new instructions that landed her here.

Trina returned her attention back on the green eye gentleman pushing her freshly dye auburn hair to the side stating,

"I don't think you can handle all of this." She ran her hand up the man's leg palming his crotch.

He grinned, "So how does it feel to be caught in a lie."

Trina could feel the man responding to her touch as he became more firm by the second. She squeezed harder sensing him peaking.

"No, I'm factual baby. I can admit you're built nicely but to get on this water slide you're going to have to grow a few more inches. Now move out my way before I have you killed to see how much you really enjoy pain."

The statement didn't shock the man at all. He approached women sexually all the time so he's used to anything coming from their mouth. But it was the look in this one's eyes that told him she wasn't joking. He fought back the urge of his inner freak to pursuit further and stepped aside but not before sneaking another glimpse at Trina's ass before it quickly vanished into the crowd

"Damn she was hot…hey excuse me sexy come here I wanted you to see what just popped up in my slacks when I saw your ass." He smiled clutching another girl by the back side.

Trina wished she could've stayed and played a little while longer with the revolting man to teach him a much needed lesson. However, the left side of her face was burning as if someone was staring through her. Not new at all to being stalked dating as far back as her "old" life. The one she let die the moment she was left for dead eight years ago.

She turned right instead, looking to the mirror behind the bar probing the background. She noticed someone in a V.I.P booth sitting off to the side that looked kind of familiar observing her every single action. They locked eyes as she made her way straight for him.

Trina stood at the rim of the man's table still holding his stare and refusing to break it.

"Now what's your fucking problem dick head do I know you from somewhere or your just some kind of pervert that likes staring at bitches in the club?"

The man laughed at the woman's attitude. The sight of his smile now forced Trina to battle her own inner freak as she whispered, "Amir! You almost had me but I'll know that smirked anywhere. Shit grey even looks good on you. I hate to admit it but you're going to look better twenty years from now."

"You're looking great also sexy, maybe a little too good. I thought you were going to get raped out there on the dance floor."

"Yes someone was going to get mistreated but it certainly wasn't going to be me. Now cut the bullshit why in the world would you have us here partying with the whole police force still on your ass?"

"What a man can't show his woman a good time because he's wanted for murder it's not the first time?"

"No baby your right and you always fix it. But why here? You know all the things I had to do to get this in here." Trina pulled up one side of her dress revealing a 380 strapped to her inner thigh as she slid into the booth next to him.

A slim average looking waitress slammed a bottle of Jose` Quervo Gold on the table interrupting,

"As you requested the biggest bottle we have in stock, will there be anything else sir?" She rolled her eyes at Trina seemingly irritated at her presence placing a single shot glass in the center of their table.

"No that will be all," Amir smirked blowing out the sparkle.

Trina waited until the waitress departed. "Ohh baby your always thinking of me, you know Jose` my favorite nigga after you," Trina shouted over the music as she poured a much needed second shot inquiring. "So what's up with the bitch she fucking or what?"

"Who?"

"The waitress?"

Amir sat back in his seat and grinned, loving the way Trina could read a woman at the drop of a dime as if she has a gift.

"I turned her down, you know real niggas never bite on an easy catch. But what I need you to do for me is just chill and try to enjoy yourself. I know you told me how you hate A.C and if you never saw it again it wouldn't be soon enough. But you didn't once say why and that's cool, I know you have your reasons. But I had no choice in the matter on this one."

"I understand baby for Pop's whoever has to die, must; anywhere anyplace."

"Correct and there are only a few more questions I need to be answered to know the real source behind his murder and no matter how hard they try to whole out, in the end, they always talk. Then I can give you my full attention." Amir ran his hand up Trina's thigh finding she was panty-less as he eased two fingers into her wet pussy. The sound from her mouth was lost in the music as her legs parted voluntarily yearning for his touch.

Amir knowing Trina's body as if it was his own brought her to the tip of orgasm then slowly stopped. Trina has a mind of her own refused to be denied gripped hold of his wrist firmly pulling him in deeper moving it back and forward and around until squirting all over it.

Amir just shook his head while he watched Drew out the corner of his eye laughing with the four women he sent his way. Amir motioned with his head towards the crowded dance floor. "That's your true love, go have fun. I know you want too, I won't be too far."

"If you insist but next time if you start something you better finish it." She popped a piece of pink Molly into her mouth before finishing off her fourth shot letting the glass crash to the table.

She made her way to the center of the dance floor feeling the drug kicking in. she shut her eyes again allowing the bass to take control of her body. Her physique fitted in her skin tight dress just right as she swayed her hips from left to right with her hands waving above her head. The sensation of her sweat creeping down the side of her face along with her dripping wet pussy forced a smiled at the thought of swimming in-between a waterfall.

"Yea this bitch Molly got me rolling like a mutha-," A lite tap on her shoulder briefly interrupted Trina's thoughts and her high.

She reopened her eyes adoring the sight of what stood before her. *"She's sexy,"* Trina became stimulated as her eyes trailed over a 5'5 almond shape grey eyed woman's figure. Her olive complexion accented her long wavy jet black hair.

"Yeah, she is thick in all the right places everything about her screams come and get me. Yup, she a freak or soon to be." The woman's full 34DD breast caught Trina's stare simultaneously as the woman took hold of her hands interlocking their fingers.

"I'm Bi", the woman whispered into Trina's right ear as she ran the tip of her tongue around the 14 karat gold hoop that hung from the lobe.

Tina feeling the four shots of Jose` warming her blood pulled the woman in closer, "Me too". Together they began to dance as if they were the only two on the floor. Grinding harder with every thump of the beat winding as if they both were a native of Jamaica.

"That's great to know," The woman replied as she ran her finger tips down the center of Trina's spine sending an almost paralyzing sensation over her whole body.

"Excuse me," Trina said which sounded more like an order than a statement, snapping out of her zone observing Amir at the far end of the V.I.P section motioning with his hands requesting her return.

She immediately removed herself from the woman's tight grasp leaving her stationary with a polite smile and eyes of lust as she abandoned the dance floor.

Amir's blood began to boil at the sight of Drew making his way for the exit with two of the girls.

"Showtime nigga," He whispered thinking, *"My dad goes in the ground tomorrow but you're going tonight if I don't get the answers I need."* He looked away from Drew for a second to spot Trina having fun on the dance floor with a female that looked almost as pretty as she did. He waved placing his stare back on his main objective.

Amir suppressed his anger displaying a counterfeit smile for Trina as she got comfortably next to him.

"It's magnificent to see when you're having a nice time."

He kissed her on the cheek pouring her another shot purposely Knocking the bottle into his lap. "Shit!"

"It's ok I'll lick it off of you." Trina reached for Amir's zipper.

"No it's nothing I can clean up real quick, so who's your friend?" Amir inquired with a slight smirk.   "Oh she's Bi" Trina quickly responded

"I could see that much, you like?"

"No that's her name and she'll do."

"Ok, then it's a date." Amir stood from the table exiting the booth just as Drew departed. "Twenty minutes," He said confirming their rendezvous as he placed a hotel key card directly in front of Trina. "I got you your own room."

"You're so good to me but if you're too late I may have to start without you."

"I wouldn't have it any other way."

Trina waited until Amir was out the club then started a little mischief of her own. She stood passing the bottle that remained over half full to a quiet woman who stood huddled inches from her booth in a small group of loud obnoxious half dressed women. They have been working on her nerves from the moment she sat down.

"Oh thank you sexy." The woman said giving Trina a passionate deep hug. They gradually separated with the woman squeezing the tip of her nipple.

"Lovely,"

Trina clutched hold of her hand bending it until the woman jerked from the pain.

"Sorry you're late I have a playmate already. But a word of advice watch the hoe you role with because thirsty ass bitches are everywhere,"

"Fuck you hoe I don't know who she talking about."

"Hey, bitch!"

Trina laughed hysterically about the eight women that were now mad, all nursing the same bottle for the whole night.

She returned to the dance floor where Bi patiently waited.

12

"**H**eather it's a confirmed match, the woman seated next to Amir in the booth is the same woman who eluded Jake from the other night." Alex read from the screen, "The odd thing is Trina Martin is supposed to be her name but according to the FBI Intel, the real Trina Martin fitting the birth date and social society number we got off the credit card she just used died ten years ago."

"So who the hell is she?"

"I can't say at the moment, I checked all the social media sites she has no Facebook, Snapchat or nothing. I ran her photo through facial recognition several times and got a few hits but nothing definite. It's as if she came out of nowhere about seven years back as this Trina but I'm working on it."

"You do that." Heather looked intently at Trina's photo locking it into memory before shifting her vision back to the screen as Amir spilled a drink on himself.

"Shit I need her to do my make-up look at that. It's like two different people. If it wasn't for this computer reading I would've sworn that she was someone else the way she's all done up." Heather uttered when it hit her. "Which takes years of practice." Heather's fingers quickly moved across the keyboard attempting to crack into the national juvenile database. "I'll say she's around 23-24 years of age, meaning she has been becoming someone else since she was a teen."

"You're right why didn't I think of that?" Alex began to search the internet for New York high school yearbooks photos between the years of 2015 and 2016.

"That's why you're the second chair."

The movement on the screen again held Heather's attention. "This is it people let's get to it, the dog is off the leash."

"I have Drew accompanied by two females in the left hallway of the club heading toward the south corridor." Det. Alex narrated into his headset giving the team play by play.

"I'll be in position in a minute and a half." Det. Jake responded racing down the hall on the opposite side of the hotel at top speed. He reached the crowded escalator taking the steps two at a time moving in and out of people.

"Excuse me, Pardon me; watch out please." He reached the bottom still in stride dashing across the slot machine section floor.

"He just made a right, entering the main hallway."

"I'm coming I swear he isn't getting away Heather I promise you that."

"No Jake I'll shield the bait you stay on the target. I know how bad you wanted to get even, now it's your time" Det. David cut in while rounding the corner at the end of the hallway. He put on a pair of dark sun glasses and waited. Seconds later he whispered. "I have the bait in my sights copy."

"Thanks." Det. Jake said a little out of breath.

"Jake that doesn't mean you can slack get a move on it the target is on the go, right behind the bait."

"I'm coming...Excuse me, sir! Dammit, get out of the way!" Det. Jake said forcefully shoving a man sending him falling to the ground. The bucket of chips he carried flew into the air scattering all over. People swarmed the free money like bees to honey robbing the man in plain view.

"Sorry." Det. Jake yelled without stopping. He sprinted through the main lobby wiping the sweat from his eyes determined to put Amir away.

"Jake I have eyes on you, in about twenty feet make a sharp right. Then another, do you see the door off to the side?" Heather questioned reviewing the hotel's blueprint on the upper screen.

"I'm entering now."

"This is a short cut, now make a left and according to this outline, this should put you several feet in front of them. Now at

167

the phones make the right and you will come out by the elevator and our target will be sixty feet on your right. And fix your wig, hat and glasses we don't want Amir to recognize you. If he does at this point he may just kill you on sight."

Jake swallowed hard with his heart beat rapidly increasing at the possibility of him dying without warning. He slowly gathered himself as instructed before stepping out into the joining hallway. He looked like anyone other than himself. He took a deep breath counting to ten to calm his nerves stating, "Heather I have the target in my sights at about twenty feet but there seems to be something wrong with him."

Amir went into action the second his palms pressed onto the door exiting the party. He fell out into the hall tripping over his own feet staggering from side to side. He gripped hold of the far wall to stable his balance, standing he spotted Drew and several other people throughout the hallway staring in his direction. He closed his eyes counting to five then reopening them, noticing three people still watching him.

"These people have extra interest." Amir knowing that when a person enters a room its human nature to give them a three second glance so the brain could register if they're a friend, foe, or threat. Any moment longer usually meant someone was searching for something else and mainly it was a weakness.

Amir smiled partly revealing his teeth his words slurring "It's… its okay I'm just a little tip...p...tipsy at the moment that's all. I'm getting old and I can't hold my liquor as I used too."

His vision rotated counter clock wise locking on the stares that still remained. He hesitated on a man standing beside the elevator with long brown hair, a bucket hat and dark sun glasses.

"It's something about him that's odd. I think I know him from someplace but where? He's not coming from the party. The way he's dress he would never get in. There's no female in sight which is abnormal in A.C. He may have had a few drinks but

he's not drunk... unless he is waiting on a hooker. Which would explain the reason for him trying to hide his identity. He's not packing or it's is in the center of his back, either way, it would be too late. " Amir continued to walk acting as if his equilibrium was slightly off closing the distance between him and Drew who approached the elevator.

Amir's sight shifted to a middle aged woman currently looking him up and down. *"By that stare in her eyes and the way she is biting her bottom lip says only one thing...this bitch is a*

Thot. "

He slid in line behind the two females and Drew as they waited for the elevator. He used the reflection of the stainless steel doors to examine the remaining man standing at the edge of the hall inspecting him out the corner of his eyes pretending to be viewing his phone.

"Now this guy looks totally out of his comfort zone. The cheap suit and the small drops of sweat forming on his forehead and hands scream out one thing.... Security or a cop waiting on some action he's not prepared for. All I know is it better not be for me because fuck action I'm giving out caskets. " **Ding!** The elevator's doors slid open.

Amir remained still and began to count down from seven as the two women followed Drew inside.

"Come on sweetheart I'll take a ride with you anywhere." Stated the middle aged woman with pure lust dancing in her eyes.

She gripped hold of Amir's arm.

"No, I'm fine sweetheart I'll catch the next one." The instant the words left his mouth Amir could sense the man behind him relax.

"You sure if you want I'll catch the next one with you, honey?"

"Well, one of you do something shit! I got some work to put in and when I put it in it goes deep." Drew said aggressively bending one of the girls over in front of him over grinding on her ass. On impulse, his hand reached out stopping the door from sliding shut.

"Go head my dear I'll be fine."

"Ok, I'm coming Mr. Nasty don't bust a vein, shit you're not the only one that needs to get lucky tonight." The middle aged woman yelled at Drew getting onto the elevator.

"Oh I'm going to bust a vein alright and it's going to a big one."

"Young man, you're just nasty as you want to be and I ain't mad at you."

Amir turned to his right seeing the man's forearm muscles tighten instantly. *"He's still not ready three...two."* Then without warning Amir with two short steps slid sideways into the elevator just as the door closed right behind him.

Det. Jake and Det. David was caught off guard by Amir's abrupt action as they looked at each other than simultaneously rushed the elevator. Det. Jake accepted to pry the double doors apart to no avail.

"Now don't just stand the fuck there get after them? Jake, you take the stairway on the right and David you take the one on left." Heather demanded.

"Copy."

They raced off, both equally eager to make the collar knowing that this arrest had promotion engraved all over it. Det. Jake being the quicker of the two sprinted up the stairs three at a time. He forced out the thoughts of the pain shooting up his legs as he rounded the fourth stairwell approaching the fifth floor.

"I got to hit the gym more." He told himself when Heather's voice came across the air waves.

"Fellas I have no visual inside the elevator there's something placed over the camera I suspect. But I still have sight of the hallways. I patched into the database and its only four stops pushed on that elevator. The tenth, seventeenth, twenty-first and the twenty-eighth floor. At this very moment, it's on the sixth floor moving to the seven."

"I'm right on pace. I'm heading to the sixth floor as we speak."

"I'm currently on the fifth."

"Well, David hurry up. This maybe our only chance to catch this son of a bitch in the act."

"I'm sorry boss."

"Don't be just get the bastard. Drew's suite is on the seventeenth floor. I believe that will be Amir's best point to strike."

"I don't believe he's foolish enough to try something in front of all those people." Det. David questioned

"Why not a hooligan doesn't care who they hurt or where they make them suffer."Det Alex interjected.

"Honestly at this point, I don't think he's a basic hooligan. He's different and we need to start treating him as such. Someone on our level if not above and then maybe we can get some cuffs around his wrist. The man has been a step ahead of us from Go!"

"Heather the elevator position? I'm now approaching the ninth floor." David questioned.

"I'm on the eleventh," Jake added short of breathe.

"It's on the tenth floor with an older woman getting off now the doors closing," Heather informed,

"I guess I'm right fellas no one else got off so it's safe to say that my theory on Amir's plot is right- wait the doors are reopening…its Amir he is getting off." Det. Alex reported

"Is he alone?"

"Yes, he just stumbled into the third room on the right across from the elevator."

"I got your ass now," Heather said. "Everyone report to the tenth floor immediately."

"But what about Drew?" Det. Alex questioned double checking his weapon to make sure it was loaded as he prepared to exit.

"What about him, he severed his purpose at this point he can die as far as I care, right now we want Amir for murder and we got him."

"You can't mean that boss?"

"Why not, have you read his file? Drew has been acquitted for murder twice. He was charged with shooting several people who all later recanted their stories or they came up missing. Then don't let me start on the robberies and drug dealing he has on his jacket dating back as far as 11 the kid's a monster." Heather grasped her jacket off of the arm of the chair and headed out the back of the van with Alex right behind her. "So yes, I'm dead ass serious."

Heather stood in the middle of the lobby with a blank facial expression as she motioned with the flick of her finger for the remainder of her team to rush the stairs. On the tenth floor, Det. Jake awaited at the entrance.

"We have the room surrounded boss waiting on your say so."

"Ok I want this floor taped off no one is to get in or go out until this is done with."

"Understood." Det. Jake raised one hand and quickly flashed five fingers then four before a short pause then three more. Succeeding their orders nine team members moving in three sets of three went door to door making sure the people stayed put.

Det. Jake phoned downstairs,

"Hello, hotel security this is Jordan speaking-"

"Fuck who you are... just listen." Det. Jake rudely interjected, "I'm detective Jake with the special homicide unit and there's a wanted murderer on the tenth floor."

"Oh my god-"

"Sssshhhh we have the suspect detained in a section and what I need for you to do is have all elevators skip this floor for the time being until I say otherwise."

"Ok, no problem Detective I'm programing them as we speak."

Det. Jake disconnected the call lifting a thumb in the air. He held it there while exploring the crowded hall of detectives until locking eyes with Heather giving her a short nod. She smiled anxiously at the thought that soon she would cross a line through

Mr. Patrick's name.

Heather turned eliminating her smile. She gave the same head jester to her point man Det. Jenkin, who detached the Vincent Van Gogh replica painting of, *The Starry Night* from the wall that hung next to Amir's suite to gain access to the ventilation system. He quickly removed the screws stepping in between the walls. There he slid the borescope through the vent's opening. He altered the tools' position.

"Copy I have the subject in my sight and he's not alone, sending live stream now."

"Receiving data." Det. Alex informed Heather handing her the iPad. She stared at the vision of Amir in the dim lit room seated in a large chair with his back to the camera. A female sat Indian style in front of him with her face moving up and down in his lap.

"Damn bitch come up for some air so I can see your face."

"Do I hear a slight bit of resentment in your voice?" Det Alex inquired.

"The only animosity I have is the fact that he's not in a cell already." Heather's blood began to boil with rage as she raised an open hand into the air.

The hit squad consisting of 20 men immediately prepared for action. They aimed at the center of the door when Heather's hand shifted slowly into a fist and it began. **Boom boom boom!**

"Police open up!"

Heather watched Amir's body jerk to the sudden sound. He removed his weapon from his hip and placed it onto the night stand beside him. The without pause he grasped the back of the woman's head pulling her back down into his lap. **Bomb boom boom!**

"Police open up we know you're in there." **Bomb boom boom!**

"Boss the suspect is not responding do you want us to ram

It?"

"What you think?"

David stepped aside and, two men with a battering ram stepped into place pumped for engagement.

Heather looked from the door to the iPad and back thinking; *this son of a bitch is not getting away this time.* She closed her eyes taking in a deep breath.

"David, as bad as I want to go in there and shoot him dead because he is clearly packing. We got to do this by the book ... Jake get the manager on the line and have a key here like yesterday."

"I'm dialing... Jordan its detective Jake I need another favor."

"And that is."

"The room key to 1029 this is a matter of life or death, do you understand me."

"Yes I comprehend detective but I don't have the power to assist you with that. All extra keys not assigned to the registered person much go through the manger."

"Jake why isn't that door open yet!" Heather yelled into the ear piece." Quickly losing her temper.

"Then get one the fuck up here now or I'm going to lock you up for interfering in police business and that carries ten years to life in prison. Can you handle being somebody's bitch for the rest of your life Jordan?"

"My god no detective but that wouldn't be necessary there will be someone up there to assist in minutes I swear."

Four minutes later a fat man in a suit and tie weighing about forty-five pounds overweight and sweating profusely stood in the door window of the staircase as Jordan anxiously knocked.

"Go away this floor is closed." Said the stone face detective.

"No open this damn door I'm not going to jail for nobody. I need to speak with detective Jake."

"There you have it they don't want our help. The officers have everything under control? Plus I don't have the key because I'm not giving it up to anyone until a murder transpires. I'm not losing my job because of what somebody thinks is going to happen." The manager stated sweating even more at the thought of being unemployed.

"You stay put you fat fuck or I'll turnover every single sex tape I have of you forcing the maids to go down on your little pecker," Jordan yelled.

"Alright I'm here but I never forced anyone to do shit."

"Jake! Detective Jake, I'm here its Jordan-" The door flew open with a p30 and a 9mm automatic pointed dead center in

Jordan's face with two detectives stepping through the opening.

"Shut the fuck up and get on the fucking ground."

"But you don't und-" **Smack!**

The forearm connected to Jordan's jaw as he was forcefully pulled to the ground. The barrel of a weapon trailed his every move. The manager didn't hesitate making it to the floor before Jordan.

"Officer please don't hurt me I explained to him that you all had it under control."

"Remain quiet before I shove this up your a-"

"Hey fellas they're with me but if they don't have that key I promise you can do what you want..."

13

Inside the hotel room, 1029 Amir continued to enjoy the warm feeling of the thick lips caressing his balls when another hard knock pounded against the door.

"Police open up, this is your last warning!"

Amir not disturbed pulled down on the front of the female's dress exposing her plump breast while sending his manhood deep into the back of her throat. He thrusted his hips up and down catching his rhythm when the phone rang stopping him in mid stroke. He quickly gripped hold of his weapon,

"Answer it and see what they want and don't say nothing more."

"Hello what do you want?"

"Hi I'm special homicide detective Heather out of New York City and I need to speak to the man your with, about a murder he may have committed back home. So I recommend that you get him to come out peacefully because we just want to talk but please don't keep me waiting."

The petrified woman placed her trembling hand over the phone relaying the message. The wicked grin she received in return said only one thing, pray. From that moment on everything, thing seemed to move in slow motion.

Amir bit down on his bottom lip as he stepped into the pathway of the door with his weapon following suite. He pulled the trigger several times just to place the position of his enemy as the nature of who he was kicked in.

The woman's cries could barely be heard through the tread of gun fire. Amir paused listening to the sound of feet scrambling for cover as he began to count. He reached eight when the counter fire erupted into the door's frame. He ducked from out the open space placing his back up against the wall once more.

Amir took in a deep breath settling himself as he quickly scanned the room for an alternative exit. He glanced toward the windowsill, "*Shit! I'm up to high to jump but I have to do something and quick.*" His eyes resumed their search discovering nothing. He raised his weapon revolving his aim as he squeezed the trigger repeatedly to buy time until it kicked back. He released the clip swiftly popping in another when it hit him…

Heather's count reached sixteen of the shots fired from Amir's weapon.

"He's empty." She said certain of it. She quickly flicked a finger with the first section of her team advancing.

Amir reloaded, raising his weapon when the door flew in off the hinges. On instinct, he jumped into the air and fired placing several shots just above the rim of the shield hitting the second and third man through the door. "Aaaahh!"

"Officers down. I repeat two officers are down." Kim screamed into her earpieces.

"Diamond formation," Heather ordered with her team quickly responding. Three rows of five detectives moved in position standing two feet in front of the injured detectives with one in the middle and two men on each side. The first row fell to the floor with their weapon locked and ready. The second row lowered to one knee equipped to strike. The last row remained standing forming a perfect diamond around the hurt detectives. Four detectives swiftly pulled the men from the room to safety.

"Clear."

Amir disappeared back behind the wall as numerous shots slammed into its structure sending a cloud of dry wall fragments throughout the room. He suppressed his wrath craving to get busy as thoughts of going out while giving up a shower of bullets echoed in his mind. He calmed himself thinking fast on his feet he gripped the scared woman by the neck placing his weapon to her temple.

"Back the fuck up or this bitch brains will be on your hands literally." Amir threatened as the detectives surrounded him. He moved pulling the female toward the door.

"Get the fuck from behind me... What I know you're not hard of hearing nigga now move or I'm going to kill her then you before one of these clowns even get a shot off."

"I don't think so," Det. David responded sharply.

"Then try me."

Det. David with his weapon locked on the center of Amir's head didn't budge as he waited on Heather who gave a short head jester to the left. Det. David not liking his order hastily stepped aside.

"Okay take it easy no one has to get hurt." Heather pleaded as she reholstered her pistol. She tailed him out into the hallway hating what she witnessed on the female's face.

"Amir, take a deep breathe please, I'm saying this as your friend so think about your actions. You don't want to do this."

"Stop calling me that, you're not my friends. You don't know me."

"Your right I don't know you but what I do know is that you don't want to hurt that woman for your own selfish reason."

"If it's my life or her life guess which one I'm choosing." Amir pulled the woman down the hallway toward the exit.

Heather's vision shifted from the woman's eyes still perceiving nothing but pure terror in their depth. She glanced toward the double doors a few feet behind Amir. She raised her hand for her men to back off.

"Okay, you win look we're standing down just don't do nothing irrational."

"I think your visit has left me little to no choice in that matter."

"No you still have options, release the girl and come with me and you can tell your side of the story to what really happened with you and your father."

"Bitch! How dare you mention him, as if you care?" Amir refusing to fight his rage a moment longer had his weapon within a split of a second pointed at Heather's face.

"How does it feel to know that your life is in someone else's hands and can be taking away at any moment?"

Heather swallowed hard looking Amir directly in the eye revealing no fear deliberating without any doubt that the man who stood before her would kill death itself if it got in his way.

"Don't do this Amir I promise you won't like the ending," She said sounding more disappointed.

"Well, I predict we're about to see." Amir's finger eased back on the trigger while looking around one last time. "I guess it's your lucky day."

He backed out using his shoulder to open the exit door. His eyes remained fixed on Heather's expressionless face which slowly transformed into a wicked grin.

Amir suddenly through his peripheral noticed a fat man lying on the floor.

"Oh, shy-" was all Amir could get out sensing someone behind him when Det. Jake's gun fired twice blowing the side of his face off.

Heather stepped through the door demanding.

"Get these two out of here." she pointed to the woman and fat man screaming uncontrollably. She stood over Amir.

"Your mind was already made up no matter what I would have said your life would've ended on this floor."

She bent down to remove his costume needing to see his birth face one last time before putting her old friend behind her until he returned in her dreams. She tugged on his beard as a single tear rolled down her face.

"Don't beat yourself up Heather he brought this on himself." Det. Alex said placing a hand on Heather's shoulder.

179

"It's not him."

"What?"

"It's not him look the beard is real and this is not fucking make up."

"But the factual ID confirmed that it was him."

"Yeah just like he wanted it to. Fuck! I can't believe this shit." Heather kicked the dead body several times

"But."

"But what Alex? We been "had" don't you get it! The situation doesn't seem strange to you at all? Up until now, we could never get a match on Amir's whereabouts or his woman friend whatever the fuck her real name is until today? Oh just lucky us we get them both? No, they were handed to us and we didn't even see it. The good old effective diversion and we went for it. Why have on a disguise if it not to prevent us from finding out who you are."

"So that we would think someone else was him."

"Precisely," Heather said when Keith's words hit her, *"Nothing gets leaked unless Amir leaks it."*

"So what we do now?"

"Start from scratch have half of Intel find out the moment we lost Amir, there has to be a blind spot where he switched himself for this guy. Then have the other half comb through every single piece of surveillance within the hotel in the past hour. Amir is still in this building I can sense it in my bones. We're going to find him you can bet on that. Now, will someone get this fucking dead man off the floor and get his prints. I want to know everything there is about him three minutes ago and bring that girl that was with him here."

"Boss."

"Yes," Heather answered heading inside the room.

"The press is down stairs in the lobby as well as a Detective Terry who's a homicide detective out of the Atlantic City both demanding a reply to the rumors of a hostage and killing up there." The Detective controlling the main entrance questioned.

"Deny everything."

In the room, the woman sat on the bed crying as Heather studied her closely. The current of tears washed away her thick mascara. The terror and uneasiness her eyes once held were replaced with years of distress and suffering written in-between the lines of wrinkles beneath them.

Heather interrogated. "Who was the man that was ready to blow you away a few seconds ago."

"I don't know him I swear."

"Then how in the hell you end up here sucking the skin off his dick."

"Well thank you, I try to be the best at what I do."

"Okay you're a "Pro" it's written all over your face. So where did you meet this trick? Black page no we close that down.
The boardwalk, online, where?"

"Neither, an parking attended stopped me and showed a pic of this middle aged handsome guy and asked will I show his friend a good time. He gave me a thousand dollars and the room key and there you have it. "

"And how long ago was that."

"What?"

"The time you got the money," Heather asked typing on the IPad.

"Oh it was ten o'clock I'm sure of it because I just finished up with my 9:30 and he always cum in twenty minutes no matter what. And the walk from the boardwalk to here takes six minutes."

"Ok thank you for being so helpful you can go but remain seated I'm just going to have an office see you out."

"Thank you, detective, he bought me for the whole night but he's gone why not catch my 2:30 hell I'm available."

"Yeah, why not."

Out in the hallway, Heather was met by Det. Jake who was waiting at the room threshold.

"Jake put an APB out on this man."

Heather handed him the iPad with a still vision of Damon handing the woman money. "His name is Damon Brake some years back he did a 5 year fed bid at fort Dix for at jewel heist that went bad. In the report, the cops believe Amir was there also but they couldn't prove it. This is our guy."

"If so why didn't he try and hide his face he got to know we're looking for him?'

"Because if it wasn't for the arresting officer leaving a note in his file there not a connection between him and Amir. But by the look on his face, this guy just doesn't give a fuck who's watching."

"Okay sending the info by Bluetooth to everyone now and The girl."

"Lock her ass up for being so fucking revolting."

"Excuse me boss but the information is in on the dead man." Detective David said extending the folder to Heather

"Okay don't just stand there read it to me." Heather headed for the stairs.

"Basically the man was nobody. A four time loser and with this strike he would have gotten life imprisonment. He was born in Harlem."

"That's how they knew he would be here and I'll bet anything that somewhere down his history line you'll find that he had disrespected Amir or his father and he used him just like the pawn he was."

"Yes, it said that he and Amir's father had a falling out over-"

"Excuse me, David, something happening… What?" Heather stepped to the side hearing Det. Jake's voice echo in her ear.

"Heather, Heather we have him. I repeat we have Damon it's a confirmed match. He's on the first floor making his way to the garage exit. Do you want me to stop him?"

"No seal off the area and make sure he doesn't leave but do not confront him. We have to be certain this time. I repeat do not confront him."

"Copy, sending you the Intel now."

Heather's vision fastened to the iPad where Damon's past movements showed on the screen. She trailed his footsteps surprised to find him and the man who was just killed getting on the basement elevator a half hour previously.

"Shit that's how they did it. The man was already on the fucking elevator." Heather fast forwarded to the instant Amir boarded the elevator. She watched closely as he tucked his head not to be seen now realizing his actions weren't for the camera. It was to take cover from his look alike on the elevator as he slid through the double door stopping at the front.

Heather continued to scrutinize the video noticing a few floors later Damon's hands shoving the dunking man in the back off of the elevator never knowing that he had been setup from the word go.

"I got to hand it to you, Amir, you always find a way to impress me." Heather walked off knowing that when you trail a fox they always return to the den.

14

Amir smirked at the thought of Heather's face the instant she realized that she had been out smarted once more. A game of wits he had to admit he was starting to enjoy.

"Bitch fell for the old rabbit in the tail pipe and ain't even know she was driving." He laughed looking in both directions before sliding his key card into room 306. Inside he scanned, certain it was empty he text Damon.

"Part 3 is complete."

"Okay, I'm on the move."

Amir unclothed and stepped into the scolding hot shower calmly removing the blood covered make-up from his body. He closed his eyes with the burning sensation that felt as if his skin was about to melt portraying as a therapy to the deaths he left behind.

Refreshed with a clear mind Amir wrapped a towel around his waist placing his weapon in the center off his back. In the living room, he paused glancing at the reflection of his muscular frame in the full length mirror mounted to the conjoined doors.

"Whatever action they want I'm ready starting with this."

Next door in room 305 Amir locked the deadbolt. "Yo, you in here?" He spoke as the familiar sound of Trina's playlist consisting of her favorite slow songs filled the air.

"Yeah turn the light on I want you to see this," Trina's voice echoed from the bedroom through the darkness. Amir click the desk light on as he entered,

"Okay I see you," he said looking Trina directly in her eyes as she bit down on her bottom lip. The sight of her laying across the plush king sized bed wearing nothing but her glistening caramel skin and black bloody pumps. Impelled him to toss the towel. He placed his weapon on the dresser when he noticed the woman from the club completely nude in the doorway of the bathroom.

"Oh my goodness, what a big gun you have and the one on the dresser isn't that bad either. Hi, I'm B-"

"I heard", Amir stated cutting the who's who short as he motioned for her to join Trina on the bed. He took a seat on the window seal giving the two some alone time. He glanced out into the scenery of the bay. *"Peaceful."*

"Kiss me" Trina tenderly spoke as her fingers ran through her playmate's hair. Bi doing as told placed her soft lips to Trina's as her tongue eased into her mouth. Bi shocked by the passion she felt found it difficult to control herself from becoming hot all over. She quickly separated at the texture of her own wetness escaping down her legs.

"Hey, where you going." Trina inquiry feeling Bi's nipple harden even though she was trying desperately to battle the

sensation. "The one thing I hate is a slut playing hard to get." Trina aggressively pulled Bi forward by the back of her neck down between her legs.

The taste of Trina's inner core was astonishingly delightful to Bi as she licked up and down on Trina's clit while moving it in and out her mouth. The touch of a hand placed on her shoulder made Bi paused her feast.

"Invite him to join us and then I can show you how to really eat pussy being that this is your first time and all."

"Dammit, how can she tell?" Bi thought keeping her composer. "Hey, Papi why don't you come here and have some fun in-between these thick lips of mine."

"Which ones." Amir inquired standing at full attention ready for action.

"It's your choice surprise me."

"I was hoping you'd said that."

185

Amir approached the head of the bed where Trina slowly placed a condom on him using her mouth. She kissed the tip of his dick letting him know he had her blessing. Amir moved behind Bi admiring the way Trina tutored her how to maneuver her face around her pussy like an artist painting a picture that would soon breathe air. He placed his hand in the center of Bi's back applying pressure until her ass stuck out giving her no way to evade his thrust.

He slowly entered her allowing just his head to enjoy her wetness. He could feel the tension from her body relax as the flow of her juices increased. He inserted nine inches into her core feeling her pussy walls expand.

"Ooohhh!" Bi yelled. The feeling of being shoved in the stomach with a bat came over her just as Trina pushed her woman's face back onto her clitoris. The clapping sound echoed throughout the room as Amir pounded away on Bi's pussy like she was late on her rent. The room lit up from Amir's phone stopping him in mid stroke. "Excuse me I got to get that."

Bi could feel her pussy throbbing the second Amir departed. On impulse, she reached out for him as Trina grasp hold of her arms.

"Boo never stop a man when he is trying to handle his business as if he is choosing it over you because the moment he stops you will no longer look at him as a man."

Bi nodded before continuing to pleasure Trina who gripped the bedpost enjoying it as she watched Amir on his phone like a hawk. She could tell by the look in his eyes that play time had ended but she questioned anyway.

"Baby I thought we had an hour."

"I did too but he finished earlier than expected, get dress and you take the money from the top drawer and go."

"I hope there will be a rain check soon," Bi stated seductively standing looking Amir straight in the eyes while giving him a nice view of her perfectly round ass.

"Bitch if you don't get your thirsty ass up outta here, fun time is the fuck over; now get."

"Come on Trina don't treat your guess bad, sis a rain check may happen you never know."

"Thanks, papi that's all a girl can ask for." Bi hastily got her things and departed. Out in the hallway, she took several steps then threw up. "I can't believe I just did that... Hell, it's over now, time to pull it together and get out of here." she headed for the staircase.

Amir and Trina stepped out dressed in all black missing Bi within seconds. They tilted their heads eluding the cameras while moving down the hall talking as if they didn't have a care in the world. An action that became almost an involuntary habit. They confirmed their ear pieces were operational,

"Two minutes and we never been here do you copy," questioned Amir.

"Crystal clear", with the words parting her mouth they separated. Amir turned right as Trina remained straight.

"Five steps"

"I'm on in eight."

Amir walked in place three times then removed his hand letting the door close behind him.

Suez peeping out from the staircase seeing the elevators close then stepped back out into the hallway. She slid the key card she stole into room 305 where she still could smell the scent of her pussy in the air. She couldn't believe what she'd done to prove she has what it takes to be the best undercover offices ever.

"In the end, they all will know." She dusted the bedpost removing

Trina's finger prints "Yes soon they all will know."

Amir and Trina took separate elevators on opposite ends of the floor down to the garage. The doors opened simultaneously with Amir stepping out into the opening. "I'm on the move."

"Okay, I'm on your one." Trina began her count down from hundred as the elevator door reclosed with her remaining on it.

Amir's photographed his surroundings to recollection. He closely scrutinized back and forth for anything out of place. *"Four people in total."* He thought to himself noticing a drunk couple kissing to his right appearing to be madly in love refusing to keep their hands off of one another. The man's hands maneuvered up the woman's short mini dress until his rose gold Rolex was no longer visible. He pulled her panties slightly to the side before pushing her face down onto the trunk of the car. *"He's too preoccupied to even think about making a move on me; he would be dead before he could even react."* Amir's sights diverted from the freak show eyeing a man to his far left with the car hood up giving off the impression that he was having car trouble.

"The black dirt on his hands and shirt match his engine. Plus he seems harmless by his small frame and little fingers but who knows these days." Amir's palms slid onto the Glock in his waistband hidden beneath his black suit jacket. He strolled as if he was running late to a business meeting while his mind was locked on the odd feeling roasting in his abdomen. His finger tighten around the trigger aware that making it home by morning to lay his father to rest beside his mother would be done by any means necessary. The rage in his blood insured himself of that.

Amir out the corner of his eye spotted a red 5.0 mustang five feet away. The two pieces of black duct tape placed on each end of the bumper indicated his getaway car. *"Kid now you're thinking."* He whispered locking his sight on the last remaining person in between him and his escape, literally.

He studied the pretty blonde woman as she sat behind the wheel of a new Camaro reading the Atlantic weekly. *"Her makeup is a little much. Maybe to hide the scar over her right eye she believed no one would notice. Her hair gave off a daring passion into the shadow of her green eyes. The kind more like a*

prostitute calling for a trick than a cop asking for backup."
Amir deliberated as his count reached one hundred by the recollection of Trina's rhythm.

As if on que Trina strode off the elevator into the garage with her hand in her pocketbook clutching hold of her .380. She cast an eye above viewing for any immediate threats. Seeing none she gazed at Amir looking for the signal that all was clear by the wiping of his forehead with his right hand. The left meant something didn't feel right. If he touched his chin it was war.

Amir's right hand moved upward conscious of Trina's presence as he began to read the woman's lips as she read over the newspaper fining himself oddly drawn to her.

"Three men were shot late last night in Patterson over a social media dispute that quickly turned deadly stated sources close to the victim. The officers reached the scene to find one African American male D.O.A, the two other young men injured by what police believe to be a nine millimeter hand gun were quickly rushed to the hospital where they remain in critical condition. The gunman after a short foot pursuit-
Amir reciting enough to satisfy his doubts judging, *"This woman is very lonely. I can tell by the wrinkles under her eyes which is way too many for her age as if she over works herself to keep busy to substitute the emptiness."* He continued to walk as his finger touched his forehead gliding across when it hit him. He looked to the scratch peeping from below her mascara. "I'll be damn"....*The sound of the footsteps replayed freshly in his mind as he visualized her jumping when suddenly her grip slipped sending her back face first into the ground. "Aaaahhh!" she yelled removing a small piece of glass from her forehead saying,*
"That's going to leave a mark."

"And it did Heather," Amir whispered. His hand touched his chin on the way to his waist removing his weapon while his other reached the center of his back doing the same.

Trina observing the warning rushed for shelter behind a car covering his Six o' clock knowing the look in his eyes.

Amir smiled as his gun leveled at Heather's head and fired. The display of her blood coating the windshield sent a small feeling of relief up his spine as he repeatedly pulled the trigger.

Heather observing her name departing from Amir's mouth as she read his lips with his pistol quickly appeared.

"Shit!" She dipped down into the passenger seat as a bullet slammed into her collar bone. Several shots trailed ripping through the interior when the headrest shattered into bits. A piece of metal punctured Heather's other eye.

"Fuck, I'm hit!" Heather whispered into the two way receiver hoping Amir thought she was dead. She quickly distinguished the change in the sound of the impact from the bullets realizing he was quickly approaching.

On call, the trunk of several cars opened with a detective ascending from each. Their weapon quickly altered in the direction of the shots just as Amir jumped onto the hood of the car fastening the barrel of the gun in his right hand dead center on his prey's head while the other rotated back and forth.

Heather sensed the ambiance of death was upon her but not because of the sight of a pistol keen to her with the trigger easing backwards. That did nothing like the several pervious times. It was the stare of detestation she witnessed for the spilt second in the groove of Amir's eyes before he hastily buried it within. She braced herself mad that she hadn't prayed in years as she prepared to meet her maker.

"Amir stop and put down the weapon or I will shoot, I swear," Alex screamed.

"Then let's get busy," Amir responded through tighten teeth picking up the speed of his circling firearm. He awaited this moment for years and now that it was here, there wasn't anything that was going to prohibit it. Not even the threat of losing his own life. The rare look of fear on Heather's face made the wait well worth it.

"Amir really, don't do this."

The sound of Trina's plea snapped Amir out of his zone. His head slowly turned with his heart quickly filling with disappointment seeing Alex with his gun placed to the side of her head as they stepped out from behind a vehicle.

Amir notorious for working under pressure slowed his heartbeat to a pace as if he was about to fall asleep. He quickly analyzed his best exit to memory. *"I can assassinate this bitch while taking Alex out with an eighty-seven percent of killing him before he get a shot off. A risk Trina will have to live or die with.*

The two detectives' inches apart at my six o'clock will get handled by Damon...Oh, fuck he's not here. He must have seen the move before I did and made it out. "

"Dammit!" He bit down vigorously on his bottom lip as he turned back to stare Heather in the eye before ending her life. What he saw her weapon now locked on him. The flow of his blood dripping down his chin only reflected a droplet of his angry as his weapons came to rest on the hood

15

The next day, back in NY Amir was lead handcuffed through the back door of the special homicide division. He remained silent exhibiting a blank facial expression. His eyes scrutinized within the precinct in search of any weakness, surely if found he wouldn't hesitate to take it.

"Jake process him in, then place him in interrogation room three. I have something to handle then I'll meet you there. Don't let him speak to anyone you got that!" Heather ordered.

"I don't think that's going to be a problem boss he hasn't spoken a word yet."

"Believe me he will... *The mother fucker is on my court now.*" Heather thought to preserve her game learning that this was just the beginning when dealing with Amir. She knew few had gotten him to this point before, but none had been able to put him away for good let alone send him upstate and she wasn't taking any chances.

The back door was about to close when Roy and his cameraman slipped inside.

"Excuse me Mr. Amir I'm Roy Townson reporting for The Sunrise newspaper and I would like to know is there anything you would like to say to the people of New York who beloved your father's hard work and devotion to the community and feel that you should due life while others say you should give your life."

"What the hell, you guys aren't supposed to be in here. I must ask you to leave now or I will have ya'll both locked up for obstruction." Heather threated pointing towards the door. "And tell whoever tipped you off I'm shutting them down now get the fuck outta here."

"Ok we'll go but I've got one more question."

"Alright, just one but I don't think he's in the talking mood."

"That fine' because the question is for you."

"Me?"

"Yes, how does it feel having to protect Amir's life now that it has a two hundred thousand dollar price tag on it? Only so that you can bring him to justice?"

Roy was speaking to Heather but watched Amir attentively as the last half of his statement parted his lips. The sight raise in Amir's eyebrow let him know his words were heard. The small grin at the corner of his mouth informed him that Amir welcomed the challenge.

"Alex, run a check and see if there are more people than usual are being booked in the station and the jail. Like, people doing dumb crimes anything to get booked and get back to me A.S.A.P." Heather spoke into her walkie-talkie not taking the mere chance that this two-bit story chaser was speaking the truth.

"Now back to you, where did you get such an outlandish tell."

"Oh, you really don't know... well, word on the streets is that there's no way Amir could have killed his father but the moment you arrested him his uncle w-."

"Wants revenge for the blood of his brother fuck that, I heard the story before and this ain't that." Amir interrupted, "If anybody says anything to me about my father's death but who did it they will die and I'm not giving anyone a pass, not him, not nobody and you can quote me on that." Amir stated speaking for the first time meaning every word.

"Oh...Oh, thank you, Mr. Amir, that's all we needed and thanks again for your honesty cut the camera off lets go. Your statement will be aired tomorrow."

Outside the camera man quickly asked, "What are you doing that was our moment, why didn't you ask him the questions."

"Did you see that man's eyes and veins?"

"No, I guess I was too busy focusing on your fucking

close up so you'll look right in one of the biggest stories of your career before you chicken out."

"Well if you did you would know you can't bull shit a bull shitter and that man is not bullshitting at all; he is the real deal.
Now let's go I have a story to write about a true killer. One this city will never forget."

"Forget? The man is about to go to jail for the rest of his life. Hell, some have forgotten him already and you blow your change to get an exclusive."

"That's where your wrong my friend, he has that look."

"What look?"

"The look of Ali, Gotti and Obama"

"And what look is that?"

"The stare of a man that won't be denied and his story is just starting."

An hour later Amir attempted to remove the remaining ink from his fingers as he was lead in the direction of the debriefing rooms.

"Now ain't this funny the hunter has just become the prey and for that amount of money I know nigga's are in line to put a shank in your back the second you hit the cell block." Jake said enjoying the news.

Amir could care less for his mind was now locked in survival mode. His muscles tightened for action as he walked down the long hall lined with interrogations room. Jake opened the door with the aroma of prison entering Amir's nose the moment he stepped over the threshold.

The loud slamming of the thick metal door was meant to give off the sense of hopelessness as it separated a person from the real world leading them to the doomed fate they would soon encounter. A technique merged with the dim lights, dark colored paint and chains that now surrounded his wrist and feet. Amir knew that anyone who didn't have the spirit to fight would surely give into this false sense of fear as he forced his feet forward. He badly wanted to turn and fight for his life right then and there pushing aside the court BS.

"This nigga here would be the first to die and every other person through that door until I walk out of here a free man or hauled off in a casket so I ca-."

"The man has done totally lost his mind I'm telling you yo. Once the word of his father being murdered hit the hood it was as if nobody was safe. Not even me."

The sound of a familiar voice interrupted Amir's thoughts and for a split second, he thought he felt his legs weaken before a surge of rage over came him. He rushed to the window of the second cell slamming his head hard into the glass.

Boom!

"Damon you fucking rat! I knew you would fold at the first sign of heat, you bitch ass nigga. I knew you weren't built for this life. Maybe in the next life, you'll fit in better you'll soon see."

"Nigga you know my work so fuck the threats. It's on, on sight that goes without saying. But this has nothing to do with fear because I'm not the one wanted for murder, you are."

"Then what the fuck are you doing?"

"I'm here to see that look on your face when you realize that the man with all the brain has been out smarted by little old me. Young buck if I was you I wouldn't do this or that. You should do this and go do that. Now I'm doing me. What's odd is you always have the same factual expression. Why everyone else looked as if their heart was about to rupture when they know it was over. Like Frankie when he found out you had played him and me. Your sister when I told her it was going to be me to send you up the river. She had that look too, but I think it was more for her failure than my success. Now, look at you about to get the needle."

"Fuck what happens to me it's what I'm going to do that should be your only worry."

"Alright, that's enough." Det. Jake gripped hold of

Amir's shoulder who hastily yanked free. He reattempted to get Amir when he caught a look from Heather and stopped.

Heather   beholding   Amir's   dead stare, mouthed deliberately so he could read every symbol, "Ch.-eck-ma-te." She then continued with her questioning turning her back on him as if he wasn't present. "Don't you mean…" **Boom Boom!**

"Don't do this to yourself, Damon."

Boom Boom! The sound of Amir banging his head continually into the glass echoed through Heather's statements.

"You mean until he covers his track of killing his own father right?"

"Boom Boom!"

"Stop it, Amir!" Heather yelled, "I thought as a man who always anticipates the cause of his actions before he makes them, would enjoy watching a great end game, even if you are the opponent but now I see not." Heather sent Jake another look who hesitated out of fear then tased Amir with sixty thousand volts. He plummeted to one knee, refusing to go all the way down as his fist slowly tighten. The shockwave rushed through every inch of his soul as he gradually rose.

"Oh, you really are a tough guy," Jake said watching Amir make it back to his feet before shocking him once more, this time at max. Amir lost control of his Blatter seconds before losing consciousness.

16

Amir sweating profusely tossed and turned back and forth trying to escape his own nightmare...He refused to weep as the darkness shielded his young frame as the ripped tank top now hanging on only by a single thread once did. He tried to escape the cave he had crept into for safety as the sound of loud footsteps promptly approached. Within seconds the silhouette of a gun could be seen slowly rising before him. He forced his eyes shut when the echoes of gun shots awoke him. "Noooooo!"

"Amir, it is okay no one can hurt you dear I promise, you're safe with me now please continue." The soft voice of Doctor Stephanie consoled.

"Are you sure," Amir questioned in a childish tone

"Dammit, he woke up again. Whoever is behind that weapon has him petrified still to this day."

"Doc why in the hell is he talking like that?" inquired Mr.

Goldstein Amir's attorney interrupting her thoughts.

"Ssshh keep your voice down,"

"But I thought that you affirmed two weeks ago when my office contacted you the day he was arrested that he wouldn't be able to hear anyone but yourself and he would be safe."

"Spoken accurately but any sound will be real to him if he is on the edge of waking up. The new technology we're using will separate your client's thoughts from factual and falsehood, kind of like the way a lie detector works. Then the authenticity of his thoughts will be placed on the screen in the center of the room for us to witness. The same way he perceives them. "

"I guess by new technology you're speaking of the wires taped to his head, chest, and fingers that got him looking more like a damn Xbox than the man he is? Well, I'm regretful to inform you, seeing how much you're enjoying this and all. I have protested this so called new method with the court this morning and I assure you it will be put to a stop by this afternoon." "Then I don't have another moment to waste, do I? And for your information, I'm here to discover if Amir is a stone cold murderer like the police report states or not."

"Of his father merely."

"Absolutely but let's not forget that I'm here because you requested a psychiatric evaluation for whatever the fuck you got up your sleeve counselor."

"Yes, Doc and I thought that would consist of you asking a few questions to find out what's going on upstairs in his brain and not having to be afraid of drinking a bottle of water next to him."

"Real funny now if you don't mind.... Amir dear you will begin to fall into a deep sleep in 20, 19, 18."

"Doc what the fuck is that dripping from the I.V into his arm."

"Nothing but general anesthesia that makes him more compliant to my questioning. Therefore I'm able to direct him to certain incidents leading up to his father's death to get the answer needed. Now please be quiet or I will have you removed, do I make myself clear?"

"Crystal doc it's your playing field I get it, I'm just spectating." "3, 2, 1."

Within seconds Amir began breaking into another hard sweat as the T.V screen came to life giving the two a view in first person to what Amir saw. He tossed and turned trying to escape his own nightmare."

"It's alright Amir don't fight, it's time to face your fears."

The screen showed a childhood Amir at the age of ten. He stood in a dim corner refusing to weep as the darkness shielded his young frame and torn tank top. The sound of large footsteps quickly advancing echoed in the backdrop.

"*Come on Amir you can do this.*" Dr. Stephanie cheered in her head as the silhouette of a gun barrel could be seen slowly rising off the back wall before him. Amir forced his eyes to shut sending the screen pitch black as the echoes of gun shots started to awaken him.

"Noooooo!" he screamed

"Amir you find, dear, stay with me okay." Dr. Stephanie's thumb rapidly moved up and down on the button refusing to let Amir awaken when she was so close to decoding this moment.

Shocked at her action, Stephanie instantly became frightened seeing the massive flow of liquid trailing into Amir's veins. She knew the drug's strength and if she was over by a drop more than what his body could handle Amir would have a severe heart attack and die.

"Come on dear don't you do this to me. I know you're a fighter I can feel it." Stephanie pleaded as the last drop entered Amir's body. She waited on edge with each second moving comparable to days knowing in less than a minute if she would become like the man she was interviewing, an executioner.

Amir's chest sudden lifted up off the couch as he began to breathe hard. The veins in his neck and arms commenced showing as his body trembled uncontrollably.

"Oh shit!"

"Oh shit Doctor what happening to him?" Stephanie grasped the ice from the table rubbing it on

Amir's neck and chest. She repeated the act going back and forth.

"God please help don't let this man die."

"Doc what the hell did you do to him?"

"Nothing this happens all the time just give me a minute he'll be fine." *God coming on I will go to church every Sunday if you come through for me.*

Dr. Stephanie fought to keep Amir still when he broke out in a cold sweat fallen back down into the soft cushions. His body gradually became motionless.

"That's good he's stable, now he just needs to stay like this for a whole minute and we're back in business."

The last second pass with Amir not going into convulsions. *"Thank you, God."*

Stephanie rarely took any chance in life. Her friend Heather was the risk taker of the two however today she was willing to do just that, distinguishing the moment she met Amir that there was something different about this prisoner and she was about to find out what.

"Amir why don't you take me back to the time when things stop being so happy in your life."

The monitor promptly showed the same childhood Amir with a slight limp in his step bouncing a basketball back and forward in-between his legs as he made his way home. He stuck his key into the lock when to his surprise the door swung open.

"Mom your home." He said wrapping his arms around her neck. Stephanie observing the large smile on the screen and now on Amir's face.

"True love, somehow she plays a big key in this but what." Stephanie took notice before turning back to the monitor.

"Boy why you so loud and yes I took an early lunch break but what about you young fella if I'm not mistaken practice isn't supposed to be over for another hour or so."

"Oh, I hurt my leg putting a Kobe move down on this one kid, mom you should've seen how I broke his ankles."

"Baby are you okay let me look at it?" Amir's mother probed sincerely instantly forgetting about her own worries while getting down on one knee to examine.

"Mom stop! It's nothing coach put ice on it and told me once I get home to add more then get some rest and that's what I'm going to do." Amir started for the kitchen.

"Don't worry about it I'll get the ice you just go ahead to your room and prepare to get some rest." She smoothly grasps hold of his arm standing to her feet kissing him softly on the cheek whispering. "I love you, dear." As she gave him a more than a tight hug

"Okay...ok mom I can't breathe."

"I'm sorry dear I just want you to know that I love you that's all."

"I know mom but you don't have to squeeze the life out of me."

"Well, you can at least say it back so I can hear it."

"Come on mom I'm not a kid no more I'm going to be driving in a few years."

"Like six years."

"5 in two months."

"Ha...Ha... that's my baby always thinking ahead. Now go lay down."

Amir cracked his bedroom door when a loud thumping sound occurred off in the distance.

"Mom, what was that? Is someone here?"

Amir's mother stopped recognizing the noise as her heart did the same at the sound of Amir's voice.

"I didn't hear nothing baby-" **Boom boom!**

The faint sound repeated interrupting her lie.

"I knew it. I asked dad why ya'll been fighting a lot lately and he said he came home early and he thought you had someone in here that ran out the back door when they heard him coming."

"That's a lie dear you know I'd never betray your father or this family in anyway."

"All I know is I'm about to see."

"Amir don't do this dear it's nothing."

"Like hell, it is if dad not here I'm the man of the house." **Boom Boom!**

"Fuck this!"

"Boy watch your mouth."

Amir raced passed his mother as she grasped hold of the back of his tank top to stop him. Amir with a look of madness his mother had never witnessed on him before but had on one other person; *like father like son.*

He refused to cease as his shirt ripped nearly off his body.

"Aaaahh!" his mother screamed falling hard to the cold tile floor losing her grip and hopefully not her son. She struggled to get up seeing Amir dashed through the kitchen in pursuit of the sound. He turned right to the den finding the door shut and the source of the noise behind it.

The sound repeated sending a volt of rage up Amir's spine. He slowly clutched the knob with a thousand thoughts racing through his brain for the first time, all of murder. He stared at his veins pulsating appreciating the way his cooked blood moved through his physique. Shocked that his usually trembling hand was still as the moon at night as he slowly opened the door. The light crept into the darkened room just enough for Amir to see a woman's head lowering as she did a line of cocaine off the desktop. The noise ensued again as her thigh slammed against the desk's draws from the powerful thrust of being fucked in the ass from behind.

The woman's head rose upward where she locked eyes with Amir revealing her identity. Barbara jolted by the presence of another person not sure who but knowing not a soul was to ever know about their little situation. Nonetheless, she was turned on by the thought of having another person join in.

"Ooooh, baby you feel so good inside me but wait there's someone here," Barbara said while still staring at Amir before giving her attention to the cocaine doing another line.

"Oh shit Ms. Barbara." Amir mouthed without speaking on the screen.

Simultaneously, Stephanie said the same aloud dumbfounded as her iPad slipped from her hand tumbling to the floor. She couldn't believe the woman she only witnessed in pictures and heard so much about from her best friend was alive before her eyes.

"Excuse me doc do you know her from somewhere." Questioned Mr. Goldstein handing Stephanie back her iPad. He already knew the answer, trained to listen to a person's body language, not their words.

"No now sssshh please!" Stephanie retorted without looking away from the screen. She watched Amir dip into the darkness of the room hiding under a nightstand the moment Barbara turned to Mr. Patrick.

"What where!" Mr. Patrick said pushing Barbara to the side. He fixed his pants up while retrieving his army issued 45 automatic from the top drawer of the desk. He rushed off in the direction of Barbara's fingers. He approached the doorway with Amir just inches to his left and raised his weapon and fired.

Amir with his eyes closed heard the loud demand as his father turned in his direction.

"Whoever is in here come out now or die."

"Daddy it's me it's me don't shoot." Mr. Patrick pulled Amir up by the back of his neck. "Boy what the hell yo-"

"Oh my God nooooo!" Barbara screamed at the top of her lungs.

Mr. Patrick glanced to see his wife laying on the floor at the threshold of the door with blood running from the back of her head. He rushed to her aid with Amir as his shadow.

"Honey are you alright."

"Mom...mom"

Mr. Patrick checked for a pulse finding it barely detectable. "Dear I'm fine, where Amir is he okay, where is he?"

"I'm right here mom what happened to you did she hurt you." Amir shot a look toward Barbara that if could kill she would be dead at first glance."

"Oh God thank you, and no I just got startled by the shots and fell back and hit my head that's all. Now help me to my feet." "Honey I don't think you should do that you're bleeding. Just lay still why I call for help," Mr. Patrick said dialing 911.

"I wasn't talking to you, you no good son of a bitch. You and that hom- (cough) that home wrecker gonna get up out of my house (cough)."

"I think I should go." Barbara quickly exited clothes in hand, half nude.

Amir sat numbly as he stared at the love of his life choking up blood as it spoiled her flavor orange blouse. He wiped her mouth with the back of his bare hand.

"I'm talking to my son the only man that truly loves me,"

"Honey you can't mean that you're just a little upset. You have to know she doesn't mean nothing to me."

"No, what you have to know is if I die there's someone who will repay you for this I promise." Amir's mom stated talking to her husband while looking Amir straight in the eye.

Stephanie could swear she observed a slight head nod of agreement from Amir.

"I'll be damn."

"What is it doc."

"Nothing."

"*Another lie.*"

Stephanie quickly scanned Amir's file seeing that his mother was D.O.A (dead on arrival) to the hospital.

"Oh *Shit, that may have been her last wish.*" Stephanie thought coming up with a way to get the answer she needed.

"Amir that day I know you were forced to witness a gun by your father but actually when the first time you touched one willingly and what did you do with it."

The screen switched to a teenage Amir standing in an alley with a man who appeared to be in his early-twenties. The man looked in both directions demanding, "Come on nigga I don't got all mother fucking day."

"What?"

"The money dammit that's what."

"Oh...oh I have it no problem."

"You better young blood or instead of selling you this piece I'll use it to blow your head off. Now up with the bread."

"Can I see the gun first so I know that it at least works?" Amir uttered nervously.

"Can you see the gun first? Yeah, you can see it." Amir found himself once again with the barrel of a gun being raised before him.

"Yeah nigga here it goes that, heat work. Don't start sweating and shit. You know what, I should bang your little bitch ass then take your shit. I'm already on the run for downing one clown as nigga what's another with a four hundred dollar bonus." The man again looked around as Amir watched his grip tighten around the trigger.

"Because my uncle wouldn't like the fact that the man he helped escape Philly to come to New York for killing his own friend only to spill the blood of his family."

"You got a point there nobody wants him on their ass if they can help it. Now where the money so I can get the hell out of here." The man handed over the weapon.

Stephanie knew it was something different about Amir as she stared at the screen trying to put a finger on it. When on interaction with the cold steel it hit her. "That's it."

"What is it doc and don't say nothing because three lies would be too many."

"Okay quickly, look at his eyes there wide open as he now looks at the man without a drop of fear in his stare. When just moments ago he was acting as if he was afraid for his live."

"Acting, how can you be so sure his fears weren't real from a screen?"

"Look." Stephanie held up her IPad which was recording the feed and rewound the scene. "Watch his eyes they widen with a twitch in the corner of it with every mention of the weapon.

Then it's gone when he realized that he's losing his cover."

"Who's to say he isn't doing that to conceal his own fear."

"I was thinking the same thing but watch his hand every time they widen."

"I will be damn his finger curls back like if he is pulling the trigger."

"Yes connecting his taught to action. Meaning somewhere along the line he was taught how to use one after his mother's death. Now if you will set your attention to the live feed. View how he is examining the weapon as if it's a German car or an exotic woman at a gentleman's club."

Amir's right hand rotated back and forth loving the way the gun caressed his palm. He pulled it back slamming one in the chamber certain it was loaded. He slowly raised his arm bringing
the barrel to rest at the center of the man's head."

"Come on youngen think about your next move if you do this." "I did."

"You couldn't have when you're still holding that pistol on me and what you think your uncle going to say when he fine out that you crossed me after he set up the deal." The man questioned with blood in his eyes.

"Who's going to tell him?"

"Oh my god! He just shot him in cold blood." Stephanie screamed as Amir fired two more shots dropping the man.

Amir stepped over top of the man firing two more into his frame to be definite he was dead. He grinned as his eyes widen looking in both directions before dipping into another alley as if nothing happened.

Stephanie needing to know more, "Amir what did you do next?"

"I object doc what does this have to do with his father's death it was many years before hand."

"Maybe everything."

They stared as Amir exited a cab three streets over from his residence. He was now wearing a ball cap and sunglasses. He leisurely strolled up the driveway until the yellow vehicle disappeared from his sight. He then raced home moving in and out of the houses the same as when he was a kid practicing for this very moment.

He glanced at his watch realizing he was shortly behind scheduled. "Shit! A man that doesn't have a plan beforehand only plans for failure." He mumbled to himself

"Did you hear that? He muttered something about a plan," Questioned Stephanie.

"No, I can't say I did Doc."

"*Liar.*"

Inside Amir hurriedly explored around knowing that the house was supposed to be empty. He doubled checked just to be certain. He took the stairs two at a time to his room as the sound of the doorbell paused him.

"Shit! She early...coming! Always plan for the unpredictable...why didn't I listen, it won't ever happen again."

"I know you hear that. He is correcting his mistakes. Like there's an unwritten hand book in his mind"

"Sorry no, I was reading over an email."

"*Another lie.*"

Amir hastily wrapped the weapon in a shirt as the doorbell rang again. "I'm coming!"

Looking around he tucked it then rushed downstairs. Stephanie couldn't believe her eyes at the sight of her best friend, years younger entering the apartment. The stare of passion danced in her eyes as she kissed a boy who just slayed a person for no apparent reason. The spectacle turned Stephanie's stomach. The two made their way upstairs ripping the clothing off one and other.

"*No girlfriend do not go for it please!*" Stephanie pleaded within. She looked away lowing the volume as Heather's clothing fell to the floor.

Minutes later Mr. Goldstein broke the silence, "You can look now but if you ask me the young lad did a fine job."

"I didn't." Stephanie opened her eyes to observe Amir staring down at her friend fast asleep admiring her beauty. He tapped her on the arm, "Babe you up?"

Receiving no response he retrieved his weapon and exited the room through the window easing onto the fire escape. He positioned a small Lego in the grove of the window than shut it behind him.

Amir used the back streets like instructed quickly moving four blocks until he reached a small two bedroom apartment. He glanced over the area carefully before making his way up the fire escape. He counted each step as he did several times in the past months. But today he would no longer be a spectator.

Amir removed the Lego sliding inside leaving the window partly cracked. He paused listening for movement... Detecting something, he clocked his weapon and headed for the back bedroom.

The door was slightly ajar with Amir spotting a man in his mid-thirty's using his hands guided himself down onto the warm mattress. He padded the space beside himself as Amir shorten the distance between them. His weapon locked on the man's head.

"Snow Bunny, what you do go and switch up your perfume on me? When I was just getting used to the old one" The man said taking in a deep breath.

"Why would I do that I love how you make that look as if you want to fuck me the moment I enter the room no matter how far away you are from me when I do," answered the woman obtaining the spot next to him coming into Amir's sight.

"Oh my god! Nooo." Stephanie yelled as everything came together at the vision of her best friend's mother looking twice her age kissing the man's neck and lips while unfastening his zipper. "If not you, then him." The man corrected.

"What, there's nobody else her-" The words got lost in her throat at the sight of Amir entering. Instantly the vision of the scared little kid flashed before her eyes.

"Oh don't look surprised you had to know this day was coming."

"Man, who the fuck are you? Say a name so I can put a face to this ass whipping." Stated the man throwing his hand up preparing to fight.

"No honey he's speaking to me and he's here to keep a promise," Barbara said standing to her feet. She took in the man that now stood before her replacing the scared little kid. She noticed his anger replaced where his tears once rested. The look of unsureness for what was to come of his life was exchanged with a wall of certainty that revenge would soon be severed. A handgun occupied his palms instead of his mother's blood with the trigger finger easing inward.

The shots exploded without pause hitting Barbara in the face and neck killing her instantly. Amir quickly checked her pulse making sure she was no more.

"Now my mother can rest in peace,"

"You damn right young blood."

"What!" Amir hastily raised the weapon locking it on the man.

"Easy star just relax you don't have to do this. I didn't see anything so I'm not a threat look." The man removed his glasses showing his all white eyes that he was blind. "But you do what you want because I'm damn sure not going to beg for me life. I done took so many that the soil crops grew from blood many of summers. But a little pointer if I may? In life, no true killer ever racks up bodies that he or she doesn't have to star. Because it makes their job meaningless when it counts though a fool may believe once they have one body why should another one matter.

Now whatever you're going to do make it quick because if my memory is right you have two minutes and thirty seconds left before the first officer will arrive."

Amir glanced at his watch while keeping his weapon locked on the blind man. He was astonished that the man was only off by a few seconds from the scheduling of the police response time.

"How could he know?"

"Don't worry your brain on me Star you'll know soon enough. I mean if you make it out of this one ask around about blind Sonny the Jamaican. I'm more than solid. But the million dollar question is if you would want to do something like this again but for money and if so here's my card. I think you got what it takes to make it in this game and to become rich. That's if you let me live." The man said smiling while easing his hand behind his back slowly moving toward the automatic 9mm resting in the center of it.

"Sonny the best auto body repair company in town... you fix cars?" Amir quizzed reading the card pondering if he should just kill the man.

"No, I fix problems key words body repair."

The sound of sirens in the distance could be heard quickly advancing. Amir applied pressure to the trigger when he asked.

"What makes you think I got what it takes to do this for a living?"

"I don't think, I know and it's not what you do in life that gives you value it's how you do them. And for you to be standing before me with the drop you're good, nobody has done that until now. And though many wouldn't agree to be blind Star is better than authentic vison. Because it gives you a different outlook of insight. When everybody assumes you're in total darkness. Like how your finger just tightened on that trigger implicating that your leaning more toward killing me than not, yet you're still indecisive. Nonetheless to answer your question when you entered the room locking your weapon onto your prey. I could hear your heart beat decelerating to a relaxing pace. Meaning two things, one that you were certain that you wanted to end her life.

And two you weren't overexcited like many others when they're about to play God. Star you're a natural at this that's why I didn't make you the moment you entered the apartment. Because you've been here several times before each time staying longer than before allowing your scent to build in the air. If it was your aroma alone I would have still made you at the drop of a dime and you would be laying right next to baby doll there."

"You mean I would be lying there and she would be still alive?"

"No I mean what I said because surely I think before I speak and note to you; interrupting people is rude. Furthermore, the bitch would be dead right next to you hell she not blind. I never leave a witness behind not even my own sister."

"You kill your sister?"

"Enough about me. What you did was mixed the three making one scent as I was saying."

"And how did I do that," *Amir questioned thinking back to his tutor's words… Amir from what you're telling me the best time to do it is when she's there with the blind trick. But be cautious because he is far from a sucker."*

"I'll enlighten you but I'm sure that you already know. Leaving your scent here is one which is no biggie if the act is done by itself. But no, you took it a step farther by seeing your target's daughter mixing the two aromas. And last but not least you made it your duty to let Heather know how much her new perfume smelled. Which you knew was actually her mother's from your surveillance. She wore it as you knew she would to impress you mixing three into one after you fucked her. Oh, don't look so surprised I can still smell her pussy juice on you."

"Man you sick."

"No I'm on point and all this tells me is you knew I would be here."

Sonny reached the butt of his gun and relaxed knowing he would need his hearing to be at a hundred percent if he was going to successfully kill the young man with such rage running through his veins. He could feel the vibration through the floor board. Then like that Sonny could sense the room was suddenly empty. He smiled at the act of swiftness.

"That boy is good but he will be great."

The scene switched to Amir removing the Lego sliding back through his bedroom window where Heather laid fast asleep. He kissed her on the cheek.

"That's it! This man is a cold hearted animal and I have seen enough. Look at how he just undress and got in bed beside her as if the events that just transpired haven't changed both of their lives forever."

"I witnessed it also doc but what does that got to do with the fact of him killing his father or isn't that the reason we're here?"

"You mean the reason we were here, this session is over. You'll have my full report by the time of the hearing. Now if you will excuse yourself …Security."

"Wait…wait please I need to know if he killed his father or not. The victim was my best friend and the person who hired me to defend Amir did so only for that answer and if I don't get it he'll surely kill him if he's innocent or not."

"Mr. Goldstein at this moment I'm not sure if death isn't the best thing for him."

"Doc I feel the same but if we don't try to get the answer we'll become the same as him."

"Alright, one more question but what if it comes back that he did it."

"Then he deserves to die to the sound of gun fire as the likes of my friend."

Stephanie could feel the pain in his words and with a slight, she began debriefing, "Amir, can you tell me the last time you have seen your father with pure hatred in your heart for him."

The screen showed the thick metal door slamming shut behind a present day, Amir. He rotated his wrist to regain the blood flow due to the tight hand cuffs.

"Hey, pal you're in the first cell on the right."

"Okay but I have to talk to someone about speaking with my father."

"No problem just get in the cell and I'll send someone out in a minute to speak with you...open cell eight!" yelled the correction officer from the intake room,

Amir paused giving the guard a quick glance before stepping in trailing the loud buzzing sound. The door slammed shut behind him interrupting the many whispers of street lies. He observed the fifty or so inmates crowed in the small holding cells as they watched him like the new kid in school.

Amir quickly dropped his head as if he was afraid. Being that he was young it frequently worked to avoid trouble. He made his way to the rear of the cell placing his back up against the wall. He stood in the corner quiet ignoring the many questions.

"Yo son what you in for?"   "Nigga what part of the city you from?"

"You banging what flag are you holding?"

"Don't I know you from somewhere Son...I'm telling you I know that cat from somewhere yo, I never forget a face that's that's ..."

"Hold on hold on." The room instantly became quiet. "I think that nigga owe me some money son, word." Interrupted Smalls as he stood up moving his arms back and forth flexing his large muscles. He was the biggest man in the room if not the jail due to his infatuation with working out. His words forced a burst of nervous laughter to fill the chamber because none knew when Smalls was playing or serious.

He was 360 pounds standing at 6'3 and most of the prison feared him. Smalls was back down in the county jail for his appeal as he attempted for the third time to get his fifty year sentence reduced to twenty which he had 8 in on already.

"C.O! C.O!" Amir yelled for the corrections officer, making his way back to the front after a half in an hour of waiting paying Smalls no mind.

"Quiet down with all that damn yelling now what seems to be your problem."

"I told the other C.O I need to speak with a lieutenant."

"Regarding."

"A special visit for tomorrow so I can get the fuck out of here."

"Visits don't start back up until Thursday so tomorrow is out of the question."

"This is not my first time here. I know the hours and believe me and if I don't have to speak with any of you I wouldn't but this is a visit I need to happen. So can you tell him that Amir needs to speak with him?"

"Didn't you just come in from court?"

"Yeah."

"Then how the hell you think the lieutenant is going to know you and you don't even know who the fuck is on."

"Just tell him that Amir needs to chat with him within the next hour."

"Yeah…Yeah, I hear you," the guard smirked walking off. "Ok play if you want." Amir returned to his position.

From across the room Lucas a hustler from Brooklyn in on a D.E.A detainer eased onto the bench beside Smalls whispering, "Yo son peep I think main man over there is trying to 69 on something or somebody."

"What makes you think that, because you know I hate a rat?"

"You don't see it."

"See what nigga? That's what the fuck I'm asking you."

"Say less, I'm just saying who the fuck just come in jail and start asking to rap with the warden or whoever without even waiting on a call."

"Come to think about it you may have a point but if so why you telling me."

"Because I was here when you came down before on writ and I know once we hit population you're going to start shaking and barking that work you got. And I think he's from Harlem like you so ya'll going to be on the same block and you don't need a nigga like that around before you find a crash dummy to do your dirty work."

"Point noticed but still why the fuck is you telling me if you know he's a rat then get busy and handle your fucking business."

"But...but."

"No buts, the second thing I hate is someone trying to gas me up because of my size thinking I'm obtuse."

"Obtuse what's that mean."

"Stupid, dummy. Now handle that or get handled one hundred." Smalls slid the blade out from under his shirt into the man's hand patting him hard on his back. "Let me see something and make it bloody."

"You ain't saying nothing I push this like you push weights," Lucas respond sizing Amir up at as he rose to his feet.

"Ok talk heavy now your starting to sound like a Harlem cat." "Never."

They both laughed as Lacus moved to the back of the cell. He inspected Amir from the corner of his eye.

Amir with his head down lost in his own thoughts didn't see the blade as it rushed from the parting crowd aimed for his heart until the last second. He moved with the momentum of the blade when his back slammed up against the wall just as it cut through his shirt piercing his rib.

"Aaaahh shit!"

Lucas smiled at the sight of the bodily fluid escaping Amir's physique. He planted his feet firmly pushing the knife deeper into his target's body.

Amir feeling his skin expanding with every thrust and not nearly ready to die swiftly fought back holding his attacker's wrist. The two provoked each other's strengths as their veins attempted to vault out from beneath their skin. They aggressively plunged forward moving the blood dripping blade back and forth.

A circle formed around them cheering mostly for Lucas who outweighed Amir by twenty pounds if not more. The two went at it as true warriors.

Amir again using Lucas' power against him pulled inward instead of matching his force as the knife cut lower into his hip as he stepped aside pushing Lucas head first into the concrete wall. Amir gripped hold of the knife swiftly ramming the blade into Lucas' back an inch from his spine.

"Aaaahh!"

"Shut the fuck nigga you want this work right?"

Amir slowly removed the knife quickly injecting it into Luca's right shower blade.

"Aaaahh! Alright... Alright, you win."

"What the fuck I say!" Amir yelled stepping to the side stabbing the man closest to them as hard as he could. The man fell gripping his thigh trying to stop the bleeding.

"What you think I don't know that's your man?" Amir questioned pulling Lucas by the neck of his shirt to the front of the cell. He pressed his face in-between the bars resting the tip of the blade at his throat, "I'm going to give you one option or you die where you stand."

"Ok, what?"

"Call the C.O and ask him to save your life."

"Cccc.Ooooo."

"Quiet down what's all the damn yelling for...holy Shit! Hey... hey, let him go."

"You still don't know when you're not the one in power." "Alright just don't hurt him."

The man on the floor knew now if he didn't do something soon his brother was sure to be killed. He tolerated the pain in his leg and rose to his feet. He dipped back into the crowd moving with his vision locked on Amir's temple. He removing the Bic pen from his waistband clenching it he jumping from the mob when Small's right fist slammed into the side of his face braking his jaw.

"Harlem pussy anybody else wants to try my man? I thought not. Amir handle your B.I son I got these niggas. Now back the fuck up and give him some space."

"Smalls you know him?" a confused Lucas asked

"Yeah pussy who doesn't know the nigga that will break your dreams if he catches you slipping and you running off at the mouth trying to fuck the new breed's name up."

"Nigga I asked you, then why the fuck you didn't say it wasn't what I thought."

"Because I wanted to see if the young cat's actions matched the stories that trailed his name in the joint and I'm enjoying the show pussy now shut the fuck up before I smack you and knock you the fuck out like your brother."

The guard's hand shook uncontrollable as he spoke into his shoulder walkie-talkie, "Cap-Captain I need you in R.N.D"

"Can it wait I have a lot to handle-"

"No, it waited long enough."

Five minutes later the Captain entered the hallway seeing his leading man dripping wet. "C.O Carton what seems so important that it could not wait." Carton just pointed.

"Amir that's you? Oh, shit C.O Carton what have you done to this man."

"Me?"

"Yes, I'll deal with you later. Now, Amir, we have been through this before and I don't want anyone to get hurt this time. So what can I do to make sure this man is released safely?"

"I just need an emergency visit from my father before I go to court tomorrow and it can't be done on the phone because it's personal."

"Done! You have my word and what else?"

"Nothing." Amir pushed Lucas to the back of the cell. He dropped the knife outside the bars sliding his hand through the open slot. He was quickly cuffed and rushed to insolation.

"Keep your head up youngen, fuck them cops and cover up because you know they're going to kick your ass when you get there," Smalls yelled.

The screen switched to the next morning as Amir did pushups with two large knocks on his head in a smaller cell alone. The four corner space was filthy and windowless with only a dirty metal mirror on the wall. A ray of light invaded the darkness to the sound of a steel slot in the door being opened.

"Okay cuff up your visit is here."

Amir with his feet, waste, and wrist chained and a black bag draped over his head walked for ten minutes in all directions. He could've sworn that he walked in a circle at least twice.

"Now turn around." The C.O said removing the cuffs and bag.

Amir doing as ordered came face to face with his father giving him his trademark grin. His appearance was impeccably sharp dressed in a grey with a yellow pinstripe suit, black Armani shoes, yellow shirt, and tie.

Amir smiled as giving his dad a kiss on his cold cheek. He looked at the casket and knew he had picked the right one indeed. The hand craftsmanship of the solid hardwood represented the ups and downs and twist and turn in his father's life. The high gloss finish signified his father's way of bringing light to any situation no matter how hard or dark it got.

Amir stood in silence taking in the last physical moment that he would ever be in the presence of the man who gave him life. A feeling of hatred shoot through his body as he whispered, "Why didn't you just give it up?"

218

Wetness formed on Mr. Patrick's tie as Amir wiped his face.

"Damn Dad they didn't even do your tie right but I got you." Amir attempted to fix it when the guards on each side of him dared their weapon.

"The warden said no contact."

Amir paying the words no mind and fix the tie the way his father would've liked as the weapon adjusted to his head. The guards watched the lieutenant standing ten feet behind Amir awaiting the sign to shoot. When the passenger side door of the hearse opened.

"Don't disturb him."

The person's voice echoed though they didn't recognize him it was in the manner in which he spoke they knew he was a man of much power as they lowered their firearm.

"Dad I'm sorry I came late that day. The only time you really needed me and I let you down. But I promise you with every bone in my soul whoever did this will pay." Amir stated a few more words that only he and his father could hear before screaming. "Now let's get this trial out the way so I can get back on my bullshit."

Amir's head slowly rose as his muscles tighten as his mind returned to Beast mold prepaid to survive at all cost then suddenly he relaxed seeing blind Sonny standing at the passenger side of the car.

"Sonny that's you."

Sonny snapped his fingers and Mr. Patrick was placed back inside the hearse.

"Who else you think could have pulled this off, you with that knife trick? Oh, it was respected but no they could care less if you kill several of them punks."

"How else would I have gotten the Captain's attention?"

"It's all gravy everything going as plan but my cousin is still kind of pissed that you made him do all that paperwork. He said he going to keep you in the hole for a week for that shit."

"You know what fuck'em."

"Hey... hey, that's my people but your right fuck'em to me he's still a pig. I used the sucker when I need him" They both laughed.

"The funeral your sister is handling everything they way your asked."

"That's it you see he didn't do it." Stated Dr. Stephanie, "Now if you don't mind leaving, Security!"

"Dr. is everything okay in here."

"Yes, I just need you to escort this inmate back to his cell in like five minutes after his meds wear off."

"No problem but that means you're all done in here right doc."

"Yes, we're thru."

"Oh Mr. Goldstein this came for you I think it's some kind of order from the court."

"I bet it is." Mr. Goldstein ripped the document free "I'll be seeing you in court doc."

17

Six months after his capture at approximately 8:36 am on a Monday morning, Amir wearing a full beard and twenty pounds of added muscle was led down the hall to a packed New York courtroom. His customary cool mind state was stripped into a man possessing a rage comparable to a caged wild lion willing to kill anything to be liberated.

His eyes estimated the brittleness of the wooden window frames while passing. *"Breakable."*

He again yanked at the extra tight cuffs around his wrist. His fingers tips rubbed the fabric of the too small county jumper studying its thickness.

"Thin but it may work."

He lightly drew against the chains.

"I' m sorry about that Mr. Amir I know they must be very uncomfortable but the big wigs upstairs' think that you're some kind of anxious killer that would murder a person at the drop of a dime given the chance. So they insisted that I lock them snug. But if you ask me you're a nice guy who's always respectful when we cross paths. I never caught you screaming at the female C.O.'s when they go by like a lot of these other guys. Man, one would think some of them never seen a woman in their entire life. Hey, girl let me stick my fat this and that into your bumper. You know I'm being nice with my words," stated Kurt a sixty-three year old correctional officer that was unfortunate to be assigned the duty of ushering Amir to and from the court.

"Really," Amir replied hating what he was about to do to the elderly man that possessed the keys to his freedom. He had taken this walk several times through these cold walls which led to the countless demise of people's lives. But never did he feel close to being one of them until now.

"Undoubtedly they are savages," Kurt continued. "Some even admitted it... I'm a savage ho come blow this pipe bitch, but let me stop no need in troubling you with all that. Seeing that it's your big day and all."

"Really?"

"Really and from the looks of all the people, that's out there one would think you're some kind of big deal. I don't know why you're in here young man and I didn't check cause I prefer to see a person for who they are and not from what a report tells me. Now, this next part you didn't hear from me. There are news reporters from all over out there to the right of the entrance. So you may want to look to the left when you enter. Just a little heads up before we walk in there."

Amir nodded in return. He could careless who was out there. His main focus was to regain his independence to once again hunt for his father's killer and that was going to occur today by any means necessary.

Amir paused permitting his mind for a split-second to think of Trina's well-being then it was gone. He had taught himself to block out everyone years ago. The moment he lost his freedom for the first time ever, realizing he could truly only control what he could touch. Therefore he hasn't spoken to anyone from the outside world except for Blind Sonny.

Amir entered the court room that had standing room only amongst multiple whispers that instantly became silent. He moved left with Kurt shielding him the best he could as numerous cell phones aimed in his direction. Kurt pointed to a table at the far end of the room where Goldstein sat reading over some last minute case law.

Amir scanned the crowd on the way to his seat which seemed to be sectioned off by groups of people who hated him each for their own reason.

In the back two rows, he noticed the family members of the people he had allegedly killed. He knew that he hadn't done one-third of the things placed on his name and even more so he was shocked by the individuals listed. Many were his associates but once the streets start talking who's going to stop it.

"I guess they're here to see me get cooked." Amir thought to wave to the section that quickly looked away.

"If you going to cry for them ride for them," he yelled. A row in front he observed Gun smoke Melvin accompanied by several of his assailants and Damon. The two locked eyes with Melvin motioning his lip to say, "I pray that you beat this so we can finish what you started the moment you step out those doors."

Amir laughed then his face became ice cold as he gestured back in their soundless conversation, "Pussy don't play with me just for that statement I'm going to rock you and your bitch and whoever in sight when I do it."

"This is about me and you remember that, because your girl is out here alone or have you forgot."

"She can handle herself or she wouldn't have been around me but you won't dare try to find out because you know I won't stop until there's not a seed left to grow your family tre-
."

Blind Sonny was seated with two females and three body guards in the front row right behind the defendant's table giving no doubt on who he supported. He placed a finger to his lips that instantly stopped Amir's threats.

Amir nodded his head in Sonny's direction as a notion of respect knowing that he was right. *"Damn I'm slipping I know better than that. Never tell an enemy your next move no matter how weak you believe them to be. But fuck that nigga and how the hell Sonny catches that with his blind ass. Hell, I'm slipping more than I thought this Sonny I'm talking about."* Amir's thoughts were interjected by the sight of his sister filling a spot behind the prosecutor's table sitting. Their eyes locked with Amir refusing to withhold his anger another instant longer,

"I see the pigs done cut you lose bitch but that won't help, you're dead to me now and later!"

"Wow…Wow." Attorney Goldstein shot to his feet stepping in front of Amir hindering his view of Sherry while giving him a firm handshake.

"Mr. Amir please this is not the time or the place."

"No you the one that's dead Amir, you can't tell? This is your pre-funeral and when it's done I'll be there when they stick that needle in your arm I promise. You fucking murderer!"

"Mr. Amir you mustn't pay her no mind she's just trying to provoke you into doing something irrational in hopes that you blow this very important day for yourself. But what I hear of you from your uncle Robert, you know all of this already so what is going on? You got to pull it together."

"What's going on is I moved with integrity and respect when I was out there. I never killed a person that wasn't in the game. But yet I'm locked up in a box twenty-three and one and the only hour I'm out is when they let two or three so called tough guys come into my cage during the yard to try and collect on my uncle's bounty. Calculating, I believe its thirty-four unsuccessful attempts at this point but there could be more. So for now on, all gloves are off anybody can get it anywhere. And speaking of my uncle, where is he?" Amir questioned through a tighten jaw not hiding his infuriation and pain.

"I understand you're displeased but you have to calm yourself before the D.A or judge arrive."

"What if I don't?"

"It will disarrange everything I'm trying so very hard to do here for you."

"Really."

"Yes, and don't you dare attempt to down play me by any means. You may be the man out there but this here," Goldstein's finger moved in a circle while looking Amir dead in the eyes, "This Is my domain so sit down chill as you say it and let me work. If not, when the D.A comes in you might as well slit his throat with that razor you have in your mouth."

"How can you tell?"

"I know a lot of things and if you will sit I will show you soon enough."

Amir looked to the clock seeing that it was twenty minutes to nine as he took his seat.

"And it was forty-one to be precise on the times they tried to kill you, not that I'm counting. And as for your uncle," Goldstein's voice dropped just above a whisper. "You see the sheriff on the right in front of the door?"

"Yeah what about him?"

"You're looking at your uncle if you know what I mean without having to say it."

"Hell even the overseer has a price."

"When haven't they?"

"Ha...Ha..." both men laughed.

Meanwhile outside Heather attempted to reach her best friend for the tenth time.

"Hello, Stephanie it's me again Heather you know the best friend you somehow forgot about. Its 8:40 and I'm due in court at 9 sharp but I need to speak to you beforehand so please call me back."

Heather tossed the phone into her purse frustrated.

"I'm guessing that she didn't answer." Questioned Jake from the passenger seat

"If I didn't know any better I would've sworn she just pushed the *fuck you* button!"

"You mean decline?"

"Yes, and it goes straight to the voicemail after the second ring almost every time."

"But why would Ms. Stephanie want to avoid you?"

"I haven't a clue. She has never missed more than two of my calls without calling me back something is wrong I can feel it."

"In that case, it has to be something serious but we can't wait for a second more without going over your report for court."

"Okay well debrief me," Heather stated seizing her moment exiting the vehicle as the reporters crowding the court house steps charged a man in a black and blue pinstripe suit approaching. Jake now use to Heather's impulsive actions was right on her heels as he read from the iPad.

"The D.A, in this case, is the man being surrounded as we speak that's Feldman Clark you two have worked together on several occasions."

"I thought he looked familiar."

"I read over several of your previous trial transcripts and ya'll seem to have great chemistry so that shouldn't be a problem. Now the defendant's counsel, he, on the other hand, is a whole different story. Out of a hundred and twenty cases he has 117 victories and 3 hung juries which ended in two plea-bargains with each defendant getting almost nothing and the other one the charges were dropped. Therefore I believe he is going to make it uncomfortable for you as possible and that's an understatement to utter the least."

"Name."

"Whose?"

"The lawyer's name what is it."

"Oh sorry, it's Goldstein."

"What! Not the beast this can't be right, I looked at every motion Amir has filed to date personally and they all read Dania

Heart's name and from the search I did she's nobody really in the law game."

"You're correct because she is really Mr. Goldstein's partner's sectary. It's an old trick lawyers use if they don't want the D.A to know who they're up against. By her being in the firm and the team's name on the letter head of the motion it leaves the door open to anyone of them to represent him?"

"Isn't that something the man is on his last leg and still he finds a way to try and throw us off. Not that it will help, at the very least he's finished."

"You think he had something to do with this misleading?" Jake probed opening the court house door for Heather.

"Yes, he's always trying to outsmart someone even when he isn't the canniest person in the room."

"Will I think it's kind of notable to have the heart to continue to fight as if the war has just begun after everyone has counted you out?"

"Then why don't you go and give him a fucking medal."

"Come on Heather now you know that's not called for-"

"Hello...excuse me, detectives." Interrupted the officer of the court standing on the other side of the glass door reading from his clip board.

"Oh sheriff Mills it's me and you again I see?"

"Yes, Heather I guess it's my lucky day. If you two will follow me this way. They have you all set up in waiting room 6 and here are your questions from the D.A and this package was left for you up front this morning. Get ready cause if I'm not mistaken you will be the first or second to testify. I will be right outside if you need my help with anything."

Heather didn't hear a word sheriff Mills spoke seconds before closing the door behind him. Her attention was focused on the large yellow envelope which read, **"Must watch before testifying."**

She had a funny feeling that something wasn't right about it as she placed the envelope on the table before her. She studied the words which seemed to her to be more of a command rather than a suggestion.

Jake sensing the same about Heather inquired, "Boss is everything okay? The sheriff offered you coffee and you say nothing and I have never seen you turn down a free trip to Starbucks."

Heather secured the door saying, "Look at those two items and tell me what you see."

227

"I see your briefing sheet and an envelope what seems to be the CD on the case. What I'm I suppose to see?"

"If you were a good detective you would have noticed how D.A Clark writes his name smooth as if he wants you to believe that he is more attractive than he actually is. Now glance at the hand writing on the envelope it's more aggressive. The T's are crossed from one end of the paper to the middle deep without a pause as if they want me to feel their pain. The W is bigger than it has to be with four hard pauses down and up, down and up but not a big enough motion to get someone else's attention without a second look. But me being the detective I am, he knew I would catch it."

"Come on boss you can't think Amir had something to do with this?" The man in jail and you said it yourself he's finished."

"Then he must have help, hell there's only one way to find out." Heather slid the disc into the player. She turned to take a seat when her heart dropped down into the pit of her stomach at the sound of her own voice screaming.

"Alex Nook."

Heather slowly faced the screen remembering the moment, recognizing this bus ride was heading to hell if she didn't do something. She witnessed herself reacting on compulsion backing her partner up. A large thumping sound echoed from the speakers.

"What the fuck just happen Heather? Please tell me he didn't shoot someone in the blind."

"Sssshhh," Heather moved in closer whispering into Jake's ear. "Keep your voice down. This was a play to get our attention." "Ours!"

"Well, mine just keep it down? If he got the disc to me that means he's connected. Shit, the television was here waiting and you know how hard it is to get one of those with their cheap asses upstairs. He could have this place bugged."

Jake becoming silent allowed his detective skills to go to work. He stared at the screen observing Heather's hands hastily exploring the wall. She switched on the light discovering Alex kneeling down next to a badly beaten man strapped to a chair. A large portion of duct tape enclosed his mouth and wrist.

"Oh,   shit   he   did!"
Heather shot Jake a stare.

"My bad boss it won't happen again."

Alex with his knife in hand cut away the man's restraints laying him flat on the floor applying pressure as he yelled.
"Heather called for help this man is bleeding badly."

Heather seeing enough ejected the cd breaking it into pieces.

"Boss if I'm not mistaken you weren't the one who called for the ambulance or found the body at Amir's house."

"I think your misidentifying the location. I responded to that call you're speaking of like everyone else. This had to be somewhere else. "

"No, if I wasn't a good cop I wouldn't have noticed the pictures of Amir and his father on the back shelf for the short second the lights were on before you ended the show. Plus there's the fact that I memorized the face of every murder victim that has come through our unit to feel as one with them. You know how you once did."

"You little shit don't dare fix you face to say that to me I never stopped."

"Then you know that was Kent Jackson." Jake's voice began to raise. "His name is on the fucking wall in red as if you didn't know the killer already. Well, I'm going to cross it off when I get back as solved. Now the question is are you going down with Alex when I do or not."

"You wouldn't dare. What about policeman code and for the last time keep your Damn voice down?"

"Officer's code is what this is all about because it's my job as a good detective to give the victim's family the closure they deserve."

"Don't give me that closure shit. He was a suspect in several of our other murder cases so what about those people families?"

"Don't put this on me. Why are you covering for Alex or did you have something to do with it also. Wait. Wait…this may mean I' could be guilty by association and don't even know it. I'll tell you one thing I'm not going down for this shit!"

"Boom!"

The table shook under Jake's fist slamming into it. The door opened in seconds as Sheriff Mills stood in the room with his hand on his weapon staring Jake up and down looking as if he was fresh meat. "Heather is everything alright in here?"

"Yes, everything is okay-…"

"No there is for sure a problem one that she is going to have to deal with quickly on her own or find out the hard way-" Jake said bumping Mill out of the way as he stormed out the door.

"Jake don't do something foolish that you will regret!"

"Heather you wanted me to stop him."

"No let him go, if I learned anything from my mother it's when a man has his mind made up let him have his way or get rid of him." Heather removed her phone now understanding what she had to do while departing. "Tell the D.A I'll be waiting in front of the court room."

"But what's wrong with this room now that your little friend is gone we could have a little fun it will be like old times until your name is call."

"Oh dear I wish I could because you was one hell of a laid." She ran her hand down Sheriff Mill's chest over his file gripping hold of his manhood.

"But no I have work to do and you need to sweep that room it feel like bugs are crawling around in it."

Heather walking down the hall put a little extra swing in her hips feeling her ass getting hot from his stare. She turned the corner straitening up her stride as she removed the evidence docket sheet from her bra she lifted from Sheriff Mill's clip board.

"Men always thinking with the wrong head." She scanned it over. "Bingo! Now it's my turn to send a message."

18

"All rise for the Honorable judge Cynthia Valentine."

"Please be seated...We're here today to address the motion filed by the defendant's counsel to suppress the charges due to lack of probable cause against Amir Patrick, am I correct?"

"Yes, your Honor." Both counsels responded simultaneously.

"I assume you're ready to proceed, Mr. Goldstein, if not too bad. I have a long line ahead of me so please let's begin."

"Yes, your Honor."

"Oh, and for the record counsel I hate nothing more than to have my time wasted with a motion that has no merit."

"I won't disappoint your Honor and I believe it's Mr. Amir's time that is being wasted here by sitting in a cell for a crime that he didn't commit. Which I will prove today that the State has no evidence of starting with my first witness Detective Jake."

"Me?" Jake inquired looking around puzzled thinking,

"Oh shit, they know we going to jail. Fuck that I'm telling."

"Him why!" Heather quickly placed her eye to the space in the thick door trying to see what Amir had up his sleeve next against the bailiff's wishes.

"Ms. you can't do that you may be called to testify."

"I'm Officer Johnson and I'm not on the list I'm just being nosey" Heather flashed her badge lying with a straight face.

"Oh, I'm sorry."

The sound of heels hastily approaching with a distinctive rhythm forced Heather to look up. From the corner of her eye,

Unforgivable Blood   By Yusuf Woods

she spotted her best friend dressed in a pink skirt suit walking across the threshold of the hallway.

"Stephanie wait!"

Heather raced down the hall to the crossway looking to the left finding Stephanie gone.

"Excuse me. Bailiff what witness room is Dr. Stephanie in."

"I'm sorry I can't give out that kind of information Det. Johnson because you're not connected with the case."

"Ain't this a bitch...*now, where did she go?*" Heather hurried off in search.

Back inside the court room, D.A Clark was up on his feet.

"I object your Honor Det. Jake is not on the defense's witness sheet."

"So the game begins Mr. Goldstein explains." The judge ordered.

"You're Honor the sheet clearly states that I would be calling the arresting officer."

"Yes, which is Det. Heather your Honor it clearly stated at the top of the report she is the leading officer."

"I don't object to that you're Honor but if you look at the end of the report as well as every other piece of paperwork involving this case. Exhibit A," Mr. Goldstein handed a stack of papers to the bailiff. "You will find they all are signed by Det. Jake therefore meaning."

"Meaning nothing more than he does the paper work your Honor." The D.A interjected

"Meaning that he also is an arresting officer or his name wouldn't be on the report. The element of doing a criminal report is that it has to be done by an arresting officer."

"I agree with the defendant counsel because the law is clear on this matter. But if the state still wants to object we can throw this case out now for falsifying documents."

"No, we don't your Honor." "Det. Jake,
please take the stand." Jake raised his
right hand was sworn in.

"Detective can you please state your name for the
record."

"Jake Willes."

"And how long have you been working for the New
York City's special homicide unit."

"Divisions."

"What?"

"We are a divisions, not a unit a division is no-."

"I get it Jake and I believe everyone here knows the
difference between the two. I'm appreciative to meet another
individual other than myself that's key on particulars. Today
should be very interesting. Now I would like you to go back
several months to the very moment that you stepped foot on the
crime scene of Mr. Patrick's murder. Do you recall that day?"

"Yes as if it was this morning. Mr. Patrick was a very
beloved person by many and one being my partner Detective
Heather who made certain every lead was checked into."

"So ya'll found the murder weapon with my client's
fingerprint on it"

"No."

"No what, that you didn't find his fingerprint on the
weapon?"

"No, that we didn't fine the weapon as of yet."

"So actually that's two no's if we're being particular
wouldn't you agree."

"Correct, if you want to put it that way,"

"Now did you witness my client kill his father."

"Objection your honor Mr. Goldstein is well acquainted
with this case enough to distinguish nobody has witnessed Mr.
Patrick's murder. Therefore he is just badgering the witness."

"Sustain Mr. Goldstein there will be no duck hunting in my court room. I suggest if you are going somewhere with this questioning get there."

"Will do, now Det. Jake on the night of the murder was this the first time you had met my client?"

"I have heard his name on several of our other cases but to answer your question yes."

"How was he when you met?"

"Excuse me."

"As a detective in a special division, I know you've been trained to notice signs of guilt. Like if a person returned to the crime scene, correct?"

"Yes, they're things that standout."

"Did my client possess any of them?"

"Honestly he showed none at all but there is still a lot of evi-"

"I have no further questions."

"I have no question, your Honor."

Jake exited the witness box puzzled as he stared at D.A Clark who mouthed "Thanks for nothing," while shaking his head from side to side.

"I'd like to call Dr. Stephanie as my next witness." Mr. Goldstein announced.

"Bailiff please show the Doctor to the witness stand."

The bailiff opened the side door to find Heather and Stephanie in a heated argument.

"That still doesn't explain why in the hell you haven't been answering my calls."

"Because we been through this before Heather with you showing up at my office and I don't know what else to say. If you want to speak to me as your friend I'm here for you always. But I can't speak about this case period."

"Dr. Stephanie your name has been called."

"Bitch you did it before what's so different about this time."

"You... Now if you would excuse me I don't want to be held in contempt of court because then I would have to call you to bail me out."

"Will you state your full name for the record Dr.?"

"Dr. Stephanie T depth."

"Okay, Dr. is it true that you specialize in this new technology that somehow gets the truth out of a person."

"Yes but the technology itself isn't as new as many people may think. It has been used in solving thousands of murder cases for over fifty years."

"Doctor, how accurate would you say this tool is that you are using?"

"About a hundred percent."

"I object your honor."

"On what bases Mr. Clark."

"That the statement Dr. Stephanie just gave to the court is false, Exhibit B. There your honor you'll find that the technology which is actually called *truth be told* is only 79.8 percent correct in the last two years and less in some years prior."

"Dr. Stephanie do you have anything to say to these allegations."

"Yes, that I have only spoken currently your honor."

"Then this conventional document is wrong?"

"No the truth be told tool has never been wrong. In these cases which is two hundred out of a thousand. If one would research deeper they will find that it was the person conducting the tool that made the mistake by applying their own opinion in the gray realm."

"And by the gray realm, you're signifying?"

"The moments when the brain's statement of the truth is unfinished."

"Elaborate."

"Ok, the system makes the brain tell the truth one hundred percent of the time. However, that doesn't remove how the brain reacts in various moments. For example when it encounters fear, pain or traumatic stress. In a lot of these moments, the mind will shut down leaving behind only a fragment of truth. From this limited truth is where people went wrong. By piecing their own stories together off of what they saw and believe in their own life.

This I had never done and would not do."

"Understood over ruled...Mr. Goldstein, you may proceed."

"Thank you, your Honor. So Dr. in your findings with my client was there any truth that he executed this crime to his father in any part?"

"You're Honor I object."

"On what bases Mr. Clark but let me warn you that you're wearing my patience thin and if you keep pushing it I may just throw the case out altogether. Because if I'm not mistaken it was you who suggested Mr. Amir go through this extreme lie detector to prove his innocence."

"Withdraw."

"To answer your question Mr. Goldstein no I didn't find anything in his mind that says he is guilty but that-"

"No further questions your Honor."

"Mr. Clark would you like to cross examine the witness this time or would you like to just sit there shaking your head again."

"No, I would enjoy nothing more than to speak with the Dry... Now Doc may I ask what was it that you were about to say?"

"That I didn't see no evidence of any kind that Mr. Amir killed his father or new about it. But what I did notice was an appalling amount of hurt at just the mention of his father's name. Which I believe could have led to him having Petit Mal seizures. Which is a rare type of seizure that involves brief, sudden lapses in attention; better known as an absence seizure. Many children appear to have a genetic predisposition to it."

"Absence seizure."

D. A Clark let the words roll off of his lips then pause looking as if he was hard in thought. He continuing. "Doctor let me know if I got this right. An absence seizure is when a person blanks out in his or her mind while they are wide awake doing things which they would not remember the next day? Because in all actuality they weren't really there? Even though they did it?"

"Roughly put but correct never the less."

"Therefore Amir could have been a part of the murder and don't remember it."

"Correct."

"Meaning that the truth be told won't work on him. That will be all your honor." "And you Mr. Goldstein."

"Yes, just a few... now doctor that doesn't explain how Mr. Amir would block out the actions of his so called friend as the cops alleged that killed his father in a robbery gone bad that my client supposedly was a part of does it?"

"No, I can't explain that it's a gray area."

"Then don't, no further questions your honor."

"Oh fuck!" Heather said removing her eyes from the crack of the witness door. "Why didn't I think of that?" She raced down the hallway knowing her friend wouldn't let her down even if she tried. "Jake meet me at the main entrance of the court house in two minutes," Heather yelled into the phone.

"But I'm alr-"

"No *buts* get there now!" Heather disconnected the call.

"But I'm already on the E-way," Jake said to no one as he headed for the exit.

Back inside the courtroom, "I object your Honor this hearing today isn't about what Dr. Stephanie thinks. It's about the test and the answer-"

"Mr. Goldstein I out rank you here in this room so you don't have to remind me of what's going on, believe me, I got this. So much in fact that I'm ready to rule. After taking in all the information I've decided."

The court room door swung open with Alex racing in behind it. "Wait!"

"Is to dismiss the charges against the defendant without prejudice."

"But your Honor my special witness has just arrived."

"Yes, Detective Alex is kind of unusual I must say but there's nothing he could allege to change my mind at this point. Because a detective has already testified that there are no prints, weapon or eye witnesses, therefore, the fact remains that the state hasn't met the burden of proof as of yet. But until then if there's nothing else holding the defendant he is free to go."

Amir smirked as he stood firmly shaking Mr. Goldstein's hand, "Thanks I owe you one, call on me anytime for anything."

"That's not necessary."

"Oh, but it is because all debts must be paid which leads me to my uncle. When you get back tell him it's my turn and he is still going to have to see me the moment he sees me."

"Amir I advise you to leave him be. His blood is old and it's dark."

"And mine is fresh and it's black so now all debts must be paid you do understand me?"

"Somewhat."

"That's good enough now if you would excuse me I got some unfinished business to handle starting with a new pal."

Mr. Goldstein shadowing Amir's stare discovered Alex on the other end of it staring back. His hand grip tightened, forcing Amir to give him his full attention.

"Knock it off, will you. I know you do understand what without prejudice means. Therefore they can bring these charges back up on you when they get more evidence and you're taunting
the fucking detective."

"Why not the games are just beginning and it's my turn."

"Well, the present day is not the time for whatever you're thinking believe me. If you don't take anything from me please take this advice. These people hate nothing more than to feel that someone has beaten them at their own game. So for a year that's when their funding well runs out on your case. You'll have to be on the straight and narrow or I swear by god they will put you under the jail for pissing in an alleyway. Your phone will be taped and they will be watching your every move."

"When did they stop?"

Mr. Goldstein shook his head with a smirk. "You are definitely your father's son. By the way, I bought something for you in case I handled my business here today as usually. Nothing big just a tailor suit, phone and a few dollars to go with your new frame."

"Thanks a lot, but you didn't have to."

"Oh, but I did young blood because you're a man trying to find his own way and who am I to judge the path you take to get there. This is one of the main reasons I became a lawyer to stop people from being prejudged. The very best of us took the long way to get right and when we do most of us give back to the next ones trying. So in a few moments, our friend is going to let you take a shower in the back to freshen up before we sneak you out of here."

"Man fuck 12 I'll wear what I got on out of here."

"No, you wouldn't because I'm not going to let you. Plus we all need friends on every levels the only way you can win in life remember that."

Mr. Goldstein gave a nod to the bailiff he pointed out to Amir earlier.

"Amir if you would follow me, Sir."

"Wait! Amir, did you give someone my phone number?"

"Maybe why?"

"Because I just got a text declaring and I quote *Amir they just arrived.*"

"Like I said it's my move...welcome to my path O.G"
Amir laughed as he walked off away.

"That's not funny this is a conspiracy and it carries the same amount of time for whatever you're planning." Mr. Goldstein stated as the door closed behind Amir. He shook his head knowing that look in Amir's eyes and whatever was up his sleeve it was sure to be deadly.

19

Several hours later as the night disregarded the day Heather stood in an office building in downtown Manhattan. She readjusted her leather gloves before stepping off the elevator onto the seventh floor with Jake following quickly behind her.

"Boss do you think this is a good Idea, breaking and entering is still against the law in every state?"

"Like I have a choice whoever sent that disc believes that they're in a position of power to threaten me and the only way to reverse that is behind that door."

"Power, position, believe whatever the case, I told you I don't want no parts of this and I thought I made myself clear." Jake walked back onto the elevator when Heather grasped hold of the back of his collar.

"Listen here Mr. *Know-it-all,* the truth is you're in this more than you think so either help me or we both go down."

"What, I don't have nothing to do with this, this is your dealing so deal with it?"

"I figured you'll say such, check your side piece."

"Why?"

"Just check it and don't you ever think you're smarter than me. Oh, I see how you been staring at me trying to read me all the time for whatever reason I don't know."

"Wait... this isn't mine."

"But it is the weapon that killed Kent and you had it for the last ten months. Just image how many times you checked it in signing your name next to the serial number of a murder weapon."

"Fuck! How? When." Jake quickly thought back remembering the night they captured Amir and Heather approached him...

"Great Job everyone now pack it up. I'm starting to miss the New York air already.

"Ha ha," The crew laughed

"Oh, Jake can I speak with you for a minute?"

"Yes Boss what seems to be on your mind?" Jake answered tying his shoe from the long run.

"I must say at first I really didn't think you had it in you to deal with these mean streets but I see I was wrong. This is the place for you and you deserve this back." Heather slid Jake's back up piece into his Exposed holster. "Now don't run off and shoot someone. Hell, who am I kidding it's you, Jake, that gun may already have a body on it."

"Ha ha." Everyone laughed

"You son of a bitch!" Jake yelled knowing he'd been played, "Okay I see I have no options in the matter at the moment but I need to know everything starting with how did you know that the janitor back there was going to let us in after business hours and why did he call you honey cakes."

"Quiet down! And that's none of your damn business and keep your head down away from the cameras. This is a privately owned practice and if we get caught were going to jail no if ands or buts about it. Do I make myself clear?"

"Crystal, but I got a thought; why don't I wait here and cover your back from afar."

"You know I would love nothing more than to leave your scared ass in the car but I need your computer skills to do this now come the fuck on."

Heather knowing the building's layout as if it was her own rushed the stairway up to the 12th floor. She opened the door then paused raising a finger halting Jake at the sound of keys quickly approaching.

"It's the security guard, isn't it? I knew this was a bad idea."

Heather watched the sweat develop across Jake's forehead and laughed to herself. She waited till silence echoed in the distance before easing out into the hallway.

"Come on it's that second office on the left."

"I can read but I still can't believe we're doing this to her."

"Grow some balls will you, reading a few files can't hurt nobody. Plus we would do it all the time when we were in college together."

"The key word in that is College and if you haven't noticed this here is the real world. She can lose her job and license for whatever you are planning to do with this information."

"The only one that's going to lose a job about this information is you if we're not in and out of here.

Heather replied pushing Dr. Stephanie's birth date into the lock pad.

"We're in."

Jake proceeded behind the desk and began to work his magic. His finger moved promptly entering several key words to crack the computer's three access codes. After a long six minutes and two security guards patrolling pass with one even trying the lock that had Jake jump under the desk.

"Welcome, Dr. Stephanie."

"Now all I have to do is find out where she hid… Bingo! Amir's sections."

Jake pushed play as a young Amir appeared on the screen hiding in the darkness. They watched in silence both with a detective's eye when Heather's heart stopped.

"Mom!"

Heather's grasp tightened on the back of Jake's chair to conceal the fact that her legs began to give out at the vision of her mother. The fact that she was being fucked from behind at the time did nothing to effect Heather's love."

"Mr. Patrick."

"Oh, my fucking goodness! Your mother was having an affair with our murder victim. I think it's time for me to go."

"Sit back down and I'm only going to say it once"

"Okay, but you don't have to be so pushy." They continued to scrutinize through the file.

"I know that bitch isn't." Mrs. Patrick said before lowering her voice resting her eyes on Sherry standing in the doorway a shame that both her kids witnessed this.

"Wait… what she just said."

"That bitch isn't."

"No don't play with me Jake, read her lips what she say after isn't."

"Isn't pregnant."

"Oh, my fucking goodness!" Heather stated shocked

Jake continued to watch disbelieving his sight when he yelled

"That's it we got him!"

"How?"

"What! You didn't just see Amir shoot that man in cold blood. And I bet you if I run a facial recognition of this guy through our database I would find that he was killed that day. Then we can get Amir for this murder." Jake said astonished at the act of violence Amir showed at such a young age.

"Ssshh…keep your voice down and yes I did see it from a tape that is not admissible in court because we're not supposed to have it let alone witnessed it."

The video continued with Heather watching herself entering Amir's house with a smile she hasn't worn in years. From her memory, this was the last time. She still could feel the butterflies from that moment as he slowly removed her clothing. Jake's eyes widen at the sight of his boss being nailed to the bed.

"Stop!"

"I wasn't staring."

"I don't care I looked great back then and good now but wait- get down I think I hear someone coming."

Jake slithered beneath the desk next to Heather sneaking one last look at the screen as Heather eyes close drifting off to asleep.

"Damn she nasty." He thought plunging deeper as the flashlight shined through the door window scanning the room and its contents.

"Do you think they saw us?"

"The light."

"Yeah, I see it that's why I'm asking."

"Not that light jackass on the computer."

"Oh shit! I got to get it."

"Who else."

Jake felt as if he was stepping out into a battlefield in Afghanistan wiped the sweat from his forehead and hands. He sluggishly took in a deep breath as if it would be his last before crawling out into the open. He jumped back into the seat while keeping his head low working his magic.

"God please don't let this man see me I'm not built for jail I swear to fucking God. Oh, my bad I shouldn't be swearing but it's to you so I should be fine right-."

"Hurry up dammit I think he's coming in."

"I know I can hear but if I don't get this back how it was we're finished anyway."

The jiggling of the door knob being rotated with the touch of cold air rushing across his face informed Jake that he would soon be behind bars.

Heather crawled out pulling at Jake's pant leg. "Come on lets go." She looked toward the exit in the opposite direction of the growing footsteps.

"Okay give me one more minute."

Heather shook her head whispering, "If I could I would lose that side piece." She advised before departing

Jake leading his class in lip reading instantly stood while closing the last window powering off when a large palm forced him back down into the chair.

"Don't move or I'll shoot ...now what the hell are you doing in here?"

Jake looked to the door then without warning he gripped hold of the man's genitals twisting hard catching him off guard while releasing him of his weapon."

"Aaaahh... my nuts." The man screamed as the flash light crash to the floor.

"Bitch shut up. Face the wall and get on your knees."

"Please don't kill me I got three kids."

"Well tell them good bye."

Jake bit down on his bottom lip unbeknown to him why but he didn't care because the taste of blood was more favorable now then in his pass. He rubbed the salty liquid against his gums using his tongue as he moved in closer when the barrel of Heather's gun slammed into the back of the man's head as she treaded out from the darkness sending him crashing to the ground unconscious.

"Jake what the fuck was you thinking."

Shaking his head his eyes widen, "I don't know I guess I was scared and panicked."

"Let's go but I don't know what that just was. I really thought you were going to kill that man in cold blood."

"Wait, the flash drive."

"Please tell me you didn't download something from her computer because there may be a method they can use to track us from it."

"No, it was just for back up." Jake lied actually he had downloaded every minute of Amir's meeting.

"Okay now come on we have little time. The other guards will be looking for him in any minute."

"Okay." Jake retrieved the drive and like that they were gone.

One year later

20

Amir stood cleaning up out in front of his store wearing his father's apron when he notices someone familiar passing.

"Yo kid...if I was you I would lay off that block for a minute," He whispered from the corner of his mouth while looking around as if he was being watched. Not seeing anyone but he knew they were there somewhere as he continued sweeping.

"Well you're not me Nigga," Stated the man in the Yankee's fitted and 24kt gold chain draped over his Gucci T-shirt as he continued to walk passed the store to the block when the disrespect sat in forcing him to stop.

"Yo where the fuck you get this kid shit from? You know my name specially two years ago when I used to put that work in for your ass or you forget the days when you had the balls to hustle and get a real dollar instead of selling chips and sodas and shit?"

"I didn't forget Damon I'm just trying to put that time behind me but I'm still a man and always will be so don't push it. This is just some sound advice about how to pick your time to get busy wisely like someone once told me." Amir placed the broom against the store wall and headed inside not wanting any part of the conversation that he knew one day had to occur. *"I should've just let him go."*

"Don't you dare turn your back on me, nigga? I used to hold you down while putting my life on the line day in and out in these streets when you had it. Now they're mine and the respect is going to be the same."

"It is?"

"No doubt," Damon responded gripping hold of Amir's arm aggressively while his other hand clenched onto the p39 automatic under his shirt. "I don't know if you heard but since you been gone Nigga's been getting shit popped like mollies on the one-four-fifth like never before."

Amir may have been out of the street for some time but there were some things a true player never forget about life and that was the move makers, the fakers, and the killers. Damon was all but a faker.

Amir slowly turned back around knowing Damon deserved better than to speak to his back for all the work they put in together. The brief memory brought a chill and a smirk to Amir's face knowing how badly he wanted to get back out there to continue his pursuit of his father's killer.

Amir shook his head to clean his thoughts noticing the same hunger and ambition in Damon's eyes he tried so hard to hide.

"*The gift and the curse.*" He thought to understand the reality of the situation. He looked Damon dead in the eyes saying,

"My Bad dog no disrespect intended and believe me I know what you're trying to do but I'm done with all that. We just on different paths now."

"Oh, I get it, all of a sudden you got some new found glasses on. After those cats done run up in this hole in the wall you call a store and tried to get theirs the fast way. But your dad wasn't having it. You need to be proud and honor his name at least he didn't go out like a sucker. It's sad to say but since you got out the joint the people around here ain't saying the same about you."

"Nigga fuck me but don't you dare speak about my father." Amir threatened with his finger in Damon's face quickly closing the space in-between them.

"Why the fuck not nigga I got a right too. I was willing to die the same as you to defend his honor. I even talk to the fucking cops about you like you asked of me and you know we don't even fuck with 12 all just to go along with whatever plan you were working. Then the team was writing to you and you never once responded or have you forgotten that too? But its ok, who knows you keep playing like a lame and one night someone else may try to get theirs the fast way off of you in there."

"What did you just say? And get your dirty paws the fuck up off of me," Amir snatched free. His veins vibrated as his muscles in his back and armed flexed ready for action when he spotted the weapon.

"If you think you can level it off try me."

The door to Damon's new Benz quickly opened with his driver Steward jumping out with his hand on his hip. "Boss is everything ok?"

"Nigga didn't I tell you to drop me off and get my car off the fuck off this hot ass block," Damon asked through tightened teeth without turning around to focus on Amir's next move.

"Yes but I just-."

"Am I dropped off?"

"Yes."

"Then go! This is between me and this lame ass nigga always has been always will be."

Several yards away on the opposite side of the street ducked low in a tinted unmarked car (D.E.A) Drug Enforcement Agency Agents Jackie and her partner Paula wrote down Damon's license plate number as the car pulled from the curbside.

"How many cars does this man got eight?" contemplated Agent Jackie, who was the leader of the six man team spread throughout 145th street closely watching their suspect.

"Team is on point it seems that our suspect may have found himself in some unwanted trouble this evening before getting to his meeting with our (C.I.) confidential informant for the control buy… over"

"Copy that, we see him," Said Conner from inside the surveillance truck located in the middle of the block. There he fed live video Intel to each Agent's mobile device. He zoomed in on his suspects as the two men noses seemed to touch.

"Paula I pray that this man doesn't flat out kill this person because you know he's a shooter"

"Yes but look at it this way Jackie we'll get the sorry explanation for a man one way or the other."

"I know, but that's not good enough. Being the first female Agent to head her own drug investigation in Harlem the stakes are higher than usual. To top it off I picked you of all people another female as my partner instead of Benson like the office insisted I do."

"Who would have tried to run the show with you wearing

the hat that's all?"

"Exactly!"

"I understand girl we just…"

"Hold that thought… team are you seeing this copy."

"Yes"

"Well ground team slowly move in but no one blow your cover unless our suspect is the shooter I repeat the suspect must be the shooter."

"But what if he's the one shot?" asked field Agent Moonie

"That's not my problem and I assure you that Det. Heather is around here somewhere. She's the one that put us on our suspect because she has a hard on for the other so she and her teams here believe me. "

"You one cold sista, and I love it," said Paula as she eased up in her seat to get a better look at the two.

Damon's stare remained cold seeing Amir's body kick into motion as his old self knowing deep down inside Amir was never going to be anybody's sucker. Damon smiled to break the tension in the air as he slowly released the grip on his gun. He watched Amir's body settle as his hand inched farther away. Then suddenly he clenched his weapon again catching Amir off guard.

Damon quickly pulled in reverse releasing the firearm from his hip as Amir hastily seized hold of his wrist freezing it at his side.

"Now what you going to do with that."

"You'll see," Damon's arm shook from the friction while his wrist remained still. The smirk on Amir's face made Damon even more frustrated as Amir knew it would. He placed his free hand of over Amir's fingers attempting to pry them open to no avail.

"Give me this," Amir flexing his power pulled the gun away.

"Go head shoot me, Nigga, at least I'll die knowing you still have the balls, to do so."

Amir felt the weapon's authority the moment it touched his palm. He absorbed the weight and texture as it brought back thoughts of his darkest secrets. He placed the barrel in the center of Damon's chest witnessing sweat forming on his hands and arms.

"So this is what you want" Amir grilled with the look of pure business on his face.

"What's a better way to die than in the face of fear itself? So don't rap me to death and let it fly, lame." Damon watched his old friend's finger ease back on the trigger thinking, *I may have pushed this Nigga too far god I'm on my way-.*"

"You know what, I'm going do something better for you just because of our past and I know my father cared about you. So I'm going to knock you the fuck out first but if you win you can live. Let's go pussy."

"All shit! Now, this is what the fuck I'm talking about, nigga you know you can't beat me."

"Yeah, I know you live off of what people say and you been dreaming of this," Amir said tucking the gun away while following Damon into the store. "Now I'm going to break them." Inside the store, a clean and sober Dave looked up from doing the weekly inventory with a smile greeting his boss,

"Hey what's go youngen-" He stopped in mid-sentence because what he saw before him was different in his god son's eyes but yet so familiar.

"Dave I'm going need you to finish sweeping up out front and watch the door make sure nobody comes in unless one of us says so."

"Boss you certain about this?" Dave inquired studying Amir's movements carefully. He had not once seen him mad let alone upset and now as his words and his body motions still remained calm but his eyes gave a different description; one of agony, blood, and war that was shortly to come.

Dave continued to study Amir as he removed his shirt bearing his black tank top while Damon quickly moved the chips and snacks racks to the side of the room stone faced.

Oh shit, it's on. "Okay, I'll see to it this moment boss."

The second the door closed behind him Dave heard a loud **Boom**. From his times at war, he knew better than to look back instead he began to clean up when the sound repeated; this time much louder.

Boom Boom!

"They're getting it in…well, let me go ahead and get this dirt up off the ground I may need to throw it on top of the other kid." Dave just shook his head.

Boom!

Amir threw another right jab while moving inward that Damon slipped just in time. He bent sideways sending a left hook hard into Amir's midsection. He quickly followed it up

253

with a right upper cut to Amir's cheek. The assault forced him back against the freezer.

Boom!

Amir bounced off the cold glass. He dancing in a circle refusing to allow Damon to rush him. He knew Damon was a great street fighter but his father taught him how to box and the two never mixed well. Amir pivoted shooting two short rights followed by a hard left jab to Damon's face and temple.

The punches connected buckling Damon as his knees gave way. He plunged toward the floor sticking his hand out preventing his fall. He pushed off rushing Amir at the knees.

Amir seeing the move coming slid horizontally but was a second too late as Damon's arms wrapped around him. He fought to maintain his balance as his body was elevated. Damon despite taking several punches to the head and face waited until Amir was in peak-flight before rotating and bringing him back down hard to the floor.

Boom!

On contact, Amir's ears began to ring as his eyes widen with stars flowing in his sights. The bells became louder as he cleared his vision when he noticed his father just inches away bleeding on the floor with blood coming from his chest. He stood up walking over to the spot where his father died.

Damon confused about what was happening as he watched Amir talking to an empty space. "Yo son who you talking too," he questioned grasping hold of his arm.

Amir snatched free saying, "I don't care if the cops were standing right the fuck there, the man's going to get the respect he deserves. You got a problem with that?" Amir clenched the handle of the gun in the center of his back waiting on an answer.

"No do you son?" Damon responded with his in the air taking a few steps back. "Here we go again."

Amir continued to speak a few more words lowering his hand caressing the air before turning to Damon with tears hugging to the rim of his eyes before they begin to fall. He instantly raised the weapon to Damon's head. "Why nigga?"

"Wow…Wow….Homie wait." Damon thinking fast knowing his life depended on it, quickly put two and two together from the Dr.'s words at the court house. *He's there but he's not.* "Amir you're in the store, your father's store. The year is 2020 and now it's you and your sister remember."

Amir shook his head answering "Yeah… Yeah, I get it good looking." he walked in a circle getting himself together. "I was lost for a minute but I'm back you know what. I think it's time we get back to doing what we were doing. But this time around we turn it up a bit. You know, no playing grind hard or

don't grind at all."

Damon stood there looking Amir up and down noticing that his eyes had returned back to normal before speaking, "Now that's what the fuck I been waiting on. For us to get back out there and lock this shit down again. You know how we do with respect, power, and blood. I got this new connect but that's no problem. He's all soft and shit never wants to meet up. I think he is scared of meeting with a nigga that's known for taking shit down. So instead he'd just text the name of the hotel and the key be at the front desk waiting. I pick up the bricks, the money will already put in one of the many bank accounts he gave me just to start all over again.

The nigga got to be holding heavy. I mean if we can handle five hundred of them things it's no problem he keeps trying to push them on me more and more. I know you said you didn't want to get in the game less you could control all of it but shit this is a big piece of the pie. Funny thing is I don't know anything about him this is really my mom's plug. She just kept saying somebody had some good cheap work and one day she bought two bricks home and it's been on ever since."

"Sound good but that's not what I'm talking about getting back too." Amir threw a warning jab at Damon's head that just missed; intentionally. "Nigga just because I was gone for a minute you think you can put your hand on me, never!"

"Man I don't think, I know."

"Nigga you don't know anything and the moment you realize that you'll do better." Amir landed a hard right just above Damon's eye then another.

"Oh shit it's on." Damon thought with his head snapping back as it seemed that Amir's hands had suddenly gotten five times faster.

Amir again circled Damon but this time he head faked before throwing a jab with both hands landing the left then the right. He lunged forward slipping Damon's upper cut and right cross as the heavy breeze whooshed across his face. Amir got low assaulting Damon's expose ribcage with several short hard shots.

He could feel Damon's body quiver behind each blow.

Damon's legs started to wobble but Amir wouldn't allow him to go down so easy. He sent a hard open palm into Damon's shoulder blade knock him upward and off balance. He rose quickly wrapping his arm around Damon's neck interlocking it with the other arm. Amir began to squeeze tighter until Damon's body began to go limp.

"Calm down calm down...Now tap out nigga and touch the shoulder or I'm going to out you." Damon's hand started upward.

"That's right go head and give into something much greater than yourself." Amir thought with his grip stiffen.

Damon becoming light headed began kicking and punching trying anything to break the powerful hold. He could feel himself losing consciousness by the second as Amir gave demands. His hand shifted towards Amir's shoulder

"If this nigga taps out I'm going to kill him anyway because that means he been soft the whole time."

Now with his fingers just inches from his arm Amir pressed harder against his windpipe. He watched the veins protruding from the center of Damon's forehead as his fingers touched his shoulder.

Amir bit down on his lip pulling with all his might to break Damon's neck when his hand shot pass his shoulder crashing into Amir's eyes before Damon collapse out cold.

"Ha...Ha." Amir proudly laughed dropping Damon to the floor. "Man down."

"Did he tap?" Trina asked stepping out from the back cocking her weapon.

"No, he kept it one hundred."

"You sound a little disappointed." Trina retorted removing a soda from the freezer shaking it on Damon waking him up.

"Ahhh...wh...what's going on and why the fuck is you pouring shit on me!" Damon shook his head gathering his thoughts

"Because of yo-."

"Because hell, stop."

"Nice to have you back."

"Fuck you, Trina."

"My money Damon that's what's up," Amir answered helping him to his feet.

"What money nigga we evened up on the last job because you passed the money and diamonds back off to me remember. And what was I doing on the floor- nigga you sucker punched me."

"Come on you know what happen, you felt that work keep it real."

"That's my story and I'm sticking to it." They both laughed.

"Plus it's one for one and I can live with that. But we might have to break that tie sooner than later if you keep acting as if I owe you. I have never been bad money in my life. All I have is my word and I pay every coin that's put on it."

"I hear you." Amir nodded with Trina quickly texting on her watch.

257

Damon chuckled, "See I may not know a lot but I damn sure know who the fuck I owe and it's not you. So go ahead and admit it Mr. photographic memory. You're slipping from that short stay inside the joint. But if you fuck with me again I'll get that rust up off of you."

"Is that so?"

"No doubt." Damon's phone chimed, reading the text he continued. "Now this is that nigga that got the bag. He hit me and said meet him downtown at the W. So if you will excuse me I have a date with paper you coming or you going to keep pushing that broom...ok nigga and by the way, you missed a spot." Damon exited the store.

Amir smiled giving another head jester to Trina as he walked into his back office. He sat in the hard leather chair that still held his father's fragrance placing his feet up on the desk. He began to count down from 10, 7, 5, 4...1"

The door flew open with Damon rushing in right behind, "Yo son just tell me how the fuck you did it."

"How I did what I'm just sitting here adding up these chips and sodas?"

"Yeah...yeah I was tripping with that I see now my mistake but you one smooth mother fuck man. You the fuck did it. I can't believe my ass been working for you this whole time."

"For me."

"Yeah nigga don't play dump I get a text saying the pickups was at the W hotel then when I leave. I get a second text to meet here and it's the same number that been hitting me up for the pass ten months"

"Okay Then who's the one playing dumb me or you? You're asking me a question about your business that you already know the answer to because you were there."

"And you were in jail I get it."

"Yes so let's play a game." Amir removed the firearm from the center of the desk locking it on Damon. "Now if you tell me how I did it you can keep the money you owe me. If you can't I'm going to shoot you in your gun hand, deal?"

"My gun hand why the hell, not the other one."

"Because if you can't use your brain now after this you'll be forced to. You have five minutes." Amir set his watch.

"Fuck it for two hundred thousand why not. Shit, we put our lives on the line for less."

"Now you're starting to understand...time."

"Hold up hold up give me a minute wait damn!"

"No we been waiting on you long enough."

Trina walked out into the room joining in the conversation. "Yeah for a minute there I thought you were going to get left behind on this mission. I can't lie, I would've enjoyed your share of the money." Trina laughed as she gave Damon a big hug whispering, "Think back you got this; remember everyone is a potential enemy," she kissed him on the left cheek before taking a seat.

Damon set his watch closing his eyes saying, "Time."

He thought back to Amir's words. *"The ones who are not your enemies are potential enemies. Because what we do involve money. Now it just comes down to when will they strike. But then again who knows I could be wrong about Frankie?"* ...*Frankie that's it he's the person that had me thinking that Amir was a potential enemy but why....* Damon continued to ponder to himself searching his brain... *Oh shit, it was him for real like Frankie said...* "*So if it was him Frankie said he didn't want the money he just wanted the names of three top drug purchasers in the city."* Okay, now that was the score with me being the *Vic.* So if he hit the lick knowing him the three became one...Him. Then he made contact...my mother.... *"I'm telling you Amir has something big going."* So the bitch was in on it the whole time.

She's not going to trust just anyone and neither are you.

Damon dialed a number tossing the phone to Trina. "Here you may not want to speak to me but I know you'll talk to yourself anytime. Okay, Amir where those bricks at now that my tab is paid."

Trina's watch started to ring.

"Okay, that's one." Amir smiled, "And for that, I got a little present for you." Amir stood up opening the walk-in freezer where a badly bruised man sat tied to a chair."

"Zeno what the hell is he doing here I'm supposed to meet him up the street in a half an hour."

"Shhhh." Trina lifted up Zeno's shirt revealing a wire in the lining of his shirt.

"Oh shit Zeno your 12 (12 aka police) Son," Damon said in disbelief.

Amir closed the door, "You can deal with him later right now they're several agents staking out the block waiting on you to make a mistake so chill for the moment. Here's your gun back you're going to need it"

"If you knew they were on me why didn't you call and say something."

"Because I need them."

"For what you don't fuck with the police."

"An Alibi." Amir began dialing with the caller picking up on the first ring. "It's time to make the call."

"Ok, I'm on the move…oh, and by the way, Uncle Robert just arrived at JFK with about twelve dudes I think he's upset with you about something you never sent. I don't know what's going on but whatever you were supposed to do please do it. That man is pure evil. He said he called and you're not answering so he came."

"Just as I knew he would because first, he has to see me when he sees me… now make that call." "I am but come on don't do thi-" Amir disconnected the call.

21

"Hello special Homicide Division, detective Kim speaking no she's busy right now how may I help you...No...No I understand yes we'll get right on it." Kim jotted down details and an address jumping from her seat. She reached Heather's second floor office out of breath. "Shit! I gotta stop smoking that loud pack stuff with my nephews and stick with the regular."

She took a deep breath before knocking twice sliding the paper beneath the door. She waited several minutes then a buzzing sound ensued with the door easing open. She slowly entered seeing Heather studying some papers while running counter informant through her computer as she talked on the phone.

"I understand all that but as of 12:00 last night my team and I have run out of funding and If I don't get it soon this killer will be off in the wind to murder again I'm certain of it...no but h-but...Okay but you know what Mayor I'm not voting for your bitch ass no more." Heather slammed the phone down on its cradle.

Kim knew how her boss was about her privacy and tried hard to keep her eyes locked to the ground and not to stare at the several crime charts behind her. She glanced at the one in the center where Amir sat at the tip of a triangle of pictures then back to the ground. When a picture of herself and several other officers caught her eyes.

"It's something off about this lead but what I don't know or it may just be me. Whatever the case I want you and Alex to handle this with him as prime detective just in case. I wrote some notes that may help here." Heather's extended hand lingering in the air for too long forcing her to look up.

"Now why in the hell are you in my business when I just gave you some of your own?"

Unforgivable Blood   By Yusuf Woods

"Oh I'm sorry boss believe me that wasn't my intention but now that I'm busted may I ask why is my name on this board alongside criminals as well as the rest of the team that worked the

Amir case?"

"First, let me ask you a question."

"That's fair shoot."

"Don't say that because you're in my office looking around invading my privacy I just might. But my inquiry to you is in the last fifteen cases following that one how many have I solved?"

Kim quickly thought and wasn't shocked by the answer she discovered. "All fifteen."

"Exactly and before?"

Pause ..."The same."

"Yes there's only one case my team and I haven't solved and that murder happened before I became an officer and I will find the killer no matter how long it takes. So I started thinking was he better than all the rest or better yet, how was he better than me?"

"And what did you come up with?"

"That he had to have help."

"Boss you cannot believe that one of us would betray you or the badge!"

"Well if that's so there's nothing anyone has to worry about but if so I'll find them?" Heather placed her notes on Kim's chest opening the door to find Jake knocking on air.

"What the hell, doesn't anybody used the phone anymore?"

"Boss I'm sorry I didn't know you were seeing someone, I'll come back."

"No Kim was just on her way out plus I have to meet with the big wig and the Chief about our budget across town in 20 minutes. But I do have a few minutes if you can walk and talk on the way to my car."

262

"That'll be great."

"Ok let me get my jacket if not them old perverts will be watching my nipples the whole meeting and we won't get anything done."

"Ok, I'll wait here," Jake said, who for over the past several months had proven himself to be one powerful detective. He hit the streets with a passion that demanded answers from the hustlers, CI's and crime bosses. He didn't want to interfere with Heather's way of doing things so he only tackled cold cases. The rewards of his triumphs permitted him to move at his own beat of a drum with his success shocking everyone but himself.

Jake solved numerous cases more than anyone at this pace. He now headed a small division of his own targeting old files supervised by the Chief. From time to time he would stop by to chat with Heather to gain advice or bring her up to speed with what he been working on and today was no different.

"Let's go, now what seems to be disturbing you."

"Me!"

"Yes, I see the new lines under your eyes. The wrinkles in your forehead. You must've lost four to six pounds from the last time I saw you, Jake. Which is becoming less and less might I add." Heather's pace picked up while her ocean blue eyes scanned the office space observing if anything had changed. *"I see Alex's desk is a mess which means he's still hard at work. Shit! Only six cases have been solved out of the seventy-four… they have to do better."* Heather stopped with her eyes centering in on a picture pinned to the bulletin board of a 13 year old black girl that was murdered almost two years previously on 125th street while walking home from piano lessons.

"Jamie we will fin-." She began to whisper when her words got stuck in her throat. She turned to Jake giving him a big kiss on the lips. "You found the person who murdered Jamie?" Heather probed with the biggest smile feeling as if a weight had been lifted off her chest.

"Yes and a few others that's what I been attempting to tell you since we left your office but you've been in your own head.

I know the look and you haven't heard a word I said."

"It's not that, I just have a lot on my mind." Unconsciously her stare shifted to the name Barbara Evans as it did every time she walked through the double doors. It was the only case to date she has yet to keep her promise too. Several years had passed since Barbara was murdered but spotting a line through her name made Heather's legs instantly go weak.

"Oh my God Jake I don't know how I'm going to repay you for this." She kissed him repeatedly then in a blink of an eye her happiness quickly turned to fury.

"Now who murdered my Mother Jake?"

"Your mother?"

"Yes, we don't have the same last name because I'm named after the *john* she believed was my father!"

"Oh I didn't know, are you the only child?"

"Yes now, who did it?"

"This what I wanted to speak with you about. But not here, when we get outside."

"Okay as soon as you tell me who done it!"

"I will, I promise the moment we're out of those doors." Jake wrapped his arm around Heather who quickly pushed him off.

"Get your hands off of me and tell me who the fuck killed my mother!"

On contact, three detectives stepped forward from the crowd that suddenly formed.

"Stand down I can handle this!" Heather ordered. "Can't ya'll hear stand down!!"

Jake nodded his head with the men stepping back into the group. Heather looked from the men to Jake and back. She rescanned the room observing everyone staring at her. She noticed on second glance that she didn't recognize the three detectives. *"Wait they're not from this division."*

The hair on Heather's arms and neck tingle from the tensions that instantly thickened in the silence.

"What the hell is going on here Jake?"

"Ok…ok I wanted to explain the situation to you in private but I see you're not going to permit that." Jake took a deep breath showing Heather his iPad bringing up a picture of a dirty Rocky lunch box.

"My old lunch box."

"So this is yours?"

"Yes, I can tell because I carved my initials upside down on the side see." Heather pointed to the letters. "But you know that already or you wouldn't be showing me it."

"I'm showing you it because your fingerprints were on it."

"Ok so, it's my damn lunch box where the fuck is this leading?"

"This was inside." Jake's finger swiped left exposing a picture of a handgun. "Have you ever seen this before?"

Heather paused thinking, "Really I'm not certain, but why so many questions? Let me guess my prints also?" Heather retorted while searching her brain for if she knew the weapon.

"Correct but that's not the issue the dirt inside was tested and it matched the years of being there since the time of your mother's death and the blood on the side of the weapon was also your mothers. Heather, I'm sorry to have to say this to you but these things were found wrapped in plastic buried at your home in the back yard. And I checked it the murder weapon" Heather's mind automatically replayed everything she just heard putting it in detective order as needed.

"He said issue meaning there's a problem. I asked who killed my mother and he never replied. My printer, my lunch box and the time frame of dirt then and my home…It all says I did

it....!" Heather skimmed the room for a way out knowing whoever was setting her up, prison was part of their plan.

"Well, today I'm not." She paused spotting Alex at the back of the room with his hand on his chest flashing three fingers in the center. On eye contact, he gave a slight nod then looked to the right. Heather followed observing Kim standing in the center of the room rubbing her leg with two fingers in the center. Kim nodded before looking off to the left where Heather perceived detective Cohen rubbing his manhood with one finger pointing to it. Shaking her head Heather looked to his eyes where his lips motioned. *"Go!"*

The room went dark with Alex hitting the lights. Kim purposely tripped over her own feet crashing into the three detectives sending them and several other detectives collapsing to the floor.

Heather rushed for Cohen who held the door open quickly closing it behind them as they departed. He clutched it shut, "Go! I'm going to buy you as much time as I can. There's a car parked at the side of the building with the keys in the ashtray. It's older so there's no GPS, therefore, you won't be tracked. There's money and a backup gun in the trunk. When you're safe call

Alex's mother's phone will be waiting and together we'll find a way to get you out of this mess."

"Ok, but how did you know this was going to happen?"

"Jake was trying to stop it all weekend. He'd hoped it wouldn't come to this but when he couldn't we went into action. You know we wouldn't let them ho ass girls upstate have you gay for the stay!" Cohen laughed.

Heather kissed Cohen on the lips "Thanks I won't forget this."

"I hope not," Cohen said licking his lips as he watched Heather's ass as she raced off. "God I hope she's innocence."

Heather let out a deep breath removing her extra-large sunglasses as she passed through the Lincoln tunnel wondering if she would ever see the city again. When a phone rang interrupting her thoughts.

"Where the hell where is that coming from?" Heather, hastily searched knowing, she had rid herself of all electrical devices the moment she turned the corner from the precinct. The sound repeated as she slowly reached in her coat pocket retrieving what seemed to be a brand new iPhone attempting a facetime call.

She pushed decline lowering the widow when a text came through...*I wouldn't do that if I were you, Heather.* The phone rang again. Heather concealed behind her shades once more answering on the three ring.

"Who the fuck is this?"

"Now is that anyway to talk to an old friend?"

"Amir I know ya no good lying ass was behind this but how?"

"The how is easy it's the why that's catchy." Amir disappeared from the picture as he pointed the camera at a T.V screen with showed him climbing into Heather's old bedroom window.

Heather couldn't believe what she was witnessing, "Nnnnoooooo!" she screamed as if it could prevent her mother's body from hitting the floor. The screen went black.

"Nnooo noooo." Heather's fist uncontrollably banged on the steering wheel. A river of tears drenched her blouse and lap. The front of her car scraped the guardrail as she took several deep breathes trying to gather herself. Calm enough she stated "Amir I'm going to show you the same lack of mercy when I kill you. But...why...why...why would you do this to me?"

"What you thought that dirty whore you call a mother was safe? Who took my loving mother away from me? Nothing happens to this family without repercussions."

"So you're telling me you killed my mother only to turn around years later to murder your own father you sick son of a bitch." *He's relaxed so maybe he'll run his mouth enough for me to find a weakness.* Heather thought to herself.

"Ha… Ha," Amir chuckled thinking, *"Heather still up to her detective ways."* Before answering, "Same old Heather always thinking about yourself that's why you don't get it. I didn't kill him that was your brother's mistake but as I said nothing happens to this family without repercussions."

"My brother I don't have a brother."

"Oh you're right, I stand corrected our brother."

"Hi there sis, and believe me it was an error that I deeply regret. I got the wrong lookout boy to guard a man with the heart of a lion. Dad was never supposed to get touched let alone be involved. The plan was to corner the market but who would've known dad was one of the top 3 drug suppliers in the city. He was disturbing to New Jersey, Philadelphia, and Pittsburgh, including the surrounding areas."

Heather stared at the phone and for the second time in minutes, she couldn't believe what she saw. She had to dig deep down into her mind to the last time she remembered him. She was in her bedroom doing homework when the front door opened….

"Mom is that you?"

"Who else the fuck would it be and you sit your little ass down somewhere real quick."

"Mom who are you talking too," Heather asked stepping out into the hallway seeing a little boy sitting on the worn-out sofa.

"What is he doing here I thought you and auntie had a deal?"

"Yeah, the fucking bitch said she can't take care of him no more talking about I spend the food stamps on drugs and didn't send them. Really some fucking food stamps and I gave this bitch my baby from birth now she go and pull this shit."

"Mom not again."

"Girl I'm going to tell you as I told her I lost my card shit! That's what the fuck happened. Hell, there should be

double on it next month, I don't know what she's complaining about but she doesn't believe it happened."

"Well he can't stay here we don't have enough food for us now and the landlord said-"

No shit! I know all that, why the fuck you think I agreed for him to go with that bitch and her asshole husband in the first damn place. This life ain't for him. He deserves better, its bad enough you're stuck here with me. But maybe he's my better half and I could stop getting high and he can stay with us what'd you think?"

"No, because it would never happen! You tried a hundred times. You'll be clean for a few days then you'll be right back at it. I'll be left to look after him and I have to stay focused so I can get into a good college and get away from this hell hole. Why don't you send him to his father?"

"Heather!"

"Oh, I forgot you don't know who his father is either."

"I know who I let fuck me raw your father died in a bank robbery gone bad as I told you. So pump your damn brakes and worry about your own fast Twot! I'm not saying anything to his father because I did enough in that situation so mind your damn business."

Heather's mind quickly shifted to the vision of Amir's mother laying on the floor speaking only in a whisper, *"I know she's not pregnant."* Finally seeing the whole picture. *"Oh shit why didn't I put this together sooner? Because I was trying so hard to forget him I couldn't see what was right in front of my eyes."* Heather pondered answering her own question.

She never could shake that look of sadness in her brother's eyes the moment those words parted her lips no matter how bad she tried. She took another deep breathe preparing to speak to him for the first time knowing it was over fifteen years since that very night. She shook her head remembering she didn't even say goodbye to him.

"Jake I'm sorry I was young and I didn't know any better we didn't have much."

"Save your words because they can't fix what those boys did to me in that orphanage." Jake removed his shirts showing scars all over his body.

"My god!" escape Heather's mouth.

"I was stabbed 12 times within my first 3 years to keep my manhood and I probably would have died if it wasn't for my brother here and Uncle Robert. Amir contacted me after reading one of the many letters I wrote to mom that you happened to toss in his trash. It's a shame you forgot to rip it up. We began to converse about pain who knew that would blend so well together.

Though I wrote in each line my anguish for you and mother I still would beg for ya'll to bring me home. At first, he couldn't understand how I wanted to be with someone who didn't want me. That's how he learned I didn't know who my father was and had nowhere else to go. He recalled the situation with our mom and his dad so he called Uncle Robert and we got tested; the rest is history. Father refused to speak about the matter due to the loss of his wife so behind his back they sent me to the best school where I traced your steps and mastered them. This is what you threw my life away for so you could study law. Why I had to endure in the worse the ghetto had to offer. Now it's time to see if you learned enough to survive as an outlaw without your mother's love as we have.

In a half, an hour an A.P.B will be placed on you for the murder of your mother and the attempted murder of a police officer."

"Boom!"

Heather watched Amir shoot, Jake, in the arm who smiled at the pain stating, "Aaaahh...That there just made jail no longer an option for you every cop in the world will shoot first and care even less later for a bad cop."

"No one will ever believe that."

"No, check your side piece."

"This ins'-." Heather just shook her head remembered

Jake's arm wrapping around her with a slight bump before she pushed him off.

"Correct because you just shot me with your gun and every badge in the city will want you dead by night fall."

"Well, the dark can't come soon enough if you're not dead beforehand…but in the meantime Amir,"

"What."

"I'd watch him closely if I were you."

"Is that so?"

"Yeah If he's doing this to me because I left him alone who's to say it really was a mistake when your father was killed and not a hit because he did the same as I. Hell we all left poor little Jake for dead and I'm the only one left living." Heather grinned at the look on Amir's face knowing she had just struck a deep nerve as he stared at Jake. She tossed the phone out of the window quickly U-turned heading back into New York. She knew at this moment her house was being searched and her bank account frozen and this was war.

"Don't worry this time I'm not going to leave you for dead alone you'll have company and I'm going to kill both of you myself…" she pulled to into a gas station buying a burner phone calling the only person she could help her even the playing field.

"Hello, Uncle Robert…."

To be continued

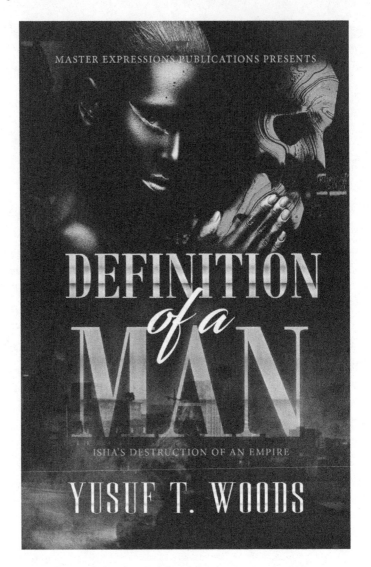

Coming soon July 2020!!!

Made in United States
Orlando, FL
29 June 2024

48409613R00168